THE HAREM MIDWIFE

THE
HAREM
MIDWIFE

ROBERTA RICH

DOUBLEDAY CANADA

Doubleday Canada and colophon are registered trademarks of Random House of Canada Limited

LIBRARY AND ARCHIVES CANADA CATALOGUING IN PUBLICATION

Rich, Roberta, author
The harem midwife / Roberta Rich.

Issued in print and electronic formats.
ISBN 978-0-385-67666-3

I. Title.

PS8635.I249H37 2013   c813'.6   C2013-903074-3
                                              C2013-903075-1

Cover and text design: Terri Nimmo
Cover images: (woman) *The Queen of the Harem* (oil on canvas), Bredt, Max Ferdinand (1868–1921) / Private Collection / Photo © Christie's Images / The Bridgeman Art Library; (city) *A View of Constantinople* by Edmund Berninger / Photo © Christie's Images / Corbis; (vintage label) © Antolen / Dremstime.com; (satin ribbon) © Zhudiefeng / Dremstime.com
Map: Erin Cooper
Printed and bound in the USA

Published in Canada by Doubleday Canada,
a division of Random House of Canada Limited,
a Penguin Random House company.

www.randomhouse.ca

10 9 8 7 6 5 4 3 2 1

*To Ken—my north, my south,
my east, my west*

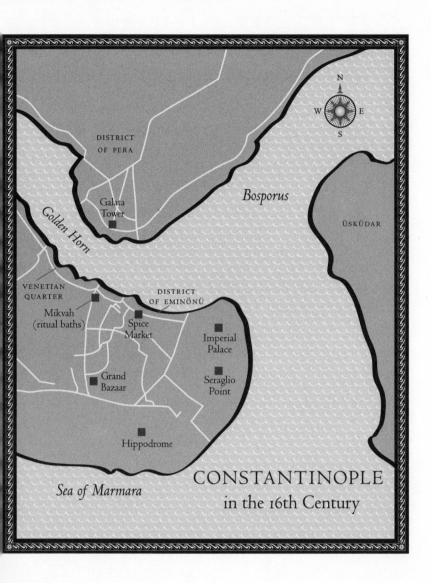

N
W E
S

DISTRICT
OF PERA

Bosporus

Galata
Tower

Golden Horn

ÜSKÜDAR

VENETIAN
QUARTER

DISTRICT
OF EMINÖNÜ

Mikvah
(ritual baths)

Spice
Market

Imperial
Palace

Grand
Bazaar

Seraglio
Point

Hippodrome

Sea of Marmara

CONSTANTINOPLE
in the 16th Century

CHAPTER I

Circassian Mountains
Ottoman Empire
1578

ONE SPRING MORNING as the sun dappled the rocks with golden light, drying the dew from the night before, making the world look as scrubbed and as fleecy as a cloud, Leah made a blunder that was to lead to her death. It was a small thing—a matter of no consequence. She failed to hear the terrified bleat of her favourite black lamb and the answering cry of its mother. A lamb in distress is always a sign of danger, but Leah was squatting on the hillside, singing an old lullaby in Judeo-Tat, the language of the mountain Jews.

As she sang, she stroked the milky blue quartz that dangled from a lanyard around her neck. The pendant, her *nazar boncuğu*, offered protection for both Jews and Muslims against the Evil Eye. Because she believed she was alone on the mountain, she sang with gusto.

There were wolves in the hills. Higher up, beyond the point where even scrubby pines grew, were the goat-hair tents of the Yürüks, so dark in the distance they looked like raptors, the tent poles like talons ready to swoop down on prey. The Yürüks were nomads; their ancestors had invaded the plains of Anatolia centuries earlier, thundering down the steppes of Mongolia on their heavy-rumped stallions, leaving in their wake destruction and death. Leah had never ventured high into the mountains to the tents of the Yürüks, nor did she want to. Her world was her mother, father, brothers, grandmother, and, of course, Eliezer, the handsome boy to whom she was betrothed. Kaş, her village, huddled at the base of the Circassian Mountains, was no more than a handful of crude houses clinging to the side of the scorched hill, a half-day's hard ride from the Yürük tents.

Herding was her older brother's job, but he was ill with fever, so the chore of driving the sheep to the summer pastures now fell to Leah. It was not a task for a girl. Look what had happened to her older sister, a girl so beautiful that their father used to joke that a path of wild roses sprang up behind her as she walked. Rivka must have shouted for help. But there had been only rocks and wind-bent trees to hear her. But Leah, with her *nazar*, a gift from her grandmother, felt she had nothing to fear.

Kagali, the family's herding dog, had wandered off to rest in the shade of the pines, and was tonguing his yellow fur as the flies buzzed around him. Two vultures, limp as shrouds, glided on a current of air. Leah's flock had long ago cropped the meadows bare of the wild sage and garlic. Now just patches of grass remained.

Leah bent down, picked up a pebble, blew off the dirt, and tucked it inside her cheek. The stone would keep her from feeling parched. Her goat's bladder hung empty at her side, long since drained of water. There was no well nearby, only in Kaş. A brook lined with flat rocks ran through Kaş. It was where the women washed clothes. Tonight when she returned, Leah would be greeted by the smell of her mother's stew and the sound of her father teaching her brothers to read.

Leah paused her singing to take a breath and at last she heard the black lamb's pleas. She hiked up her kaftan, tying it around her waist to free her legs. She took up her brother's crook, which lay beside her. As she stood and listened, the lamb's bleating grew weaker.

Leah raced up the ancient path, which had been beaten like a welt in the ground by centuries of footsteps. There had been no rain for three winters. The earth had split into fissures, each one an open mouth, greedy for water. The lamb's bleating seemed to be coming from a crevice at the top of the hillside.

When her chest began to heave from the upward climb, she spit out the pebble, afraid she would choke. She thrust two fingers into her mouth and gave a long, piercing whistle. She waited for Kagali to dash into sight. He was as big as a ram and so savage he was kept chained at home when small children were nearby. His collar, embedded with sharp iron spikes, was crusted with the blood of wolves foolhardy enough to attack the flock.

Leah reached the crevice and crouched at the edge, peering down and listening, the ewe beside her. She knew the lamb's shrill, tremulous cry, so like that of a newborn infant. She had pulled this winter lamb by his tiny hooves out of his mother's belly many days ago when the moon was still full. It was her favourite—a black lamb with one blue eye and one black. Squinting into the crevice, she saw that he was struggling to free a hind leg that was jammed between two rocks. The ewe stood helpless beside Leah, her front hooves working the stony ground, sending a shower of pebbles down onto her lamb's withers.

Suddenly, the dry perimeter gave way, causing the ewe to lose her balance. She twisted as she fell into the gully, and landed with a thud on top of a boulder. Even from above, Leah could see thistles had torn a ragged slash on the poor ewe's udder, scoring her from belly to teat. When Leah returned home that evening with the flock, her mother would pack the wound with flowers from yellow coltsfoot and dress it with mosses. She would heal it by reciting a passage from the Torah, blowing forty-one times over the gash.

Each year after spring thaw, Leah's father daubed the ram's chest with a mixture of fat and soot from the cooking pots. In this way, he could tell which of the ewes the ram had serviced. The ram's sooty mark was still on this ewe's back, a black smudge where he had mounted her.

Leah fell to all fours and peered down at the ewe and her lamb, heedless of the rocks cutting into her knees and palms. If she lost both ewe and lamb, her father would scold her. And rightly so. She should not have been singing songs. She should have been paying attention to the flock.

She inched her way down into the gully using her hands to brace herself along the sides, unleashing an avalanche of rocks. The heat in the crevice intensified the smell of the lamb, still milky from its mother's teat. The dust and the buzz of insects in the narrow space made Leah dizzy. Her face was sweaty and coated with a dusting of grit. Eventually, she reached the bottom.

Stuck between the two boulders, the lamb was unable to move. It was only then that Leah noticed his foreleg, the bone protruding, white as an ivory backgammon tile. As she was reaching for the lamb, she heard the sound of cascading pebbles and looked up. She expected to see Kagali's yellow eyes peering over the edge of the crevice. But she saw only the vultures circling high in the air.

Leah shoved and pushed at the boulders until the lamb's leg was free. The ewe was crying frantically. She straddled the lamb and grasped her delicate foreleg. Quickly, she manoeuvred the bone back into place. She tore off the hem of her kaftan and used this strap of material to bind the lamb's leg. Then, with the bleating lamb tucked under one arm, she began her awkward ascent. As she reached the top, the lamb struggled and twisted out of her arms as she toppled him over the edge. Leah hauled herself out of the crevice after it. She paused to catch her breath. Now she would have to return for the ewe.

She glanced around. Where was the rest of the flock? And then, a few paces away she noticed a heap of yellow fur—Kagali, splayed under a clump of wild grass. His tongue hung from his mouth; his eyes were open and fixed. His flews had fallen away from his teeth, which made him look as though he were snarling. The dog seemed to be staring at something just beyond her shoulder. "Kagali?" Leah drew closer to him. Why didn't he spring up to greet her? She put her hand on his snout. As she leaned forward, she noticed that the dog's throat had been slit cleanly and with such force it had nearly severed his head.

For a moment she froze, refusing to believe what she saw. Kagali's fur was matted with blood from the red, gaping wound in his neck. Had it not been for Leah's hesitation, this moment of stunned paralysis as she worked out the obvious—that no wolf could have inflicted such a wound—she might have escaped.

When she looked up, she saw a man in dun-coloured hides—a man with legs as thick as the ridgepole of her father's house. A man so big he blotted out the sun. By his high cheekbones and his flat black eyes, which stared at her expressionless as stones, she knew he was a Yürük. The bones of a large animal strung around his neck rattled in time to his panting. Leah would not think of her sister. Her mouth opened to scream.

"Be quiet, or I'll slit your throat too."

He towered over her, his knife hanging at his side still

wet from Kagali's blood. A man without a proper head-dress, just a filthy cloth tied around his head. Broken sandals on feet so black Leah could barely see where his sandals ended and his feet began. A man covered in scars. A man who reeked of goat cheese and yogourt. Whose beard glistened with grease. Who looked as though he had been smothered in mud and dirt, stung by insects, ripped by thorns, scarred by the hooves of trampling horses, and had survived it all.

"Who are you?" he demanded in a voice that seemed to come from the low clouds above her head. He spoke a coarse dialect she could barely comprehend.

"Do not kill me," Leah said.

"Who are you!" he roared.

"Leah, daughter of Avram, the shepherd."

"Louder!"

She repeated her words.

"Where do you live?"

"Kaş." Too far away for her father or brothers to hear her screams. "I am only a child." It was a lie. She was fourteen, but skinny for her age. He seized her by the chin, looking into her eyes. "Your father cares nothing for you or he would not send you into the mountains alone."

Leah avoided his gaze, looking instead at his camel-hide tunic, which moved of its own accord. It took her a moment to realize that waves of lice made it seem alive. A few paces away, the man's horse nickered. Nothing was real—not the man nor the horse. All was a dream, like seeing the world through the wings of a moth.

"My brother tends the flock, but he is with fever."

The man grunted. His fingers clamped harder on her. A reckless anger took hold of her. Knowing the words were foolish before they were out of her mouth, she said, "You killed Kagali. You should not have done that."

"Brave, for a girl."

The man grabbed her by the waist and turned her upside down, shaking her as though emptying a sack. The heel of yesterday's bread fell out of her kaftan and bounced on the rocks. Kagali's corpse was so close to her face she could smell his blood.

He tossed her to the ground. She lay there, the air knocked out of her. Several paces away, she heard the bleat of the black lamb. She watched the man pick up the bread from the ground and cram it into his mouth, gnawing and sucking it. Leah fumbled her *nazar* from under her kaftan, rubbing it back and forth between her fingers, trying to calm herself with the smoothness of the stone and the tracery of veins in its depths.

When the man hunkered down hunting for bread crumbs, she tucked the *nazar* under her kaftan and scrambled to her feet, thankful she had worn her old sandals and not the new ones her father had made for her that flopped because the straps were too long. If only the earth would open up and conceal her. If only she could crawl back into the crevice and disappear. She steadied herself against a large rock and took a gulp of air. She used to be the best runner in her village, faster even than the boys.

Leah bolted.

Behind her, she heard the Yürük run to his horse and heave himself into the saddle. She raced downhill toward Kaş. Her father, uncles and brothers would sever this savage's head from his shoulders just as he had severed Kagali's.

A hundred paces into her sprint, a stone gave way under her foot and she lurched and fell and skidded, grit filling her nostrils and mouth.

The Yürük was off his horse and on her in a flash, seizing her by the waist. He drew his fist back and struck her above her ear. Her head jerked sideways from the force of the blow. The sun exploded in her head. Grabbing her hair, he forced her head back, exposing her throat. She thrashed and bit his hand, grinding it between her teeth, but it was no use. As he heaved her over his shoulder, the matted fur of his hides cut off her air. He clambered over the dry rocks toward his horse, carrying her with little effort as she tried to kick the part of him where his legs joined. He growled something in his guttural tongue that she could not make out.

Just as a wolf drags fresh kill to the lair for its pups, he would carry her in fetid hides to other tribesmen. They would use her, and when they had taken turns they would kill her with no more thought than she would give to wringing a chicken's neck. Crying, she bounced upside-down against his back, her head thumping against his goatskin bag. In front of her appeared the legs of his stallion, strips of dried meat hanging from the saddle. As the Yürük heaved her from his shoulder and over the pommel onto his horse, her lanyard broke and her *nazar* fell and caught in one of the strips. Leah reached down and grabbed the stone before it shattered under the horse's hooves. The man threw his leg over the saddle, picked up his reins, and spun the horse around in the direction of Kaş.

With each stride, the pommel dug deep into Leah's tender belly. Blood rushed to her head, banging in rhythm to the horse's gallop. She grew dizzy. And then the light dimmed and faded. When she regained consciousness, she was flat on the ground, stones poking her back, her kaftan rucked up around her waist. Above her spread the sky and clouds. The sun was setting. She did not know how long she had been lying on the ground. Her ear throbbed. She put a hand to her head and felt a knob the size of a winter apple.

The Yürük stood, his feet planted on either side of her, a grin exposing toothless gums. She kicked and twisted. In his rage, he seized a rock next to her. He raised it over his head, about to smash it into her face. Leah began to pray. *God, if it pleases you, let this savage kill me quickly. Better to die than to be dishonoured.*

Leah thought of her family. If she was murdered, who would tend the sheep when her brother was ill? Who would spoon mutton soup into her grandmother's mouth? Who would help her mother bake bread? Who would play back-gammon with her father? And what would become of her betrothed? Who would bear his sons? Did not the Torah say that destiny favours those who are resourceful and brave? She pivoted to one side, squirming out from between the Yürük's feet. She scrambled on all fours and then regained her balance and ran, stumbling, as fast as she could. The sun was over her right shoulder, so Kaş must be straight downhill. She raced to an outcrop of rock where she should be able to see her village in the valley. She stared down, thinking she was in the wrong spot. These blackened houses below, with smoke rising from crossbeams, could not be Kaş. But there were the familiar houses arranged in a semi-circle around a well, her family's house nearest to the stand of pines with the donkey tethered in front. The door hung by one hinge; the roof was on fire. Among the ruins, Yürüks rummaged, heaping booty into a mound—carpets, rounds of hard cheese, *kilims*, quilts, sheepskins, and cooking pots. Women and children ran in all directions. In the midst of the chaos was her grandmother standing stock still next to their house, as though in a daze.

Leah ran faster than she had ever run before, falling and getting up, again and again, all too aware of the Yürük who had mounted his horse and was pounding behind her. As she approached her village, she saw her grandmother carrying Leah's baby brother in her arms. She had nearly reached them when there was a sharp *crack*, like the snap of a bull-whip. Her grandmother was too hard of hearing to look up. A burning timber from a neighbour's house crashed upon her and the baby, crushing them so swiftly they had no time to cry out.

Leah wanted to drag the timber off them, kiss her grandmother's lined face, take her baby brother in her arms and bury him in the hills in a grave with a pyramid of stones on top, but there was no time. She had to find her father. Where was he? He had always protected them. Why had he allowed this to happen? Leah heard shouting and yelling. She turned in the direction it was coming from. In the field beyond the houses, a mob of horses and Yürük horsemen charged after something, bending double in their saddles to seize an object on the mud-packed ground. A rider snatched up the object and hoisted it level to his horse's withers. As he was about to heave it over his saddle, the rider next to him wrestled it from him and sped away.

The nomads were amusing themselves with *buzkashi*, a game played with the headless carcass of a goat. They had revelled in this sport for as long as anyone could remember. But something was not right. Leah tried to identify the oddly familiar object the men were fighting over. She strained to see. Dear God. She refused to believe what her eyes told her. It was the body of a man, the legs cut off. Wound around his neck was a scarf of blue wool that Leah had knitted.

It was her father's body, bruised and lifeless, covered in mud and horse excrement. One horseman gained possession of his limbless body, dragging it to a pile of stones on the side of the field, and with a triumphant cheer that seemed to tear a hole in the sky, he claimed victory. The game was won.

Leah had no time to fall to the ground and be sick. No time to bury her head in her hands and weep for the father who had fed her *plov* and *borekas de handrajo* from his plate, and had given her his blanket on winter nights when the wind whistled through the chinks of their dwelling.

Hear me, O Israel, the Lord is our God, the Lord is one. She'ma Yis'ra'eil Adonai Eloheinu Adonai echad.

A shadow fell over her. The Yürük had caught up. He seized her, pinning her arms to her sides. If she did not manage to wriggle free, he would hurl her to the ground. When he was through, his seed still trickling down her thighs, another man would take his place and another and another.

Have mercy on your daughter, Leah. Steady me in your arms to keep me upright. Send the wind to my back so that I may run swiftly. Pour your strength into me, so that I do not falter. If you shield me from these savages, my voice will grow hoarse so loudly will I praise your Name.

CHAPTER 2

District of Eminönü
Constantinople

WHEN HANNAH heard the clatter of wheels on the cobblestones and the tinkle of harness bells outside her window, unaccustomed sounds in this neighbourhood of people on foot or on horseback, she peered through the shutters. To her astonishment, there was a carriage in front of her house. Throwing the window wide open, she leaned out.

It was not the Imperial Harem's best carriage, nor its worst. Yes, the Sultan Murat III's *tughra*, the intricate calligraphy of his name, was painted on the carriage door in gold. Yes, the bay mare wore ostrich plumes on her head. Yes, her martingale, the chain draping the beast from breastplate to noseband to prevent her from tossing up her head, was finely crafted, but it was made of silver not gold and the mare was past her prime, spavined, and a single animal, not one of a matched pair. No liveried driver sat up top in the narrow seat of the landau, just grizzly old Suat, a slave from Circassia, his mouth as usual pressed into a scowl, his lips a slit of disapproval. His turban was askew and finger-marked from the constant readjustments required while lumbering through uneven streets. He slumped in his seat, reins slack on the horse's rump. Many times, in her still clumsy Osmanlica, the language of the Empire that she had learned from her neighbours, Hannah had tried without success to coax a smile from Suat's toothless mouth.

Even with the carriage at a standstill, the bells jingled in rhythm with the mare's heaving sides. They were intended to warn everyone on the street that an Imperial carriage approached and all within hearing distance must scuttle away lest they glimpse a woman from the harem. But who except midwives like Hannah or women of the worst sort would be foolhardy enough to venture into the streets after dark? What on earth could be so important as to warrant coming to Hannah's door so late? Not a birth at the Imperial Harem, that much was certain.

Two years ago, shortly after Hannah and Isaac had arrived in Constantinople from Venice, the very same carriage had come to her door to take her to the Imperial Harem for the confinement of Safiye, the Sultan's beloved wife with whom he had been besotted since he had first set eyes on her many years ago. Some said she had bewitched him. How astonished Hannah had been that night to hear the carriage come to a halt in front of their house, a dwelling far grander than anything they could have afforded in Venice. In Venice, they had lived in a cramped one-room flat hidden behind the heavy wooden gates of the ghetto.

Her Constantinople neighbours had peered curiously from behind their latticed balconies as Hannah rattled off in the carriage that night.

She had not been prepared for the sight of the Imperial Harem—the black eunuchs, the vast rooms, the brilliant blue and white Iznik tiles, the swooping roofs of the pavilions, the delicate sherbet made with snow packed in burlap and then transported by cart from Mount Olympus, several hundred kilometres away.

Only the blood and the screams of the birthing mother had been familiar. Poor Safiye had laboured valiantly but her travail ended in disappointment. How had Hannah—a Jewess, a foreigner, a newcomer to the city, a fugitive from Venice—come to the attention of the palace? She had her friend, Ezster Mandali, to thank. Ezster, a Sephardic Jew, a pedlar to the harem and confidante to the Valide, had recommended Hannah's skills to the Sultan's revered mother. Someday, may God be listening, the palace would buy silk tents from her husband Isaac's workshop. Naturally, the palace had several midwives already—capable country women with placid smiles who steadied mothers on the birthing stool and allowed Allah's hand to do the rest. This was not Hannah's way. Hannah relied on herbs, used different instruments, and asked questions of those with more experience than she possessed. She gave courage to the faint of heart, poured strength into the weak, and gave hope to the discouraged.

When Hannah had alighted from the carriage the night of Safiye's confinement at the Imperial Palace, a fleet-footed slave girl from Aleppo grabbed her hand at the entrance to the harem and together they raced through the gardens, past the Valide's private hamam, the steam baths, until they reached the Sultana's birthing kiosk, specially prepared for the event. It was draped with panels of embroidered silk set with rubies, emeralds and pearls, depicting harmonious scenes of the heavenly gardens of paradise. The quilts and bedcovers were red. Suspended over the divan hung an embroidered bag which Hannah knew contained the Qur'an. At the foot of the divan was an onion stuffed with garlic and impaled on a gold skewer. This was to ward off the Evil Eye. The gold washing bowls, porcelain ewers, and other utensils rested on low lacquered tables. A variety of sweetmeats and sherbets were arranged on thin grey-green celadon dishes. Hannah later learned the Sultan and his family all ate from such dishes as a precaution. The glaze of the tableware turned black upon contact with poison.

Hannah should have felt awed by the splendour of the pavilion, the ceiling supported by marble colonnades, the floors of cedar and sandalwood giving off the most delicious fragrance, the gossamer textiles, the richly dressed attendants, slaves and concubines, but all she could think was how grateful she was to have her birthing spoons, the silver forceps that had helped her liberate many an obstinate baby from its mother's womb.

Several women surrounded the Sultan's wife, Safiye, as she laboured on her birthing stool, all of them trying their best to relax her by rubbing her back and her hands, by holding golden beakers of lemon water to her lips. But the space at Safiye's right was empty. Her mother-in-law, the Valide, was conspicuous in her absence. It was a known fact that the two women had no affection for each other. Idle tongues speculated on the reasons why.

Hannah went to the basin of hot water in the corner and washed her hands. She wrung out the cloth the slave girl handed her, moved through the other women surrounding the Sultana, and took the open space to Safiye's right. She wiped the woman's forehead. The Sultana grasped the arms of the horseshoe-shaped birthing stool while the usual palace midwife, a stout woman from Amasia, cried out three times without conviction, "*Allah Akbar*"—God is most great.

Hannah nodded to the midwife, who took her cue and retreated to a corner of the kiosk.

Safiye was mad with pain, her eyes rolled back in her head. A young odalisque stood by helplessly, patting her hand. Hannah noted with approval that the birthing stool was fashioned of walnut, the sturdiest and luckiest of woods. The odalisque caught Hannah's eye and gave a small shake of her head. It told Hannah what she needed to know: the Sultana's travail had been long and unproductive.

In Constantinople, birthing was always a social occasion. All the women of the harem, from the most beautiful concubines to the lowest slave girls, were present in the room. Surrounding them were storytellers, eunuch dwarfs, jesters, jugglers and musicians. That night an astrologer sat off to the side, studying his chart. To Hannah's annoyance, he muttered, "Not an auspicious time to be born."

Crouched on a rush mat in the corner was an old woman performing a lead pouring. As the molten lead sizzled in her pot, the crone gave a toothless grimace and shrugged, indicating that the lead had hardened not into bright, clean shapes, which would have been a good portent, but into misshapen, twisted forms. Hannah was grateful that Safiye was in the midst of a birth pang and not aware of the ill omens surrounding her.

A dwarf dressed in a red turban and green kaftan approached Hannah and pulled a silver coin from behind her ear.

"Please," said Hannah, "let us all stand back and give Her Excellency some air." She turned to an old woman with a long nose like those from the town of Sinope on the Black Sea. Hannah knew she had been the Sultan's wet-nurse years ago, and asked, "How far apart are the pangs?"

"Since the last call to prayer, two minutes apart. We have tried everything. The child has no way to come out. The *djinns* have sewn her womb closed." *Djinns* were the tiny demons that tormented and interfered in every event, causing endless misfortune.

"Shush," said Hannah, hoping the wet-nurse was mistaken.

"A mother's mind is easily discouraged by the words overheard during her travail." She felt a surge of protective affection for Safiye. If this crowd of onlookers could not be optimistic, could they not depart and allow Hannah to get on with the task of saving this stubborn baby?

Safiye had more to worry about than simply birthing this child. Her only son, Mehmet, aged fifteen, was delirious with typhus and might not live to hear the call for morning prayers. If there ever was a time when the Empire required a male heir, it was now. Hannah stood for a moment studying the contorted face of the woman writhing on the stool. It was a lovely face but not a Venetian one. Long black hair, blue eyes, a rarity in this world of dark eyes and flat, high cheekbones. Rumour was that she was from Rumelia and had been brought to the palace when she was twelve.

Many busybodies thought Safiye overly interested in affairs of the state and other matters of no concern to women. Some feared the Sultan relied too much on his wife for advice. Whatever the truth of it, she would not be eavesdropping at the grilled window of the Privy Council, listening to state secrets, anytime soon. If Safiye survived, this birth would weaken her for months to come.

Kübra, a slave girl dressed in a plain blue kaftan with a long braid down her back, approached Hannah and said loudly, "Safiye must scream more softly. The Valide is trying to pray and finds the noise unsettling."

Hannah opened her mouth to protest, but the girl, bending low as if to readjust her belt, said in a whisper only Hannah could hear, "The Valide wishes me to convey her thanks for your assistance last month in a certain matter." The girl cast a sympathetic look at Safiye and walked off in the direction of her mistress's private quarters. Hannah was touched by the Valide's message, but tried to put the embarrassing event out of her mind and concentrate on Safiye.

The dwarf, swaying from side to side, turned clumsy cartwheels around Safiye. He bobbed up behind her birthing stool and then performed a somersault, as though fired from a cannon. How anyone could imagine that a woman in labour would enjoy all of this noise and confusion, Hannah could not comprehend. At home in Venice, the birth room was a hushed, secluded space, with only a midwife and perhaps the labouring woman's mother and mother-in-law. Here the entire harem believed a mother's suffering was cause for celebration. Perhaps if the confinement was an easy one such antics would comfort and divert the labouring mother, but when a labour was difficult, it could only make matters worse. And suppose in the end, there was no reason to rejoice? Suppose the confinement concluded with a dead mother or a dead baby? Or both? A crowd would only amplify the sorrow.

Hannah motioned to a nearby musician playing a stringed instrument. "Play something soft and soothing. Her Excellency is tired. Help her to relax between her pangs."

Hannah rubbed almond oil on her hands and bent her head close to Safiye's ear. "I am Hannah. I have come to cajole this baby out of you."

The Sultana tried to smile but her lips quivered. "I am in so much pain. Is there something you can give me?"

Hannah took Safiye's hand. Opium would deaden the

pain but it would also weaken the birth contractions, and this child had already dawdled in the birth passage too long. "Let us first see what can be done without opium. The poppy sometimes slows the baby's breathing."

"In that case, I will manage."

"Brave and wise," said Hannah as she squatted in front of the birthing stool. She waited for a pang to pass and then felt Safiye's abdomen, moving her hands up and down and around. The child's head was in a good position. A steady pull from the birthing spoons might ease it down farther. Hannah pressed her ear to Safiye's belly. The baby's heartbeat was slow and faint.

Hannah loosened the drawstring of her linen bag and took out her birthing spoons, which had been fashioned in Venice by a silversmith. They resembled two soup spoons with shallow bowls and gently curved handles, fastened together in the middle by a removable pin. Hannah blew on them for luck and cradled them in her hands to warm them. Her reflection in the spoons showed a drawn, white face with large black eyes, surrounded by a cloud of dark hair. She recited the prayer she always murmured at such times: "If it pleases God, may I do no harm." Then she said softly to Safiye, "The birthing spoons are of no use if you are sitting upright. I know it is not the custom to give birth in a prone position, but if you lie down I can reach inside you and grasp the baby's head."

When Safiye nodded weakly, Hannah motioned two slaves to help the Sultana onto the divan and settle her into a reclining position.

Safiye's eyes widened when she saw Hannah's birthing spoons. "You plan to use those?"

"Do not be frightened. I have done this many times before."

The jugglers ceased tossing balls; the astrologer looked up from his charts; the dwarf's gymnastics came to an abrupt halt. Everyone was staring at Hannah as though she were a magician.

Hannah announced, "This is an instrument to help ease the child into the world. You will see."

A look passed between Hannah and Safiye.

The Sultana nodded. "If it will help my son."

All labouring women wished for a son. None had more need of one than Safiye. Hannah unhinged the spoons and worked first one and then the other into Safiye's passage until Hannah could feel them slipping into position, the baby's temples cupped in the shallow bowls of the spoons.

"Now, push."

Safiye gave a grunt and tried her best.

Hannah gently compressed the spoons and as the womb contracted, she pulled. The baby's head emerged. Hannah felt a wave of relief. The Sultan was a small man, built low to the earth, with a large head and broad shoulders. If his baby shared these traits, it would not bode well for his wife's confinement.

At the next contraction the shoulders should have slipped out, then the rest of the tiny body. But that did not happen. There were two more pangs accompanied by much pushing and groaning, yet the shoulders would not emerge.

Hannah said, "Do not lose courage. You and I are working together and with God's help will get this child born."

The Sultana groaned in reply.

Not for the first time, Hannah was struck by the absurdity of a fully formed baby trying to pass through such a tiny orifice. It was a blasphemous notion, which many might construe as a criticism of God's design. "Take a deep breath. Rest while you can. Your pangs are good and strong. It will not be long now."

"I am trying," said the Sultana.

"I know you are——"

Just then, Safiye screamed and arched her back, her hands clutching at her breast.

A babe could suffocate if it lingered too long in the passage. Hannah did not waste time listening for a heartbeat. She withdrew her birthing spoons and reached her hands into the passage, thanking God for her small fingers. One tiny shoulder was caught fast on the sharing bones, the girdle that held the pelvis together. *May it signify a healthy, broad-shouldered boy*, Hannah prayed. A lusty heir was all that was lacking in this palace of sloe-eyed, heavy-lidded, voluptuous beauties, but the child was jammed inside its mother like a chimney sweep caught in a chimney pot atop one of the grand palaces in Venice.

"Another moment and we will have your baby out, *cara*." Hannah should not have addressed the Sultana with such familiarity, but the endearment came involuntarily to her lips.

She rotated the head and compressed the infant's shoulders to draw it out. Newborns were always malleable, their little bodies as soft as warm wax. A moment later, she felt rather than heard the burst of noise, like the small explosion of a cork withdrawn from a wine jug. The child had been so compressed that its shoulder had come loose of its moorings. The small bone of the upper arm had slipped from its socket. The baby slithered out, screaming. Hannah held it tucked under one arm and studied its angry red face. Poor mite. The shoulder joint was an angry red knob. No wonder the infant wailed so.

Perhaps a shoulder dislocation was not an unusual problem, but it was Hannah's first experience with it. There must be something she could quickly do to persuade the shoulder back into place. She searched her memory for advice from other midwives.

Safiye clenched so hard at the folds of Hannah's skirts that her knuckles were white. "Please help my baby," she whispered.

The musicians played more loudly, shaking their tambourines and beating their drums to camouflage the child's screams. If they would only cease their terrible racket, maybe a solution would occur to her. The baby was in agony, the tiny red face a mask of pain. To do anything would be better than to do nothing. She must act.

Hannah set the baby down on a cushion. The child was slippery with blood and mucus and the white waxy substance that covers all newborns. Covering her hand with a cloth, Hannah grasped the baby's upper arm and rotated it until she heard a soft popping noise. This noise, coupled with the child's screams, made Hannah's ears ring and her body grow hot and then cold. She swallowed, wishing for a breeze off the Bosporus to penetrate this pavilion, which had grown stuffy with the aloes burning in a gold censer and the breathing of too many people and the crackling and spitting of hymeneal torches. So much pain, so much blood. But the child was no longer crying.

Safiye lay with her eyes closed, sweat dripping down her face. "A healthy child?" she asked.

"A happy outcome. You are blessed." Hannah held the baby up to face the crowd, clutching its slippery body firmly under the arms. All eyes were fixed on the newborn.

The band fell silent, tambourines on the floor, drums abandoned. The fiddlers stood with their horsehair bows hanging at their sides. A number of the women of the harem withdrew handkerchiefs from the long folds of their tunic sleeves and began to cry quietly. Everyone was exhausted and relieved. No one dared to praise the beauty or vigour of the child for fear of attracting the Evil Eye.

Hannah laid the baby down on a cushion and rubbed it with a cloth, watching the little chest rise and fall. Finally, the diviner murmured, "Ugly little thing." There were a few grunts of assent, then a silence so profound that Hannah could hear the gibbering of the monkeys from the menagerie far away in the Third Courtyard.

The only other sound was the infant, breathing noisily, its tiny pink body still filled with birth fluids. Hannah withdrew her iron knife from her linen bag, preparing to cut the birth cord. Then she realized her error and put the knife down. The Sultan must perform this ritual. He would name the boy. He would face Mecca, his son raised in his arms, and he would recite the Call to Prayer and the Declaration of Faith. Hannah signalled to Mustafa, the Chief Black Eunuch, who had just entered the pavilion and now approached the Sultana's divan.

"Would you advise the Sultan of the birth of his s—"

Hannah's request was cut short by Mustafa's hand on her arm. He pursed his lips and shook his head, glancing at the infant. Hannah followed his gaze. For the first time she saw what she had been too busy to notice before but what had been appallingly obvious to everyone else in the room—the swollen lips of female genitalia.

There was no need for the Sultan's attendance. No need to announce the royal birth by firing off the cannons outside the Walls of Justinian. No need to do anything, except to bathe the little princess and nurture her until she was of an age to make a good marriage. Raising a girl, as the old proverb went, was "like planting a fig tree in the neighbours' garden."

Hannah cut the cord and then handed the child to the young wet-nurse. The girl carried the child to a golden basin filled with warm, fragrant water and gently washed her. Then the wet-nurse placed three sesame seeds on the infant's navel for good luck. She swaddled the child and wrapped her in a blanket. She tied a blue-beaded amulet to the baby's shoulder over the spot that had caused such anguish. Someone placed a bottle of sherbet with a piece of red gauze tied over the top next to Safiye. Had it been wound around the bottle's neck, it would have signified the birth of a boy. A braid of garlic was hung over the golden cradle to keep away the Evil Eye.

One more thing had to be done. Hannah turned to the exhausted mother on her divan. "Try to stand up so the birth cake will come free."

Two slave girls helped the Sultana to rise. An attendant handed Hannah a bowl, which she placed between Safiye's legs, and the birth cake fell into it with a gratifying plop. How messy this part was and yet how necessary. The cake must be complete. If it was torn or disintegrated, it meant segments left behind in the womb. Hannah flipped over the contents of the basin with a pair of ivory tongs an attendant handed her, feeling ridiculously like a soothsayer studying entrails for omens.

"Good. We have it all out."

The slave girls lowered Safiye back onto the divan.

When she was comfortably settled, Safiye reached for the baby and clasped her to her breast. Hannah smiled at the sight of the two of them, Safiye tearful and happy, oblivious to everyone's disappointment that the child was female. The baby was pink as rose-water sherbet and breathing strongly now. A slave girl removed the soiled linen from the divan and brought in fresh towels scented with sandalwood with which to bathe Safiye.

The Sultana was exhausted, every movement an effort, and barely able to cradle her tiny infant.

Hannah said, "Shall I bind you now or would you prefer to wait?" In accordance with custom, the wet-nurse would suckle the child for two or three years. To prevent the

Sultana's milk from coming in, Hannah must wrap strips of linen tightly around Safiye's breasts. It would be painful for a few days, but then her milk would cease.

"I prefer to wait. You have earned my mother-in-law's gratitude as well as mine," Safiye murmured, her eyes never leaving the baby's face.

So she had heard Kübra's whispered thanks from the Valide. Even in the midst of her travail, Safiye was attuned to the actions of the woman who held the power of life and death over every woman in the harem.

Hannah knelt next to Safiye and whispered in her ear, "You have a lovely princess. Next year I will deliver you a little prince. I am certain of it."

"I am happy with my daughter. I shall name her Ayşe. I shall have the pleasure of her company all of my life. Whereas a son? Who knows what might happen?"

Hannah said, "It is a wise woman who is content to receive what God has bestowed upon her." The Sultana was referring to the cruel custom of fratricide, which had been the practice of the Imperial House of Osman for a hundred and fifty years. When her son, Mehmet, if he survived, took the throne from his father, he would be obliged to have any younger brothers and half-brothers strangled to prevent a war of succession. It was a custom that appalled Hannah.

She replaced her birthing spoons, her cloths, her herbs and potions and salves in her linen bag and rinsed Safiye's blood from her hands. The baby was dozing in her wet-nurse's arm. In a short time, little Ayşe would be nursing contentedly.

In forty days there would be a celebration in the hamam. Hannah would be invited to attend because she had delivered Ayşe. A duck's egg would be broken into a bowl and rubbed onto the baby's skin to accustom her to water and keep her safe from drowning.

And yet, far more serious dangers than drowning faced the princess and, indeed, everyone in the realm as Hannah and every subject in the realm knew. The great Ottoman Empire was in as much peril as if an enemy army were camped outside the walls of the city. The Empire, the mightiest the world had ever seen, stretched from Budapest on the Danube River to Aswan on the Nile and from the Euphrates almost to Gibraltar. It included the Balkan Peninsula, Transylvania, Moldavia, and Wallachia. It encompassed the Black Sea to the east and the Red Sea, and the Persian Gulf to the south. Fifty million souls, freeborn and slave—Muslim, Jews, and Christians—lived within its realm, but without a healthy male heir, there would be civil war. The enemies of the Empire—most of Christendom, including Habsburg Naples and Sicily, and even the Muslim neighbour to the south, Persia—would tear it from gullet to groin like wolves bringing down a stag.

Two years had elapsed since that memorable night, the birth of the Sultana's princess. Mehmet had recovered from typhus but he remained sickly. His circumcision had been postponed many times because of frequent bouts of ill health. The Sultan continued to rule, though he rarely left the palace and seemed content to leave the affairs of state in the capable hands of his mother. And worst of all, the Empire remained in a perilous state.

For two long years, there had been no births, no pregnancies, no stillbirths, not even a royal miscarriage. Safiye had failed to bear a son. The Sultan had failed to sire another heir, whether by Safiye or any of the harem girls. The Grand Vizier Mehmet Sokollu, was not happy. Mustafa, the Chief Black Eunuch, was not happy. The Valide was not happy.

Only Safiye with her precious two-year-old daughter Ayşe, whom she petted and spoiled like a doll, was happy.

Hannah's beloved husband, Isaac, came up behind her and wrapped his arms around her waist. Together they looked from the window of their home into the street below where the little mare snorted and stirred restlessly in her traces outside the front door. Theirs was a district of twisting streets, a neighbourhood of foreigners— Armenians, Greeks, Jews, Circassians—any number of people from remote corners of the Empire.

Isaac rested his chin on her shoulder. "Do you have to go out so late?" he asked, knowing she had no choice when the Imperial Palace called.

"Whatever tonight's crisis, it is not a birth," Hannah said. "I will stay up until you arrive home safely."

"Please, go to bed. You need to rise early tomorrow."

Hannah's friend Ezster had confided behind a cupped hand one afternoon in the *mikvah* why there had been no more harem pregnancies and why it was unlikely that there would be any in future. The Sultan could not perform with anyone other than Safiye. It was believed the Sultana had placed so powerful a curse on his genitals that he was useless with other girls. If Ezster was correct, then God Himself was powerless to set matters right.

But if Hannah was not being summoned for a birth, then what was she summoned for? An odalisque, a royal concubine, suffering from a difficult menses that Hannah could treat with hot compresses and a tisane of camomile? Or perhaps Safiye required an elixir to aid in conception? No, something more serious. Was it a repetition of the Valide's embarrassing difficulty?

Prepared for any eventuality, Hannah tucked into her linen bag an assortment of herbs, and, just in case, her birthing spoons. Almost as an afterthought, she packed a fresh peach, newly picked from her garden. From a few streets away, she heard the thud of the watchman's metal-tipped staff on cobblestones as he made his rounds, admonishing those without serious business to return to their homes before he locked the city gates.

Isaac watched his wife packing. "I am so proud of you, Hannah. I know life in Constantinople is difficult for you and yet you make the best of it, even earning the trust of the palace. Imagine! You are so valued that the Valide herself calls you out in the middle of the night . . . although I wish she would restrict herself to daylight hours."

"The Valide does not value me half so much as I value you, Isaac. Without you, this transition in our lives would have been impossible," she said. Although Hannah spoke calmly so as not to alarm Isaac, she was worried. No one, especially women, travelled the streets at night if they could help it. It must be a dire emergency to justify the appearance of the carriage at her gate.

He smiled and kissed her.

Hannah and Isaac went downstairs and stood in the street, waiting for Suat to dismount and open the carriage door. The stars hung so low it seemed as though they had been hurled into the heavens by an unseen hand.

Hannah looked back at their house and spacious grounds. They had bought the property from a prosperous arrowsmith whose workshop had handily converted into a workspace for looms, trays for mating moths, drying cocoons, and all the paraphernalia of silk-making, including an orchard of mulberry trees in the back. The purchase came with a parrot, Güzel, which Hannah could hear screeching even from a block away. Soon after they took possession of the house, it became apparent why the arrowsmith's wife had left the creature behind. This beautiful bird from Afrika, with lustrous grey plumage and a tail of vivid red, knew no greater pleasure than to lure an unsuspecting person to its perch. Then it would stretch out its scrawny neck waiting for a caress. As soon as a finger appeared, the bird would slash with its black beak, leaving behind a bleeding cuticle or punctured thumbnail. The creature would then fill the house with shrill, human-like cackling while it squatted on its perch, shifting its weight from one scaly leg to the other.

Isaac turned Hannah toward him and straightened her veil. As a Jewess, she was not required by law to wear a veil, but at certain times it suited her to pass for Muslim. Now, she wanted to avoid the attention of roving gangs of Gypsies only too happy to gawk at the Imperial landau and the woman inside. She wore a silk dress and pearl earrings. The silk was from their workshop, of course, spun from their own worms, woven by Isaac on their loom. The cloth had been dyed in a vat of madder and oak kermes and turmeric to give it a reddish hue.

Suat held open the carriage door. Hannah gathered her skirts, and Isaac handed her into the compartment and closed the door behind her. He leaned up through the carriage window to kiss her goodbye, patting the velvet pouch around her neck, adjusting it so it nestled next to her skin. Isaac wore a matching pouch. Even Matteo, their son, wore such a pouch. Without the constant warmth of their bodies, the silk eggs would fail to hatch and provide a new crop of pupae for the next mothing season.

Isaac smelled of lemons. He regularly rubbed lemon juice on his hands to remove dye used for the silk. In the light from the pine-pitch torch, his eyes shone.

"Good night, my darling," he said. "All will be well. Administer a poultice, mix up an herbal decoction, place your cool hand on an anxious forehead, and soon you will be back."

Isaac's optimism usually steadied her, but now, when all the signs pointed to an urgent situation—the time of night, the closed carriage, the impatient way Suat was glancing from the mare to their house and back again—it made her nervous.

Constantinople had been the start of a new life for her and Isaac. They had used the ducats Hannah had brought from Venice to purchase their ample house. Jews were permitted to buy property in the city. Even more startling, Ottoman law permitted married women to own their own property. Hannah had not imagined such a thing was possible.

"Give Matteo a kiss for me," she said.

A feeling of peace came over her as she thought of Matteo, her three-year-old son. Early this morning through half-closed eyes, she had seen him at the doorway of their bedroom, trailing his blanket. She pretended to be asleep. He folded himself over on all fours, head down, knees pressed together. Then he rabbit-hopped to their bed. Without saying a word, he squeezed himself between her and Isaac and pulled the covers over all of them. She hated to leave knowing that he would likely wake in the morning calling for her, but what was she to do? Hannah could not possibly refuse a summons from the Imperial Harem.

Before she had a chance to blow Isaac a kiss, as was their custom on parting, Suat clucked to the mare and they were off. Hannah was flung back, hitting her head on the roof of the carriage as they lurched into the narrow cobblestone street.

Later that night, when she returned from the palace, she would recall the look on Isaac's handsome face as she was leaving. She would wonder if they ever again would enjoy the intimate conviviality and the gentle jesting that had always typified their marriage before that night. The events at the palace were about to change everything.

CHAPTER 3

Constantinople

H ANNAH SETTLED back on the cushioned seat for the long, jarring ride to the palace, the residence of the Sultan and his family, as well as the administrative centre of the entire Empire. Once they were out of her neighbourhood, she ripped off her veil, which always made her feel like a baby born with a caul over its face. They rumbled past the *Misir Çarşisi*, the Egyptian spice market, a low structure shaped like the letter T. During the day, the smell of garlic, peppercorns, frankincense, and saffron emanated from the building. It was here that Hannah purchased remedies for every malady, even gunpowder to cure haemorrhoids.

Such a still night would be populated by *djinns*—those fiery, evil creatures whose chief delights were dumping slop buckets on people's heads from upper-storey windows, snatching turbans off dignified pashas during public ceremonies, and stealing babies out of their mothers' arms and hurling them onto hard tiled floors.

The district of Eminönü was silent now—no familiar wheeze of the blacksmith's bellows, no raucous clanging of hammers on metal, no insistent cries from fishwives and butchers, no calls from the porters at the dock loading and unloading the ships. The only sounds were the squeaks of the mare's harness and her hooves clattering on the cobblestones.

When they reached the street of the felt-makers, the throb of a drum interrupted the silence. The guards were locking the old Roman Gate of Septimius Severus at the confluence of the Golden Horn and the Bosporus. Among the refuse heaps lining the alleys, Hannah could just make out the scurrying feral cats. From roofs and treetops came the caterwauling of the felines that prowled the city chasing rats at night. Hannah hated the scrawny, diseased creatures, but she hated the alternative of a city swarming with vermin even more.

She pressed a handkerchief across her nose and mouth against the stench. She could have been blind and still able to tell from the odour of sheep's urine used to tan hides that they were now on the Street of the Tanners. The tanners were a wretched group of artisans who defiled the quarter by pouring their filthy water into the open sewers.

They should have put it in barrels and disposed of it outside the city walls as ordered by the authorities, but few of them ever went to the trouble.

When the carriage reached the district of Sirkeci, the street grew so narrow—it was no more than an alley—that neither the moonlight nor Suat's torch could penetrate the darkness. Suat, who exhibited a propensity for driving too fast on the winding streets to demonstrate he was accustomed only to the wide boulevards of Seraglio Point, was forced to slow down. The horse stumbled and then refused to budge despite the crack of the whip on her back and Suat's urging. Grumbling, Suat climbed down from his seat and, one hand on the horse's bridle, the other flat-palmed on the rough stone walls, moved forward, feeling his way along the narrow street. After several minutes of slow progress, they neared the water. Breezes from the sea greeted them as they swept along the south shore of the Horn. It had been about an hour since Hannah had climbed into the carriage and still the giant fortress of the Imperial Palace loomed in the distance, high on a hillside overlooking the Bosporus.

As they neared the port, Hannah heard the squeak of ropes on restless boats and the drunken shouts of sailors. At the harbour, the smell of the salt-ladened sea air and fish from the markets filled her nostrils. A few moments later, they drew nearer to Seraglio Point, which jutted like a rhinoceros horn into the Bosporus. The Sea of Marmara lay to the south and the Golden Horn to the north. Only as they approached the palace, set high on the bluff, did the air turn sweet and fresh.

On the right they passed the Hagia Sophia mosque. To Hannah's left, moonlight cast a silvery wash over the high palace walls. The Sublime Porte, the main entry into the palace, with its twin turrets and gatekeepers' quarters of large octagonal towers with pointed roofs on either side came into view, rearing up like a creature rising from the sea. The carriage passed through the Gate of Salutation, entered the First Courtyard, the wheels gliding on the marble paving. Hannah replaced her veil.

During the day, this central courtyard of the palace was open to all the Sultan's subjects. It seethed with crowds of people seeking redress for grievances. Several hundred agitated Ottomans usually surrounded the pavilions while busy scribes wrote out their complaints. Empty now, the vast space echoed with the clatter of the mare's hooves. Five heads were displayed on spikes on either side of the Gate, a warning to all who passed of the Sultan's absolute power and the consequences of not yielding to it. The heads were stuffed with cotton if the executed man had been high-born or with straw if he had been of low station. The carriage passed numerous armouries, the buildings of the Imperial Mint, and stables housing three thousand horses.

Hannah averted her eyes from the Fountain of the Executioner, where the executioner washed the blood from his hands after beheadings. At the entrance to the harem, the carriage finally halted. Craning her neck, Hannah could see a gigantic, formless shadow against the white and blue Iznik wall. To her surprise, as her eyes adjusted she recognized Mustafa himself waiting for her rather than one of his minions. Mustafa, the Chief Black Eunuch, the guardian of the harem, wore a black sash, black tunic, and a towering black turban with a gold quill on top. A girdle of diamonds encircled his hips as befit one of the richest men in the palace. Only the Sultan and the Grand Vizier were more powerful than Mustafa.

Though she had met him many times, his inky blackness continued to astound her. She had not encountered Nubians in Venice and she could not help but study the man every time she saw him. How was it possible for skin to be so dark? Had Mustafa been standing in front of a black basalt wall, she would not have seen him. Hannah had been frightened of him the first time she met him, but had come to admire his brilliant eyes, satiny skin, and gentle nature.

Mustafa was a master of self-control. Only his occasional gruffness and his halting steps revealed that he was frequently in pain. For the Arab slavers to remove what God had intended a man to have was an appalling crime. Perhaps he still had the desires of a man, yet there had never been a whisper of scandal about him regarding the girls of the harem. To Hannah it seemed as though his joy came from his chest of jewels and his political power. There were those who claimed he owned a magnificent *yali*, an estate on one of the Princes' Islands, with a huge house overlooking the Sea of Marmara, where he retreated when the pain rendered him unfit for human companionship. It was the kind of story one hears in the harem, a place where idleness and boredom incite tongues to wag.

Mustafa approached the carriage and bowed his head low, the golden quill in his turban glinting in the shadow of the Gate of Salutation. As always when Hannah noticed the quill and thought of its purpose, she did not know whether to wince or to blush.

She stood as Suat dismounted from the driver's seat, opened the carriage door, and placed a small set of steps in front of the carriage. She held out her hand to Mustafa, who took it in his plump one. It was scented with attar of rose. His skin was as soft as a girl's. He steadied her, helping her to alight. As she bent toward him, her velvet pouch swung forward and grazed his chest. Mustafa also wore a velvet pouch around his neck. While hers contained silkworm eggs, his, it was rumoured, contained that shrivelled part of his body that had been taken from him as a young boy, a part he kept with him at all times so that when he died, he could be buried whole.

She released Mustafa's hand once her feet touched the marble paving stones. Was it right that Hannah permitted Mustafa to touch her? It was a riddle she had not solved. Jewish law was strict: unrelated men and women were forbidden from having physical contact. Did the law include someone like Mustafa, not entirely a man, yet certainly not a woman? His voice was high, his torso thick, his hips almost womanly. His hand was warm and comforting in hers. Whether right or wrong, Hannah had not the heart to avoid contact.

Mustafa smiled, his lips as fleshy and pink as a conch shell, his generous cheeks creasing, flashing teeth as white as the Chinese porcelain in the new palace kitchens. Was his smile heart-felt? He beckoned her to follow him into the Imperial Harem.

Hannah was naive, as Isaac had told her often enough. She was no wiser than a child when it came to the politics of the palace—a place of conspiracy, intrigue, sudden deaths, disappearances, and poisonings. Not a dish of food passed the Sultan's lips without the Chief Taster trying it first. People in the palace whom Hannah met and laughed with one day were gone without a trace the next time she inquired.

As they walked, Mustafa's shadow leapt against the tiled walls like a puppet in Karagöz, the popular marionette theatre. His shadow appeared more graceful and lively than he did, swaying on his pattens, high shoes designed to be worn in the steam baths. Clearly, she was not here to prepare a girl for a couching. Mustafa was not carrying his red volume, *The Book of Couchings*, in which he recorded all of the Sultan's trysts.

Mustafa asked, "How is the best midwife in Constantinople tonight?"

"You mean the best in the entire Empire?" They always bantered like this.

"You are right. I stand corrected."

"I am very well, thank you," she said, wishing he would hurry up and tell her why he had sent for her.

They made their way past the gardens, with their beds of tulips with names like Glitter of Prosperity, Beloved's Face, Rose Arrow, and Increaser of Joy. In truth, she disliked these

Ottoman tulips with their etiolated petals, which looked as though they had been trimmed to dagger points. How much lovelier the rounded, chalice-shaped tulips of Venice, their glossy pink petals as inviting as the palm of a baby's hand.

Hannah's penchant for all things Venetian, nay, her aversion to all things Turkish, was a characteristic against which she struggled. The tulips were a perfect example of what Isaac referred to as her "failure to appreciate the splendours of the Ottoman Empire."

They walked past the menagerie of elephants, tigers, and monkeys. The odour of what the jungles of Afrika must smell like pervaded the gardens, a musk-heavy but not unpleasant smell, disguised in part by the spicy scent of carnations and fresh white bread baking in the ovens nearby. Night air was known to be unhealthy but Hannah took a mouthful anyway, enjoying the coolness. On the other side of the menagerie, Hannah saw a familiar sight. The spider monkeys awoke inside their gilded cages, shrieking and rubbing their genitals in that disgusting way of theirs, then spitting like the wizened old carpet sellers in the bazaar. Hannah would have giggled had she not been so preoccupied.

There is no need to worry, she told herself. The worst that had ever befallen her in the palace was a nibble from the giraffe in the menagerie. The creature had an unsettling habit of arcing its long neck and reaching over to nuzzle her, which made her want to bathe. The first time it had occurred, she jumped and gave a scream, not out of fear—there was little about the gentle beast to frighten her—but out of surprise at the touch of its flabby, prehensile lips. Now, instinctively, she made a wide circle around its low enclosure.

A careless worker had left a pile of bricks in the path and Mustafa took her arm to guide her. "Building, always building," he said. "This time it is ten new kitchens with lead-domed roofs to replace those destroyed by fire last year. The ovens will be large enough to roast an entire herd of oxen."

Hannah said, "A sultan never dies when he is building." She had heard the expression often and decided to try it out herself.

Mustafa paused for a moment and turned to look at her. Had she offended him by referring, however obliquely, to the Sultan's death? Mustafa's face revealed nothing. This was the way of Ottomans. Venetians were direct and never shrank from telling you what they thought about family, religion, and politics. Ottomans, especially around foreigners like Hannah, kept their own counsel.

"How many people live in the Imperial Palace?" Hannah hoped it was not a rude question.

"Five thousand, from the Sultan to the lowliest pot scrubber in the scullery to the odalisques to the Valide herself. All must be fed." Odalisques were taught to play instruments, to embroider, to sing and dance, to learn the erotic arts—all in the hope of one day becoming concubines for the Sultan. They were lovely girls, some purchased at the slave market near the Hippodrome, some sent as gifts for the Sultan from governors of the far-flung provinces of the Empire.

Hannah and Mustafa skirted a small apricot tree where a peacock wearing a gold necklace roosted, crushing the young boughs with its weight. They arrived at the outer entrance to the harem, the Arabalar Kapısı, where beeswax candles flickered in onyx sconces affixed to the high walls.

Hoping to prompt the usually voluble Mustafa to reveal more, Hannah said, "It is late. Suat had difficulty passing through the streets."

Mustafa offered no comment.

Unable to restrain herself, she asked, "It must be an urgent matter for the Valide to call me out at this time of night. A birth, perhaps?"

"Not a birth, unfortunately. I have a different task for you." He stood in front of the Gate of Felicity, the entrance to the harem, making no move to reach for the collection of keys that dangled at his side. "Do not look so apprehensive. You will know what is required. It involves that orifice you are so familiar with."

At last, Mustafa took an ebony key from the chain at his waist. Even then he hesitated, looking as though he were weighing what to say, before speaking. "A new slave girl has arrived," he ventured, as he fitted the key into the lock and gave it a turn. "This girl you are about to meet is the Valide's gift to her son. Leah is—how to put it—rebellious? She is a tough little thing, filthy and evil-tempered. You must excuse her appearance. We have not managed to tame her sufficiently to bathe her or comb the knots from her hair."

This was very odd. The harem had scores of slave girls to wash, scrub and render presentable any new arrivals, even intractable peasants. In any case, most girls from the slave market were only too happy to find themselves in this earthly paradise of marble and gold cloth and jewels and savoury foods. Why would Hannah be called to help with such a matter? They walked through the Gate, passing by the open door of the guard room of the black eunuchs' living quarters where they ate and slept when not on duty guarding the ladies of the harem.

"What is it you wish me to do?" Hannah asked as they walked through the courtyard, the mosque of the black eunuchs on her left.

Mustafa made no reply.

"If she is so difficult, why was she purchased?" As soon as the remark passed her lips, Hannah realized it was not only far too direct but also a criticism of Mustafa, who had no doubt purchased the slave girl on behalf of the Valide. Isaac often cautioned her to be more circumspect in her dealings with those in the harem.

"Meet her," Mustafa said, "and you shall have your answer."

They arrived at the inner gate of the harem, which was framed with a black-and-white stone arch and gold callig-raphy adorned with quotes from the Qur'an. Mustafa's slow gait and the way he nervously felt for the clanging keys on his girdle betrayed his uncharacteristic anxiety. Hannah tried to see past the gate but saw only a yawning maw of blackness. Many slave girls had passed through these portals, but none had left—at least not alive. There were only two ways to depart: in the mourning shroud of the dead, or in a burlap sack snugly tied at the neck and weighted down with river stones, to be hurled into the Bosporus by the palace death squad, the deaf mutes. Just as the eunuchs in the harem had had their private parts cut off, the deaf mutes had been rendered deaf by spikes rammed in their ears and mute by having their tongues cut out. In the dark of the night, these thuggish brutes drew silken cords around tender young throats, thrust their bodies into sacks and tipped them into the waters.

Mustafa's torch sizzled and spit shadows against the walls of the corridor. Trying to see past him was like trying to see past a giant, swaying cart rumbling down a narrow, rutted road. He wobbled in his pattens. They were crafted of inlaid silver and mother-of-pearl. They reminded Hannah of *chopine*, the high, elegant shoes the grand ladies of Venice favoured to keep them elevated from the mud of the streets. Her own feet, in leather slippers turned up at the toes, made a shushing noise on the hard marble, a counterpoint to his staccato clatter.

Mustafa addressed her in a hushed tone. "She will not speak, nor eat. She does nothing but sob and moan and act as though she had arrived in the worst prison in the world instead of heaven on earth." He put a hand out to steady himself against the wall. "You remember Nilia, the Nubian slave girl who works in the baths? This vixen you are about to meet scratched Nilia's face when she tried to bathe her."

There were robust eunuchs to hold the girls for the some-times harsh beauty procedures, or discipline them when they violated one of the many rules of the harem. Why not use one of them? Hannah twisted the velvet pouch around her neck. The ceiling felt lower, the air mustier, and the walls closer. When would Mustafa disclose her task?

Suddenly Mustafa's torch burned out, but he continued walking. His voice seemed to come from far ahead of her. "Before we waste any more time on this girl, I must know for certain whether she is a virgin. Otherwise, I will be only too happy to sell her to the Arab brothel-keeper down by the docks. Let *him* try to civilize her."

Hannah leaned to one side, feeling Mustafa's presence only because of the shift in the air and the sound of his fumbling with the enormous ring of keys. She heard him insert a key into the lock of a small door. She heard the creak of rusty hinges and felt the cold metal of the door as she groped her way in behind him.

Fate has a way of making us accomplices to evil, Hannah thought, while Mustafa struck at a tinderbox and lit a candle in a wall sconce which lent a flickering light. Pinpricks of light drew attention to the golden quill jutting from his turban and the gemstone on his thumb.

I have learned my lesson, Hannah thought. I want no part of whatever cruel scenario is about to unfold. She remembered another night long ago in Venice and what had flowed from her reckless decision to disobey her rabbi and accompany the Conte, her son Matteo's natural father, to his home. She and Isaac were not, in fact, Matteo's real parents, though they kept this a secret from everyone in Constantinople. On that night, the Conte's gondola took her to the palazzo on the Grand Canal where the screams of Matteo's mother greeted her. Hannah had been called to help the Conte's wife give birth. And she had saved both mother and child. Afterwards, there had been nothing but the silent, lonely ride back to the Jewish ghetto.

The events of that night had turned her life to chaos. When the Conte and his wife died of the plague, Hannah rescued the boy from his uncles, who wanted him dead so that he would never inherit his father's estate. From this experience, Hannah had learned that one ill-considered act could propel her on a dangerous course from which there was no escape. She was grateful to have Matteo, of course, whom she and Isaac had adopted as their own. But still, her folly haunted her, and a small voice inside her wondered if tonight, yet again, she was taking a path she might later regret.

The flickering light from the sconces on the wall reflected on Mustafa's skin, oiled with butter as he peered into the small room.

"Where is the girl from?" Hannah asked.

"She comes from some horrid place in the Circassian Mountains. I expect one village is much like the next." Mustafa gave a wave of his plump, ring-covered hand. "The Valide admires these Circassian girls, but some are as wild as the mountains from which they spring. Although I must admit they can be lovely. And this one is as remarkable in her looks as she is in her—what shall we call it—spiritedness?"

His voice was wistful. Perhaps Mustafa still desired the pleasure a woman could give to a man. What torture he must endure to be surrounded by the most beautiful girls in the Ottoman Empire, unable to lay a finger on any of them. She hoped he had a woman he visited from time to time, a woman who knew the secrets of how to pleasure a eunuch.

"Did her family sell her?"

Mustafa had once told her that poor sheepherding families—one could only pity them—often had to sell a child to the slavers who passed through their villages. The droughts had been severe for the past year. As the pastures dried up and turned brown, daughters of the peasantry flowed into the city's slave market.

When Hannah concluded years ago that she could not conceive, she thought of purchasing a young, healthy girl as a servant and then giving her freedom when she came of age, but Isaac would not hear of it. He had been a slave one terrible year on the island of Malta and believed that everything to do with the buying and selling of human flesh was wicked. It did not matter that Hannah would have nurtured the child and freed her from slavery. For Isaac, this was not enough.

"This girl was not sold by her parents. She was captured," said Mustafa. "You know what those marauding Yürüks are like. They would have left nothing behind but the chimney stacks."

Stolen from her family, just as Isaac had been stolen from her. It was not difficult to imagine the dreadful things the girl had been subjected to. Isaac had confided to her so many of the harsh privations of his enslavement. Even now, he sometimes awoke in the night in a pool of sweat, the sheets sticking to his body. Isaac was a grown man and a very strong one. This was a girl, perhaps little more than a child.

Hannah waited, but Mustafa let his comments hang in the air.

"How uncharacteristic of you, Mustafa, to reveal so little. They say you know the details of every girl in the harem. The girls joke that you are so well informed that a mouse cannot poke its twitching nose out of a hole without you knowing the number of whiskers it sports."

"Do not believe everything you hear. I know very little—especially about this girl."

Not even Hannah's attempts at levity, it seemed, would loosen his tongue.

"The Valide will present this girl to the Sultan very soon. Many hopes rest on her. First, however, we must know for certain whether she is intact. The Valide requested you specifically to conduct this examination. It is a great honour, as you know." Ezster had told Hannah that the Valide was keen to find her son, the Sultan, the perfect girl, but dear God, why did Hannah have to be involved?

As Mustafa fumbled for another key from around his waist, Hannah realized why she had been called. Any of the palace midwives had the skill to ascertain whether or not a girl's hymen was whole. But in a palace of intrigue, lying, and double-crossings, the Valide trusted only Hannah to tell her the truth.

"And if she is not a virgin?" Hannah asked.

Mustafa unlocked the door of a small room. "The dock

workers and sailors are not fussy about where they plow and cast their seed. Off to a brothel she will go."

Hannah had seen the pox-ridden, half-starved girls in cages by the docks. She would not wish such a fate on anyone.

Her concern must have showed on her face, for Mustafa said, "Do not look so worried. The exam is a formality, I assure you. Leah is not more than fourteen, I would guess." He smiled. "The Sultan caught a glimpse of this little peasant when she was brought in yesterday and has talked of nothing since. She is a *gözde*, a girl in the eye of the Sultan. Hence the urgency."

Mustafa held open the door of the room. He gestured her in, then looked around. It took a moment for Hannah to realize she was in the dormitory where they kept the newly arrived girls, a spartan room, dimly lit, but no doubt much more comfortable than the simple hut the girl had probably grown up in.

"I have moved the other odalisques to another dormitory so we may have privacy," said Mustafa. "Leah?" he called.

A slim shaft of moonlight entered through a high clerestory window framed with gossamer curtains swishing in the breeze. When Hannah's eyes adjusted, she saw a sleeping mat rolled up neatly on the floor. Stacked in the corner were a stool, a divan, a prayer rug, and a scattering of cushions, one of which had been slashed. A flurry of goose feathers floated in the air. Through the high window drifted the fragrance of jasmine and roses from the palace gardens.

"Where is she?"

Mustafa touched his pine-pitch torch to a candle in the wall sconce, sending an arabesque of smoke to the ceiling, where it flattened and dispersed like a low-hanging cloud. "Where, indeed?"

The scent of rancid beef tallow filled the room. No expensive beeswax candles in this quarter of the harem. Hannah glanced at the ceiling but saw only the timbers. She squinted, searching the corners of the room.

Mustafa spied the girl first. He gestured to the window far above his head. Crouched on the ledge, half hidden by the billowing curtains, was a form radiating predatory stillness. It took Hannah a moment to realize she was looking at a girl and not a wild animal. Her eyes were opened wide in terror. Her hands curled around the window ledge. Behind the fear was the determined aggression of a creature that has been cornered, a creature expecting brutality and therefore coiled to spring. God knows what she had been through thus far in her short life.

Mustafa pulled the stool under the ledge and climbed on it. He teetered as he stretched up to grasp the girl's thin, muscular leg. Hannah held her breath, afraid he would give a sharp yank and bring the child crashing to the floor. Instead, he murmured soft words of encouragement as though coaxing a kitten out of a tree. The girl shrank farther back onto the ledge, one hand reaching behind her to clutch the iron grille. Mustafa continued making cooing sounds. Moving closer, his face upturned, he reached up again to seize her leg. She kicked at him with a determined little foot. Mustafa's turban toppled off. The *aigrette*, the elaborate filigreed gold pin set with rubies and diamonds that held his turban in place, came loose, and the turban and quill clattered to the floor. A muscle twitched in Mustafa's cheek as he climbed down from the stool and bent to retrieve his turban and quill. No doubt he was regretting that he had not forced a gold-foiled opium pill between the girl's lips after she first arrived.

"Mustafa, let me try," said Hannah, but Mustafa replaced his turban on his head, squared his shoulders, mounted the stool again, and extended a hand up to the girl.

For his forbearance, he was rewarded by the sound of a throat being cleared and then a splat of saliva on his cheek. This insult was followed by a stream of curse words in Hebrew and instructions on what Mustafa could do with his quill.

God my rock, protect me, Hannah thought. This girl, who seemed more suited for the Sultan's menagerie than his couch, was a daughter of Israel. For a Jewish girl to speak so was an embarrassment for all Jews. It was Hannah's conceit—she supposed that was the right word—to believe that Jews acted better than gentiles and better than Muslims. *Judge not that thee be not judged*, as one of her gentile neighbours would say. The words echoed in Hannah's mind. Leah must have suffered greatly to act in this way. Sympathy would serve better than a sharp reproof.

In Hebrew, Hannah called up, "You are lucky Mustafa did not understand what you invited him to do with his quill."

The girl gave a snort. "You speak Hebrew?"

"I would not be much of a Jew if I did not."

Again in Hebrew, Leah shouted at Mustafa. "May hyenas crawl up your asshole and eat their way to your throat!"

He got off his stool and backed away from the window ledge, then looked at Hannah.

Hannah, pretending not to understand what had been said, took a cloth from her bag and gave it to Mustafa to wipe his cheek. Then he got back up on the stool and this time lunged for the girl. Quick as a snake, his fingers wrapped around her ankles. Leah struggled against his hold, lashing out, thrashing and bucking. A smell of sweat wafted down, the acrid scent of an animal fighting for its life. Mustafa held fast. Hannah could not look. She did not want to see the girl fall and hear her land with a thud on the stone floor.

When she heard nothing but the growls and the grunts of a struggle, Hannah finally turned. The girl had lost her grip on the grille of the window. Now her fingers were curled around the curtains. Mustafa was bent over, still balancing on the stool, his hands braced on his knees, panting.

"I am too old for such antics. I shall call a couple of eunuchs. They will subdue her before she harms either herself or us. If that does not succeed, there are always the Janissaries." The Janissaries were the elite private corps of soldiers who guarded the Sultan. They would lose no time in hauling the child unceremoniously to the floor and packing her off to the prison cells under the slaves' hospital.

"Give me a chance," said Hannah. "Leave me with her a moment."

Mustafa stepped down from the stool. "May Allah be with you." Then he bowed and backed out of the room.

Hannah heard him turn the key in the lock as he left.

Why must Mustafa lock her in? She had had a horror of being locked in small rooms ever since she was a child and heard the story of a man, thought to be dead, who had been thrown into a coffin, the lid fastened shut, and buried alive. The beating of fists could be heard several houses away but no one dared come to his aid. Now she knew how this man had felt.

Just as she was about to take Mustafa's place on the stool, something landed on her head. The girl was flinging what looked like a cloud of filaments onto the floor. Yarn? Shreds of her garment? Charred lamp wicks that a lazy servant had tucked along the window ledge?

The girl's face appeared from behind the curtain. Hannah saw large, wide-spaced eyes staring down at her. Green, the green of the sea, the green of the first trees to bud in spring. Green eyes in a land of black-eyed women. Not even the Valide herself could claim this distinction. The girl was indeed extraordinary.

On Leah's face was the look of both predator and prey, of falcon and rabbit. Her gaze never left Hannah's face. Hannah knelt and scooped up a handful of the strange substance from the floor. It was hair. Long, lovely, shiny strands, as glossy and black as a horse's mane.

When Hannah looked up again, Leah's eyes were still on her. There was the glint of iron. In her hand, Leah held a knife.

CHAPTER 4

Jewish Quarter
Rome

THE SMELL OF DEATH made Cesca giddy. It had a sweetish odour rather like the water in a vase of lilies that had not been changed for several days. The windows in the bedchamber were too narrow to admit a breeze. The oil lamps sucked all the air from the room. For what Francesca—or as most people called her, Cesca—had in mind, none of these details made the slightest difference.

Inside were all the women, including Cesca and the widow, Grazia. Outside in the garden were the male mourners—Jews clad in shades of black and grey, curls hanging down on either side of their faces, beards showing the remnants of last night's soup, their skin colourless from too much time in the prayer house.

All except for one man.

Like a white heron among a flock of crows stood Foscari, the nobleman from Venice—tall, fair, blue-eyed, and beardless. There was a deliberate grace to him, an economy of movement as he stooped to listen to something the rabbi was saying, cupping his hand behind his ear as though he were hard of hearing, although Cesca knew he was not. And then there was the matter of his nose—silver, attached by silk threads wrapped around his ears, flashing in the intermittent rays of the sun.

Why, she wondered, would a gentile trouble himself to attend the funeral of a Jew? And not just any gentile but a marquis. And not just any marquis but the Venetian ambassador to Constantinople. Surely such a man must have better things to do than attend the funeral of an obscure moneylender.

In a semicircle around the bed, Cesca stood with the other women who were darting glances at Grazia, waiting for her to approach the corpse and begin the ablutions— wash the body, stuff the ears, nose and mouth with cotton wool, tie the ankles, cross the hands on his breast, and wrap him in a shroud. The widow Grazia should step forward and begin the task, but she did not.

"I cannot, Cesca," Grazia finally said, turning to her. "You must do what has to be done."

"As you wish," Cesca replied, approaching the bed. To her relief, none of the other women moved toward the body to help her. This would make it easier to carry out her plan. "Go outside, all of you. I will look after him." She had almost said "it." *I will look after it.* That was all he was now— no longer Leon, no longer human, no longer anything but an unpleasant household task to be performed.

The women hesitated. They stood for a moment, their arms at their sides.

Cesca put an arm around Grazia's shoulders and gave her a nudge toward the door. "Go. I can manage."

The other women took Grazia by the arm and trooped out to the garden, where they stood apart from the male mourners. Cesca locked the door behind them.

With Grazia and the other women gone, she would have the solitude she needed to wash and wrap the body. It amused her to remember that this morning when she threw cloths over the mirrors, a custom required when sitting *shiva*, the period of mourning, she had noticed that even after everything she had done, her eyes remained as guileless as lapis lazuli.

Leon had died young. His black beard, without a hint of white, reached the middle of his well-fleshed chest. Death had scrubbed the colour from his face and left it a dull grey. He wore a prayer shawl, black frock coat, and breeches.

Cesca had donned a stained wool skirt this morning, knowing what lay ahead. She would not sacrifice her good dress. The rabbi would perform *keriah*, using a knife and slitting her mourner's clothes, not on a seam that could be mended but in the middle of the cloth, making it unwearable.

This was the way of Jews. Cesca had studied their habits well. For two years she had worked for Leon and Grazia as the "Shabbat goy," performing chores forbidden to be done by Jews—extinguishing candles and lamps on Friday night, lighting the fire on Sabbath morning. The services she had performed for Leon's sole benefit she preferred not to dwell upon.

Jews were profligate in some ways: two sets of pots and dishes to keep milk from mingling with meat, and costly beeswax candles wasted squinting over books. But they seemed to Cesca miserly in other ways—refusing to buy fresh cherries in July, walking thousands of paces out of their way to save a *scudo* on a pail of goat's milk.

Grazia was not like this. She had been a Christian, the blue-eyed daughter of a baker, who had fallen in love with Leon when she was fifteen and, to her family's horror, converted to Judaism.

Was Foscari acquainted with the custom of *keriah*? Through the open window, she glanced into the garden, searching in the crowd of men for his well-barbered head of sleek chestnut hair. Evidently not. He was wearing his handsome white jacket, buttoned in spite of the heat, not a bead of sweat on his brow. She looked away when she saw him gazing at her, but not before she observed one blue eye close in a wink. Something stirred in her. It had been a long time since she had had a well-made man in her bed. Had she known what lay in store for her at Foscari's hands, she would not have given a long, sensual wink in reply.

Cesca closed the window and turned to the task at hand. She would make quick work of Leon, then the men would lift him onto a palanquin and carry him down the hill to the Jewish graveyard outside of town. While Leon was being released into the waiting arms of his pagan god, Cesca would help herself to what she was after in his study.

She took a step toward the bed, leaned over the corpse, and lifted its arm. Taking a deep breath, she began to undress him—yanking off his white *tallis*, his prayer shawl, tugging off the black gabardine breeches, and jerking him out of his jacket. Even in death, his body repulsed her— the long feet splayed outward, the fingers curled up at his sides. She tossed a sheet over the corpse and dipped a cloth in a bowl of warm soapy water, then wrung it out so that it was nearly dry. She wrapped it around her hand like a glove. Nudging aside a corner of the sheet, she picked up an arm and began to wash it with purposeful strokes.

Her gaze fell on his face. There was swelling over his right eye. Grazia believed it had been caused by a blow to his head on the corner of the table as he toppled to the floor after his heart gave out. When Grazia found him, he had one leg folded underneath him, the other rotated at an awkward angle.

Cesca passed a hand over his eyes but they would not close. They resisted her, staring sightlessly—as dark and cold as they had been in life. This was why mourners placed coins on the eyes of the dead, but she had none, and even if she had, she would not have wasted them on Leon. Studying his cooling body, she wondered at herself having been frightened of him—his pale, lashless eyes that had tracked her as she dusted, swept, polished, and set the table with silver and crystal, all the while feigning interest in the account books he kept for his business as a money-lender, brow furrowed in a scholarly frown.

In fairness, Cesca had also watched Leon. One afternoon she was quietly trimming candlewicks when Leon thought she was at the market. When she heard the hinges of his strongbox squeak nearby, she fastened her eye to a knothole in the baseboard, which gave her a view of the study.

The only light shone from high above his head—a lumpy and ill-made candle. The wick was braided from the worst class of rags, cast-off cotton perhaps or a charred scrap of linen. It was hard to imagine the exemplary Grazia—her feather-light pastry, her flawlessly straight seams and crisp table linen—fashioning such a thing. No matter, Leon did not care as long as no tallow fell on his gold.

He had lifted the lid of the chest wrapped in iron bands, which was set high on a simple wooden platform to protect it from water damage—the Tiber River flooded the Jewish Quarter during the rainy season each year, rendering the main floors dank and wet. He removed a canvas pouch from the chest. As the rough boards of the floor dug into her knees and hands, Cesca heard the clink of coins and watched as Leon opened the pouch. Next, she saw the flash of gold as Leon counted his money, letting the coins trickle between his fingers. Once counted, he replaced them in the pouch and locked them in the chest.

With the thought of that gold so close at hand, her

movements quickened. She washed Leon's armpits, the inside of the elbows, the veins etching a trace of blue on the pallid grey skin. She finished, then let the arm drop and moved to the other side of the bed.

When she lifted the other arm his jagged fingernails caught on her dress and pulled at her bodice, as though he were clutching for her breasts one last time. His nails were so long that they curled under. Cesca found a small pair of scissors in a drawer and began to trim them. She would toss the parings in the fire so that his spirit did not return to seek revenge.

Out of the corner of her eye, through the window, she saw Foscari. He was talking to Grazia, his face the very picture of sympathy. Then, he reached high into the apple tree and plucked a fruit from its branches. As he ate, he leaned forward so the juice did not drip on his jacket. Foscari had arrived the first time one rainy night last week to borrow money from Leon. Cesca had overheard Leon tell Grazia that Foscari needed ten ducats to cover some gaming debts.

Cesca grasped the corpse's right hand. The gold wedding ring set with a diamond caught the light, gleaming. The nail beds were as deep and rectilinear as a coffin. Ink stained the callus on his middle finger where he had grasped his quill. The broad webbing between Leon's fingers made his ring easy to slip off, and the diamond flashed as she dropped it into her pocket. Once the body was wrapped in the winding-sheet, no one would know the ring was missing.

Seeing Foscari wipe a drop of juice off his chin made Cesca hungry. When she was a child, there had been three years of abundant harvest, then one year of terrible famine—"the starving time," her mother called it—a time when they ate bark, roots, grass, acorns, white clay, even boiled up leather shoes and boots. A memory floated to the surface of her mind. She was a child, perhaps four or five years, holding her mother's hand in the middle of a square in Rome. Cesca wore a tattered green dress with an uneven hem.

Surrounding them was a huge, jostling crowd. The man next to her, a tanner judging by the stink of him, nearly trampled her in his haste to get to a scaffold. It was so high in the sky that she could barely see the hanged man swinging from the noose. The ravenous mob surged forward. Her mother swung Cesca to her hip and, making swift jabs of her elbows, shoved her way to the front of the crowd.

The tanner got there first and began hacking at the body. With his skinning knife, he severed a piece of leg and crammed it into his mouth. When Cesca's mother begged him for a taste, he tossed her a bloody hunk of thigh. Her mother held it to Cesca's lips. "To live, you must eat, my darling." When Cesca averted her face, her mother coaxed her, cupping her hand under her mouth, speaking to her in a murmur until she eased in a small piece, encouraging her to chew and swallow. At first she wanted to spit it out, but the blood was warm and salty, the flesh springy and dense. Cesca's throat relaxed. She swallowed and then, like a fledgling in a nest, opened her mouth for another morsel. Never had she felt her mother's love so strongly.

Cesca returned to the corpse, swabbing Leon's white, hairless thighs. His flaccid penis lay between his legs. She had not seen it in the light of day. Under the quilt, there had been only an unseen shaft of flesh, pushing and insistent. Leon imagined she enjoyed these encounters. And so she did, but not in the way he thought. Their grapplings were a welcome respite from scrubbing pots and dipping candles. In Leon's bed her mind could wander. She could dream of the country, of hills and wheat ripening in the sun, of orchards heavy with cherries, peaches, and apples. Of her future.

From the pile of rags in the corner she took a long strip of muslin and tied his jaws together, heedless of whether his tongue was tucked into the back of his throat. She poured herself a glass of wine from a jug on the floor and drank it down. Then, crossing herself, she fumbled about under the shroud and, head turned aside, stuffed balled-up bits of rag into his orifice.

Cesca searched his room for the knife she knew he kept there. She picked it up. With the tip of the blade, she nudged his phallus into the valley between his legs, below the soft hillock of his belly. Then she gave it a jab. Leon had no more use for it than he had for his ducats. A pretty little farm in Bassano del Grappa, just a few rolling hectares. What an obedient little donkey I appear to be, Cesca thought—one of those biddable beasts who labours without complaint for years for the pleasure of kicking my master once.

CHAPTER 5

Imperial Palace
Constantinople

CROUCHING ON THE LEDGE with the knife upraised, Leah slashed at her head with jerky, erratic movements. She flung down more and more hair to join the pile on the floor, pausing only long enough to hurl a curse at Hannah in Hebrew to the effect that Hannah and all of her family were the offspring of promiscuous, fornicating pigs who rutted without regard to prohibited degrees of consanguinity.

"It is a delight to hear Hebrew spoken so fluently," said Hannah. She had an idea. "I know what it is like to be a stranger in a strange land." Was it her imagination or had the girl lowered the knife a little? Hannah was afraid to move, but spoke in a steady voice, eyes fixed on the girl. "Like you, I came to this city because I had no choice. It was difficult at first—the language, Osmanlica, from which all vowels have been stolen, the odd provender stuffed with pistachio nuts and cinnamon, the Sephardic Jews who are so different from the Ashkenazi that they hardly seem to be Jews at all. But I have made my life here and so must you. Every day will become easier, until one day you will regard the harem as your home. You will be taught many things—embroidery, the rules of etiquette, not to point one's feet toward one's elder, never to speak first to one's superior. You will, in time, become accustomed to your new surroundings." How hypocritical Hannah felt urging such a life. The harem offered luxury and privilege, petting and cosseting, but would Hannah want such a life for her daughter should she be blessed with a girl one day? To be pampered but to be as useless as the flightless silk moths Isaac carried on heavy trays to the garden—fluttering, quivering, diaphanous creatures that beat their wings in the afternoon sun, then spun their cocoons and died at night?

Could the odalisques not be taught something more useful than never-ending embroidery to decorate cloths that required no further embellishment? Every scrap of fabric in the harem was replete with idealized landscapes of pavilions, gardens, cypress trees and water, birds, tulips, carnations, trailing vines and peacocks, fruits and nuts. To expend such time and patience on items destined for a baby's bottom or for the declivity between a woman's legs as a menstrual pad! It all seemed such a waste.

"Will I be taught to write Osmanlica? I would like that," Leah said, finally lowering her knife.

"Mustafa does not permit it." He would not condescend to give a reason, not that anyone would dare ask, but Hannah had guessed: he feared the girls would write love letters, tie them to pomegranates from the trees in the garden, and toss them over the harem wall for young men to find. And likely these bored young females would do exactly that. Who could blame them? Wouldn't Hannah do exactly the same thing in their place?

"Where is your family?" Leah asked.

"My husband and son are here. The rest of my family live in the ghetto in Venice." Hannah had a few cousins and a younger brother, Samuel, all of whom she missed. Her sister Jessica had died tragically before Hannah left Venice, under circumstances Hannah could barely bring herself to think of.

"You are better off than me," said Leah in a small voice. She peered at Hannah from behind the gauzy curtain. Her beautiful face was in need of a good scrubbing. "What do you miss the most about Venice?"

Everything, Hannah thought but didn't say. Isaac claimed that with the passage of time, her vivid imagination had transformed Venice from a city of fetid canals and Jew-haters to an earthly Babylon. Hannah noticed the girl's posture had relaxed, though she made no move to leave the promontory of her window ledge.

"The ghetto is what I miss. The smell of cooking— sardines in brine, baby artichokes fried in garlic, warm bread and pudding. Here in Constantinople all I smell is the reek of sheeps' entrails, the cloying stink of overripe persimmons, and beef tripe rotting on the butchers' tables—" She caught herself. This kind of talk would not assist the girl. "I have been cursed with an oversensitive nose. The smells here are no worse than the ghetto at home, just different. When I was a child, my father used to tease me by saying that had Jews been allowed such an occupation, I would have made an excellent perfumer. He was right, but I am happy to be what I am—a midwife."

"You are a kind woman."

And you, dear heart, could use some kindness, Hannah thought. You have suffered more than most women twice your age and yet, look at you. Not bowed, not broken, feisty as an alley cat.

"Leah, you cannot control your life any more than you can control the tides. When you flail and thrash and growl and grumble, when you struggle against the inevitable, you will drown. But, if you let go and float, you will be borne aloft. Allow me to help you."

Hannah heard the exhalation of long-held breath. She climbed onto the stool and softly touched one of the girl's ankles, pressing her thumb on the knob of the delicate bone. As she did so, she said, still speaking in Hebrew, "No one here will harm you if you obey. Come down before the eunuchs arrive. They will not be as gentle as I will."

Now that she was closer to the girl, Hannah could see her heart-shaped face and trembling mouth. Through the worn material of her shift, Hannah noticed her delicate clavicles. The girl was far too thin, her belly distended from malnutrition. Her skin was stretched as tightly over her kneecaps as hide on drums.

"Come down," Hannah said. "Even a mountain lion must eat. I have a peach in my bag."

Hannah released the girl's ankle and held out her arms, listening for sounds of further throat clearing or, worse, the whoosh of a knife slicing through the air. There was only silence. Hannah stood on tiptoes. The girl bent over slightly, and Hannah took her hand and squeezed it.

"Be a good girl now."

There was a flash of iron and the knife hit the tile floor and skittered against the wall.

Leah eased herself to the rim of the window ledge and held out her arms. Hannah swung her down and set her on the floor. She weighed more than Matteo but not by much.

Then Hannah took the white peach from her bag and held it out to Leah. The girl snatched it, sniffed it, and then began to take huge bites, letting the juice trickle down her chin.

"From my garden," said Hannah. "The first of the season."

They heard the sound of the door bolt being drawn back and Mustafa entered, flanked by two eunuchs in blue turbans.

"They will not be necessary, Mustafa. Leah is tranquil, as you can see for yourself."

He glanced at the girl. "Good. Then I will leave you to your work." He turned to leave with the eunuch guards, but first bent down and scooped up the knife and tucked it in his sash. The air stirred. One of the girl's tresses tumbled from the ledge and settled on the floor. "May Allah be with you," Mustafa said. He bowed and backed out of the room, closing the door behind him.

"Do not lock the door, Mustafa. There is no need," Hannah said. She heard several voices in the corridor as he addressed the eunuchs. To Hannah's relief, there was no scrape of the bolt.

Mustafa called through the door, "Two eunuchs are standing by, Hannah. If you need them, you have only to shout."

"Leah will be sensible," Hannah said, catching the girl's eye as she spoke.

Before Mustafa's footsteps receded, Leah said, "I hate him. His simpering voice, his fat hips, the way he waddles."

"Mustafa no more wished to be a eunuch than you wished to be captured and sold into slavery."

Leah wiped her face on the sleeve of her shift, which was a colour that was no colour—the hue of stray dogs, of kitchen rags used too long to scour pots, of poorly cured cheese.

"Do you know how the Arab slavers make young boys into eunuchs?" Without waiting for an answer, Hannah said, "When Mustafa was nine years old, he was captured by a slaver outside his village near Lake Chad with several of his cousins while they were swimming. The other boys and Mustafa were bound around the chest and upper thighs. Their private parts were cut off and the boys were then buried in sand up to their necks and given no water or food for nine days. When Mustafa was dug up, he was more dead than alive. He was the only one of the boys to survive." She paused. "You have noticed the gold quill in his turban? He must insert that into himself so he can make water."

Leah's lovely face lost its hard look, her bottom lip quivered.

"The Arabs took him by caravan to Alexandria, where he was sold at ten times what a normal boy would have fetched. And then he was sold on through various markets until he reached Constantinople."

Hannah intended the story to give the girl heart, to show her that adversity could be overcome, but Leah looked so upset that Hannah was sorry she had told her.

"Why has Mustafa sent you?"

"To examine you to ensure you are a virgin." Hannah gestured to the divan. "Slip off your clothing and tell me how old you are."

The girl remained standing. "I have seen fourteen summers," she said, making no move to remove her shift.

She appeared much younger. Mountain girls often looked young because of their meagre diets of *plov* and gruel. Many had deformed pelvises from inadequate food.

Leah was not ready for the Sultan's couch. Surely she had not even commenced her flowers. Dare Hannah suggest to the Valide that the Sultan wait a year or two until the girl was older? She paused to reflect. What a ludicrous idea. God's Shadow on Earth be denied? If he wanted a girl, he had only to raise his finger and she was his. Nor would substituting another girl in Leah's place be an option. Hannah had heard the tale, as who had not, of a Circassian slave who years ago sold her rendezvous with old Sultan Selim to another girl. The Circassian slave was never seen again. One thought gave Hannah hope. The Sultan, who was surrounded by the loveliest girls in the Empire, was like a gardener who refused to pick any flower except one—Safiye.

Leah climbed onto the divan, squatting as though tending a fire, knees hugged to her chest, her child-fragile neck inclined, head resting on her knees, chopped hair raised like the bristles on a hedgehog. She rocked back and forth to give herself comfort. As Hannah watched, all traces of Leah's wild self disappeared. She looked now like the terrified and exhausted child she was. Hannah dug in her bag, found a vial, and poured a few drops of almond oil into her hands. She rubbed them together to warm them. She had no stomach for the job that lay before her, but she had no choice.

Leah's toes were splayed as though they had never known the confines of sandals, much less the soft kid slippers with upturned toes favoured by the ladies of the harem. Where was the dazzling and eager virgin to awaken ardour in the loins of God's Shadow on Earth, ruler of half the world? Where were the ample breasts, the pearly skin, and the voluptuous figure of a fully formed woman in her prime childbearing years? Hannah reached in her bag again and drew out a cotton sheet. She unfolded it, let it billow and then float down to settle on the girl. Leah drew it up to her chest until it covered her chin. Even in her present state, a scalp red with angry gashes, legs dotted with insect bites, Leah was beautiful. A beautiful child. What could be done to help her?

Hannah spoke softly. "Lie back."

The girl sat rigidly.

Hannah waited.

Slowly, Leah eased herself into a reclining position, then curled into a ball, her face turned toward the wall. Hannah wondered if the girl had been violated by the Yürüks, a tribe notorious for their brutality.

Hannah spoke in a coaxing and gentle tone. "You are from the Circassian Mountains?"

Leah turned toward Hannah and nodded. Around her neck was a leather lanyard, which had been broken and then clumsily retied. She reached for it and showed Hannah a *nazar boncuğu* of milky blue stone, an amulet against the Evil Eye. "My grandmother gave this to me," she said, rubbing it against her cheek.

"Which town are you from?" It made no difference, except to encourage the girl to talk. Hannah knew nothing of Circassia and could not have named one village in the entire region. She knew only that it lay somewhere beyond the Black Sea. A few hundred Jews lived there in poor, isolated settlements. The men herded sheep; the women wove rugs on backstrap looms during the winter to sell at spring market.

"It is nothing but starving dogs, burnt huts, and charred bones now."

"And your family? What of them?"

"I saw my father's corpse desecrated in a *buzkashi* game."

Dear God. The Yürüks were the fiercest of the nomadic tribes, their horses the swiftest, their men the most savage. "Mercy upon you. I am so sorry." Hannah laid a hand on Leah's shoulder. "You are a brave girl."

"My grandmother used to say the same thing."

Hannah arranged her equipment on a linen cloth next to the divan—bandages, herbs, vials of oil, silk thread, needle and scissors. The birthing spoons remained in her bag. *May they not be needed for this girl for many years*, she prayed.

Hannah glanced at Leah's face. The girl stared at the ceiling, blinking and fighting back tears.

Hannah asked the question she dreaded the answer to. "Were you violated?"

"The Yürük who captured me dragged me to his tent high in the mountains so that he did not have to share me with the other men. He threw me down in front of his fire. He ordered me take off my clothes. He stared at me so long I thought his eyes would scorch the skin off my bones."

Hannah wanted to put her hands over her ears so she would not hear the rest. But if the girl had been dishonoured, there was no point in putting her through the ordeal of an examination. "And then?"

"I picked up a knife from the ground and cut off a lock of my hair. I handed it to him. Among the Yürüks, this signifies a plea for compassion." Leah fixed her green eyes on Hannah, who could imagine the directness of Leah's gaze discomfiting even a Yürük.

"He tied my hair around the hilt of his dagger. He did not strike me again. He made a bed for me in the corner from a smelly camel skin. Then he told me to sleep. In the morning he fed me sheep's yogourt sweetened with honey and announced he would make his fortune from me."

Hannah's heart was breaking. "You need not tell me the rest."

"He sold me to Arab slavers. After several weeks, I do not know how many, I was on the slave block in Constantinople where Mustafa bought me for the harem."

"You were lucky, in a way," said Hannah.

"I know," Leah answered. "I was."

Hannah thought the girl was ready. "Shall I examine you now?"

"I can save you the trouble. I am not a virgin. I am—or rather, I was—betrothed to Eliezer, a boy from the next village. We loved each other and so did not see the point in waiting. And now, I am glad we did not wait, because he is dead, killed like everyone else in my village by the Yürüks." The girl began to sob.

Hannah ran a hand over her cheek and thumbed away a tear. "You have been through a great deal for one so young."

"What will Mustafa say when you tell him?"

Hannah had to tell the girl the truth. She would find out soon enough on her own. "He will sell you back to the slavers."

Leah went silent. After a while, she said, "Maybe it is God's wish that I die. Maybe I should hurl myself off the roof of the kitchens."

Hannah pulled Leah by the shoulders into an upright position on the divan. "Life is a gift from God. To squander it is wrong."

"Even if I end up in a brothel?" The girl grabbed at the sheet falling off her and wrapped it around herself tightly. "Tell Mustafa that I am intact. Please."

Her green eyes remained fixed on Hannah. If Hannah lied and was discovered, she faced execution. Her head would be displayed on a spike in the First Courtyard. If Hannah told the truth, the girl was doomed. What should she do?

"There is only one thing I want," said Leah.

"And what is that?"

"My mother." At this the girl's head collapsed on her knees and she began to sob quietly. It broke Hannah's heart to hear her and watch the quivering movements of her thin shoulders. Hannah's own mother had died in childbirth when Hannah was younger than Leah.

For many years Hannah had longed for a daughter. Not a girl like this child, though, so troubled in her mind that perhaps not even love and a gentle touch could save her. No, Hannah longed for a duteous, quiet girl who would sit by her side and learn to sew and unravel the silk cocoons in Isaac's workshop. A daughter to whom she could pass on her secrets of midwifery and herbs. A daughter to whom she could give her silver birthing spoons. Hannah sat on the divan and drew the girl to her. She took her in her arms and rocked her.

"I dreamed of my village of Kaş last night. I smelled

the mildew on the walls. I felt the hard pallet on the dirt floor. I heard the breathing of my parents, my brothers lying next to me. But when I reached out to touch them, there was nothing but air."

They sat together like this for a long time until Leah grew calm. Hannah reached into her bag and withdrew a stoppered bottle containing a weak solution of alcohol infused with stinging nettles and lime water. She had planned to use these ingredients in a liniment for an elderly neighbour, but Leah needed the remedy more. Taking a clean cloth and saturating it with the liquid, Hannah pulled the sheet away from Leah and rubbed the wet cloth over the girl's limbs.

"This will sting, but it will take away your bad memories."

Leah did not flinch. Instead, she relaxed under Hannah's touch.

Next, Hannah took a sachet of dried passion-vine leaves from her bag. "I will instruct one of your attendants to mix this with a little water and some sugar to mask the taste. You will drink it at night. It will help you to sleep without nightmares."

Leah nodded.

There was the tap-tap of Mustafa's steps outside. The door opened and Mustafa's head appeared. "Finished?" he asked.

When Hannah nodded, he said, "Come. The Valide Nurbanu, the Sultan's mother, wishes to hear from your own lips that the girl is a virgin."

Hannah rose and the girl grabbed her arm. She looked up into Hannah's face one last time, as if to say, *Please, help me.*

My child, I do not know how. Had Hannah thought this or said it aloud? She was not sure.

Hannah collected her things and followed Mustafa out the door and down the corridor to the Valide's apartments. The whole time, she was thinking to herself, *why risk my life for a girl who is neither kin nor kith? So what if Leah is a Jew? If she dies in a brothel or flings herself from a rooftop, of what concern is it to me?*

Hannah knew the harem servants could work miracles. Leah's thick eyebrows could be plucked with a silk thread into a line as fine as a stroke of the calligraphy pen. Her pubic and underarm hair could be coated with a paste of quicklime and ointment, and then scraped off with the edge of a honed mussel shell. A layer of luminescent flesh from rich foods cooked in the palace kitchens would cushion Leah's bony elbows, knees, and clavicles, making her appear older and more voluptuous. In time, the girl's hair would grow back, although not even the Valide could order it to be waist-length before she was presented to the Sultan.

All of this could be accomplished with ease, but how could a maidenhead be made whole?

CHAPTER 6

Jewish Quarter
Rome

CESCA SPREAD THE SHROUD on the bed. By
rolling the corpse back and forth she managed to
position it in the middle. She folded the shroud
into the shape of a triangle, tucking in the ends so that no
part of Leon showed.

A few steps across the hallway was Leon's study. On the
table was the promissory note Cesca had seen Foscari sign,
leaving behind as a pledge a ewer that Cesca could see at
a glance was merely plated silver. Leon had bent over his
strongbox, counted out Foscari's money, and then slid the
ducats across the table, averting his eyes as though it pained
him to see the gold pass from his hand to Foscari's. At the

time, Cesca had wondered why Foscari sought out a moneylender in Rome rather than in Venice where he lived, but she had given the matter no further thought. No doubt nobles had to be discreet about going to Jews for money.

Cesca dragged out Leon's strongbox. Using the key Leon kept tucked under the corner of the carpet, she undid the lock. There, next to a bag of crimson powder, she spied it—the canvas purse. A shroud has no pockets. If she did not act now, when would God place such an opportunity before her again? It would be churlish to spurn His offer. She snatched up the pouch. But there was no delicious heft, no merry tinkle of coins, no shiny ducats straining the seams. She loosened the twine around the neck of the pouch and turned it upside down, shaking it like a cat toying with a dead mouse. The crinkle of parchment and two sheets slipped out and drifted to the floor. She kicked the worthless sheets out of her way. Had there been a fire burning in the grate in the study, she would have flung them in. Where were her gold coins?

She pawed through the strongbox, pitching items to the floor—a cheap garnet ring, a glass brooch, a small pair of scales for weighing gold, a jeweller's loupe, letters tied with a silk ribbon, a tattered yarmulke. She had planned this moment down to the tiniest detail, going over it in her mind so often it was as though Leon's ducats were already snug in her pocket. She felt the righteous anger of a woman who has been robbed. Rage gathered at the back of her eyes and moved to her forehead, and travelled to her arms, her torso, her legs—like a forest fire gathering momentum as it burned downhill—until it consumed her whole body. Her dream, which had seemed so attainable—take the ducats and sail off on the next ship—was shattered. She snatched up the empty canvas pouch and threw it to the floor and ground her heel into it. Have my ducats sprouted wings and flown into the sky? Have they grown legs and run off down the road?

She picked up the first of the two sheets of parchment off the floor. The tiny script was probably Latin, that much she could figure out. Once, Leon had explained that all merchants and moneylenders wrote commercial contracts in Latin so that a trader in, say, Venice could read without difficulty a contract from a merchant in Constantinople, Amsterdam, or Leghorn.

Cesca had learned to tally figures but never to read. For the first time in her life, she could see the sense of learning to decipher ink squiggles on a page. She shook the parchment and held it to the light, twisting it this way and that, as though by scrutinizing it she could force it to reveal its secret. It seemed to be a promissory note. Foscari had signed a pledge document much like this one. It also had a motif of oak clusters on the top. She had glimpsed it as it lay on the table, the ink drying. She smoothed the paper out and held it to the light from the window, noticing something she could understand—numbers.

There in the middle of the page were the figures 100, written in numerals in Leon's precise hand. The signature at the bottom of the page was a maddening scrawl. Even an educated person could not have made it out.

Cesca was about to pick up the second document, which had a border of peacocks in blue and green ink, when she heard voices and the rattle of the bolted door. She dropped the documents in fright. For a moment she could not think what to do. Her mind had been so focused on the money, she had forgotten the mourners outside. They had come to collect the body for burial! Hastily, she shoved both parchments into the pocket of her skirt. Later, she would find those ducats. She gathered the scattered items from the floor and thrust them into the strongbox. When she tried to slam the lid, the yarmulke caught in the hinge, preventing the clasp from closing. Yanking it out, she tossed it under Leon's desk. She slammed the top closed, replaced the strongbox on its platform, and slipped the key back under the corner of the carpet.

Assume an appearance of calmness, Cesca thought. She brushed some dust off her skirt and smoothed her hair. She forced herself to breathe more slowly as she opened the door and proceeded down the hall to admit the mourners. Her instincts told her that in some obscure way these two indecipherable documents held the secret of what had become of her ducats. All nobles could read. Foscari was a nobleman. He could explain what the papers signified. With her hair arranged prettily, she would go to him. She had no one else to turn to. Had there been more to Foscari's relationship with Leon than she realized? Could she trust Foscari not to betray her to Grazia?

With his aid, she would find her ducats and when she did, she would buy a dress of Atlas silk, a prosperous farm, and a respectable husband. Never again would she be hungry.

CHAPTER 7

Imperial Palace
Constantinople

A s HANNAH FOLLOWED Mustafa through the corridors of the Imperial Harem, her courage began to desert her. It was madness to lie to the Valide about this peasant girl. She thought of the Fountain of the Executioner in the First Court. Of what importance was the life of a slave girl compared to the erotic whims of the Sultan and, hence, the future of a great empire?

A heavenly fragrance greeted Hannah as Mustafa ushered her through the wide doors of the Valide Nurbanu's private apartments.

"Watch," he said. "Then do as I do. Remember, your

head must never be higher than the Valide's. You must not sit unless she commands you to."

Hannah nodded. Mustafa had tactfully chosen to ignore the fact that Hannah had visited the royal apartments before, although clearly he remembered that night very well. There had been no time for instructions about protocol during that visit. Hannah had raced to the Valide's side, hovering over her, unmindful of the impolite shadow she cast on Her Highness, Hannah's toes pointing every which way, even directly at the Valide. Tragically, the royal womb had become twisted, and Hannah had had to perform all manner of indignities on the most powerful woman in the Empire in order to assist her. The Valide on all fours. Hannah behind her, her fingers inserted into two royal orifices, tugging and pushing and pulling until the womb settled back into place. Hannah had never spoken of it to anyone, not even Isaac.

Hannah's heart was beating so loudly now she was afraid the Valide would hear it. Kübra, the lovely slave girl with a long, black braid hanging to her waist, was present. Hannah felt very small and insignificant in this room, the ceiling high enough to fly a kite, expansive enough to hold Hannah's entire house, workshop, and gardens. Trompe l'oeil paintings in greys and blues depicted arches, colonnades, and sparkling fountains of an imaginary palace so skilfully rendered Hannah felt she could walk into it—feel the splash of the water and hear the birds overhead while she sat next to the fountains. Emerald-encrusted mother-of-pearl wainscotting adorned the room. The entire tiled floor of the vast reception room was carpeted with thousands of rose petals—white, pink, red, crimson, and gold. Dozens of ladies-in-waiting flanked the Valide, some fanning her, some carrying trays of *dolma*, grape leaves stuffed with ground lamb, and *börek*, flaky pastry filled with spinach and cheese. Others held tulip-shaped glasses of pastel sherbets.

An evening breeze off the Bosporus stirred the petals on the floor. It felt not quite real, as though Hannah were walking through a dream. She waited as Mustafa descended on all fours and crawled the length of the room to announce Hannah's presence to the Valide, who, Hannah could see from the corner of her eye, was seated on a dais. *Trust no one in the palace*, Isaac had often cautioned. *Remember the swift justice meted out to those who vex the Valide.*

Mustafa reached the dais and some words were exchanged, but Hannah was too far away to hear. Then Mustafa pivoted, still on all fours, and beckoned Hannah forward. Hannah carefully put down her bag in the entranceway before dropping to her hands and knees. She crawled to the raised platform at the far end of the massive reception room. A fragrant, invisible trail of perfume followed her. When she reached the dais, she warily raised her head.

The Valide Nurbanu was seated on a chair of inlaid ivory, her feet immersed in a gold basin of water large enough to bathe twins. Carp nibbled away at dead skin from her feet. This was the latest fashion among the ladies of the harem, Ezster had told Hannah.

"*B-Bismillah,*" Hannah stammered. *In the name of God, the most compassionate.* The word was awkward on her tongue.

"*Bismillah*, indeed," the Valide answered. "We meet again."

As Hannah's eyes travelled from the Valide's feet and up to her face, she saw how composed the woman was, notwithstanding their previous encounter. Hannah kissed the hem of the Valide's *pelisse*, then glanced down, studying the marble floor beneath her.

"Rise," the Valide said in Venetian. She nodded to Mustafa to include him in the invitation.

Hearing the Valide speak in the beloved rhythms of the Venetian dialect reminded Hannah that Nurbanu, in her former life, had been Cecilia Baffo-Venier, the illegitimate offspring of two of the noblest families in Venice. Hannah ventured to look at her. Her Highness was smiling now, showing her perfect white teeth. Rumour was that one of her ladies-in-waiting scrubbed them every night with a pointed stick dipped in a paste of lemon juice and salt. Hannah thought it wise not to meet her eyes for too long, and looked down again at the carp flashing silver and gold in the low-sided tub that held the regal feet of the mother of the Sultan. The Valide squirmed in a way that made Hannah wonder if perhaps the two of them had something in common—ticklish toes.

Two slave girls helped the Valide rise and steadied her while a eunuch dried her feet with a gold-embroidered cloth. They led her to a divan covered in rose-coloured silk. There, Valide Nurbanu rested, one wrist crossed over the other, a glass of sherbet by her side, while a girl massaged her feet with oil. The Valide's *pelisse* reached her ankles. It was a lush, vibrant red dyed with cochineal. The fabric shimmered. Every dyer in Constantinople would kill for this most precious of red powders, made from the crushed bodies of insects from New Spain. Cochineal, Isaac said, was wonderfully fast. If only he could see with his own eyes this astonishing crimson—a ridiculous notion since no man outside the Valide's household was permitted in her private chambers.

Although she was not young, Nurbanu was so lovely that no one who gazed upon her alabaster skin and long, graceful neck questioned why the late Sultan Selim had been so enchanted with her. Her black curls were swept up into twin coronets in the Venetian style. Here and there, diamonds winked and sparkled in her hair like a constellation. Surrounded by women and eunuchs, there was, of course, no need for the Valide to wear a veil.

When Nurbanu was twelve, she had been kidnapped off the coast of Páros in the Aegean and brought to the palace as a concubine for Selim, who fell so in love with her he could not eat. The cooks in the palace kitchen and the Imperial Taster swore that not a morsel of food, not so much as a roasted chickpea or pistachio nut, passed Selim's lips for two months. Nurbanu's political shrewdness was legendary. Selim had depended on her to the exclusion of his chief adviser, the Grand Vizier. The Valide's enemies, Ezster claimed, were legion. Gossips contended that the Valide remained loyal to Venice in spite of the growing conflicts between the Empire and the Republic. Others said it was a pretense, her way of extracting lavish gifts from the Venetian ambassador in exchange for advocating Venetian interests. Nurbanu was just thirteen when she bore Selim's first son. Hannah had a thought. Perhaps if Hannah told the truth about Leah, the Valide would be sympathetic? No. It was impossible.

Mustafa bowed low before the Valide, approaching her divan cautiously and kissing her hand. She dismissed him with a flick of her jewelled fingers. He fell to his hands and knees and slowly crawled backwards out of the room, his belly grazing the floor, leaving a trail of displaced rose petals in his wake.

It was Hannah's turn to approach the royal divan. She was so frightened she would happily have changed places with any other person in the room, including the young girl who was netting the carp out of the gold basin and stringing them through their gills to carry them off to the kitchens.

The Valide reclined with what seemed to Hannah an unnatural calmness, eyes fixed on her. Damp circles formed under Hannah's arms. They say that the body odour of an animal excites the instinct of the predator, causing the eyes to narrow and the mouth to water in anticipation. She must relax and show no fear. The Valide picked up her glass of rose-petal-flavoured sherbet and began to sip. Hannah could almost see the translucent skin of her neck flush pink as she swallowed. A pair of large, silky-haired dogs lounged at Nurbanu's feet, front paws crossed in an unconscious imitation of their mistress.

"On you be peace and the mercy of God and His blessings," said Hannah with her right hand on her heart, as was the Muslim custom.

"Be seated," Nurbanu said in Venetian, gesturing to a large silk pillow across from the dais. "I am so pleased that Mustafa persuaded you to join me."

It was a great honour to be asked to sit in the Valide's presence. Commoners were usually required to remain on all fours, their chins touching the floor. No doubt the Valide intended her graciousness to put Hannah at ease. Hannah arranged herself on the cushion, careful to point her feet away and to keep her head low.

The Valide's face, so Venetian in its paleness, the fine dark eyes and eyebrows like raven's wings, and her fluent Venetian, reminded Hannah so much of her beloved Venice. The sound of the familiar dancing vowels and polished consonants was like sunlight sparkling on the Grand Canal. Hannah nearly forgot her nervousness and disgraced herself by blurting out how she missed the city of her birth and longed to return.

"Your Highness, I am honoured to be here," Hannah said.

One of the dogs stretched and yawned, revealing pointed teeth that looked as though they could devour her whole.

"The Venetian ambassador sent these brutes as a gift," the Valide said. "Can you imagine? These huge, nettlesome creatures, a gift? My scribe had to send him a reprimand." She paused and then, hands in front of her face as though holding up a scroll of parchment, pretended to read. "'I require two *lap* dogs, not these hulking, long-haired monsters. Send others and let them be *white* and let them be *little!*'"

Hannah was mystified. Was not one canine just as horrid as the next?

"I sometimes wonder whether anyone listens to me. My needs are not so complicated nor so difficult to fulfill and yet . . ." She shifted on the divan where she was seated and then locked eyes with Hannah. "But you and I have a more important matter to discuss." The Valide reached over to a tortoiseshell tray of spicy meatballs resting on a stool next to her. She plucked one from the tray using her thumb and the tip of her index finger and placed it on her tongue with such delicacy it was as though the food had floated through the air and into her mouth of its own volition.

In response to the delicious smells of roasted walnuts and lamb, Hannah's stomach rumbled. The Valide pretended not to notice but nodded to Kübra, the slave girl. Kübra was, so the gossips of the harem reported, blessed with feet identical to the Valide's. When the Valide ordered a new pair of pattens, it was Kübra's task to wear them until the silver *repoussé* strap over the instep was sufficiently soft. By this method the royal foot was spared all chafing and discomfort.

Hannah accepted a plate of *mezes* from Kübra and a glass filled with sherbet. "Thank you." The liquid sherbet was cold and tangy with a touch of lemon and pomegranate juice. She savoured it, swallowed, and then spoke again. "To hear my language again. And spoken with such grace. It warms my heart, Your Highness."

"Such a pleasant change from Osmanlica—bestial grunts and wheezes that masquerade as a language." There was a pause while the Valide waited for Hannah's response.

Caution, warned a small voice in Hannah's head. Of course she detested Osmanlica, but she must give no reply that sounded treasonous. Making herself understood in this language of the Turks was an ordeal. She would canter at full speed into dead ends before lurching to a stop. Her stammers and stutters were supplemented by extravagant hand gestures, vigorous movements of the head, exaggerated shrugs, and much pursing of the lips. Isaac urged her to make more of an effort, to study more and to seek out women with whom she could practise. It was *her* tongue now, he said. Isaac, who could learn any language within a matter of a few months, had no comprehension of her struggle. Once, in the midst of a quarrel, Hannah screamed at him that Osmanlica sounded like glutinous maize soup bubbling over a camel-dung fire. Isaac had laughed until tears ran down his cheeks.

He often lectured her on the virtues of Constantinople. She was able to cast off the red headdress that had marked her as a Jew in Venice. Yes, Jews here paid a head tax, but they were free to practise any profession, own any type of business, and buy property, Isaac argued.

All true enough, but it did not prevent Hannah from missing Venice. Even the Jews here were different. The Sephardim, the Jews from Spain and Portugal, were more relaxed, more sensual, more refined, and less learned than the Ashkenazi from eastern Europe. The Sephardim spoke Ladino instead of Yiddish. They had names that did not even sound Jewish, like Spinoza, Cardozo, and Mendoza. They looked down on the Ashkenazim like Hannah and Isaac, whom they thought boorish and fashioned from coarser clay than themselves.

Hannah took another mouthful of her sherbet. The palace chefs perfumed sherbets with jasmine, attar of roses, bergamot, and cloves, all of which were designed to impart fragrance to the secretions of the odalisques' private parts. If she and Isaac coupled tonight, would he notice? In her nervousness, a tiny giggle almost escaped her lips.

"Hannah, you have not answered me," said the Valide. "What is your opinion of Osmanlica? We are fellow Venetians. You can speak frankly."

True, they were both from Venice, but barriers of social class and religion made it odd to refer to the two of them as "fellow Venetians." Perhaps the wide expanse of sea and nostalgia for the familiar conferred on them a familiarity they could never attain in Venice.

Hannah took a deep breath. "You and I, Your Highness, slip naturally into Venetian with the gratitude of bathers slipping into the Sweet Waters of Asia on a humid August night."

The Valide smiled.

"Besides," Hannah added, "as anyone will tell you, I am a poor linguist. Yesterday in the market I asked for six aubergines and the vendor handed me a bunch of radishes."

Valide Nurbanu laughed. "I think this is your way of saying you detest Osmanlica and all those who have the misfortune to speak it?"

The Valide might have lived among the Ottomans most of her life but she had not lost the directness of speech that Venetians were famous for.

Hannah said, "I cannot walk abroad in your city as I did in Venice without either my husband or one of the workers in our workshop to accompany me. But hidden in a carriage, I may come and go as I please."

A look of incredulity passed over the Valide's face. "Such liberty compared to those of us in the harem! But who would wish for it? Not I."

Her Highness had no need to leave the harem for either companionship or intelligence. Ezster had told Hannah that the Valide had a network of spies as intricate as the gold mesh holding her hair in place. Nothing escaped the Valide's notice, from the menstrual rhythms of the girls of the harem to the number of chickens roasted in the palace ovens, to the Grand Vizier's military campaign against the Safavids in Persia.

The Valide gestured to Kübra to replenish her sherbet. "I find it fascinating to hear other points of view. Tell me more about yourself, Hannah."

Hannah revealed details about her family, their business, the neighbourhood in which they lived. Encouraged by Nurbanu's interest, Hannah had the boldness to speak of Isaac's silk workshop, where he fashioned billowy silk tents in which the rich enjoyed picnics. Hannah described his tents as so delicate that the slightest wind made them billow and dance, deceiving the picnickers into thinking there was a strong breeze blowing off the Bosporus even when there was not so much as a puff of air. Hannah did not mention to Her Highness the glut of silk in the market nor the unsold bolts in the warehouse.

"Another reason for my happiness here is that I can use my skills as a midwife without being branded a witch."

"And yet," said the Valide, "our palace cradles are still empty." She took a sip of sherbet, then replaced the gold-rimmed glass on Kübra's tray. "It is not a happy state of affairs."

"It is fortunate that Safiye was able to bear Mehmet, may his health continue to improve, and her little Ayşe."

"You are well aware"—the Valide paused, touching her lips with a napkin—"that I was . . . unable to attend Safiye's confinement."

Unwilling was what the Valide meant. It surprised Hannah that Nurbanu would bring this up; it had happened so long ago. "My daughter-in-law was in a great deal of pain, I imagine." The Valide made the words *I imagine* sound like *I hope.*

"There were difficulties. Her labour was long—two days—but all seemed well, until the infant emerged with her shoulder out of place. With God's help, I was able to manipulate it back into position and stop her anguish. Poor Safiye suffered as well."

"Two days of pain, and for what? A girl." The Valide tossed a meatball into the open jaws of one of the dogs. "Childbearing is the greatest of all gambles, is it not?"

"Very true," said Hannah. Soon, the Valide would inquire about Leah. Hannah felt her stomach tighten.

"Even in the glittering casinos of Venice's Grand Canal, neither the turn of a card nor the roll of dice can compare to the dangerous game of chance we women are forced to play."

Hannah had never taken part in a game of chance in her life but she was playing a dangerous game now. What were the odds that a lie about Leah would be discovered? On the other hand, had not the Sultan rejected all odalisques and concubines his mother and sister had placed before him for the past several years? He might decline Leah as well. This was Leah's only hope.

"Hannah, Safiye clutches on to my son as tightly as a fish-wife holds on to a snapper. My son could at any time, may Allah not be listening, sicken and die. He could be assassinated." The Valide sighed. "The enemies of the Empire are everywhere. The Chief Taster died a very unpleasant death last year from a bowl of pistachio nuts and honey laced with quicksilver." The Valide plucked a pastry filled with walnuts and honey and fresh cream from a tray at her elbow.

"I understand."

"Safiye has tried for years to produce a second son. She has failed. Miscarriage after miscarriage, then another girl. On it goes—vexation after vexation, disappointment after disappointment. In spite of this, the Sultan remains devoted to her. It is very tiresome. The Sultan must put her aside and find a girl who will bear sons."

Unlucky Safiye. Was she nothing more than a burden to be discarded? How miserable Hannah's life would be if Isaac had decided that Matteo was not sufficient, that he wanted a son from his own loins. There was nothing but his love for her to stop him from thrusting her aside. The law would place no obstacles in his path. And yet Hannah knew he loved her too much to abandon her.

The Valide held out her hands so that Kübra could wash off the pastry crumbs. "Here we have the very crux of the problem." The Valide opened her hands palms up as if in supplication. It was a disarming gesture for the most powerful woman in the Ottoman Empire and hence the world. "You are renowned for your skill in delivering babies, but have you ways of turning a man's thoughts to procreation? The Sultan can perform perfectly well with Safiye, but with another woman, no matter how lovely, his royal member is as flaccid as . . ."—the Valide, to Hannah's amusement, blushed—"last season's carrot."

She leaned forward and let her hand rest on Hannah's knee. Hannah had the presence of mind not to disclose her surprise.

"My daughter, Esmahan, and I have searched far and wide to find Leah. I made sure my son had a glimpse of her through a hole in the floor of his sleeping chamber when the slavers delivered her. The girl has engendered in my son's heart the kind of lust against which there is no shield." Nurbanu's mouth formed into an expression that was not quite a smile. "But while his heart may burn for his little slave girl, there is a great difference between Allah giving a man desire and providing him with the ability to satisfy it. One only has to watch the eunuchs gazing upon the girls in the hamam to divine that."

Hannah winced inwardly at the comparison. Not certain how to respond, she finally said, "I try to educate myself in all matters concerning childbirth and conception. I have knowledge of herbs." *Herbs to enhance fertility*, she could have added, none of which had had the slightest effect on her own body. She also knew of herbs that thwarted God's will and prevented conception.

The Valide Nurbanu stirred on her divan and pushed up the sleeves of her kaftan, making her gold filigree bracelets jangle. "Young Mehmet, Murat's only son, remains weak from his bout with typhus two years ago. If he should someday succumb, and if anything—may Allah not be listening—happens to the Sultan, there is no one to rule the Empire."

There was a long pause while Nurbanu re-crossed her legs on the divan. Her trousers under the red *pelisse* were made of a fabric so diaphanous that Hannah could see a mole on her ankle. "I have often puzzled about the mystery of conception. Why, for example, God breathes life into some unions and not into others. Some physicians believe that a man's seed is like that of any seed and simply needs a willing vessel—the warmth and moisture of a woman's womb in which to grow and flourish."

If only it were so simple, thought Hannah.

The Valide Nurbanu drummed her fingers on the ivory tray by her side, prompting one of the dogs to twitch its ear in a disquieting way. Hannah waited for the Valide to ask the question that was making her knee jump.

"So this girl from the mountains on whom I have pinned my hopes. I trust she is a virgin? The slavers assured me that she was, but they are Arabs and therefore liars. I trust you, and only you, to tell me the truth. You understand how important this is, the condition of her hymen?"

Hannah said, "For Jews the issue of virginity is also crucial. The Book of Genesis says of Rebekkah, daughter of Bethuel, 'And the damsel was very fair to look upon, a virgin.'"

"I know that Leah is fair to look upon, or will be when she is attended to. My question remains: is she or is she not a virgin?"

"She has suffered a terrible shock," Hannah said. "Her entire village was burned to the ground, her family murdered before her eyes."

"How fortunate for her that I purchased her."

Hannah rearranged herself on her cushion; her legs were falling asleep but she dared not stretch them. "Leah needs time to accustom herself to the palace and its ways. She is overcome with grief."

"Her spirits will improve when she is cared for." The Valide grimaced slightly. "I suspect she was as filthy and brown as a goat when you examined her. Will she be worth all the creams and perfumes and attention we will lavish on her?"

"I think not, Your Highness."

"Really?" The Valide picked up a fork and stabbed a pastry with too much force, sending it skittering to the floor. One of the dogs pounced on it and wolfed it down before Kübra had a chance to grab the beast by the collar. "Leah is to be a gift to my son. She will be presented to him—and soon. I repeat: Is she or is she not a virgin?"

"Leah will know nothing of the womanly art of pleasing a man in bed," said Hannah.

"Nonsense, her inexperience will make her more appealing. Time is of the essence," said the Valide. "Not too much delay or the Sultan will forget her, nor so little that he fails to experience lusty anticipation."

The Valide spanked her hands together in a way that demanded a response. "Answer my question—now," she added, as if the gesture were not enough.

Though, of course, Hannah had never laid eyes on the Sultan, she knew him to be a man old enough to be Leah's grandfather, with a pendulous belly and hooked nose. There was no taking the words back once they had left Hannah's lips. "She is a virgin, Your Highness."

"Wonderful!" the Valide exclaimed. "I want to see the chubby fist of a princeling waving at me over the side of that cradle." She indicated the corner of the room where a cradle rested against the wall. "Not a lot to ask, is it?" Nurbanu arched an eyebrow. "If you succeed in breaking Safiye's spell, you will have my undying gratitude."

"I shall do my best," Hannah replied, trying not to think about the lie she had told and its possible consequences.

"I do not have to tell you that if her meeting with my son goes well, you shall have a handsome reward."

Hannah bowed her head. Isaac would be well pleased with her.

"Mustafa reports that you have a tranquil effect on the girl. When the Sultan summons the girl to be brought to his divan," she added, "you shall be present at their couching."

CHAPTER 8

The Aphrodite
Mediterranean Sea

T HE WIND PLAYED with Cesca's hair, unknot-
ting her careful chignon and whipping it about
her shoulders like an untidy cape, just as it had
every morning for the past three weeks since she had
boarded the *Aphrodite* at the Port of Venice.

She gathered up her blond hair and twisted it around
her hand into a figure eight. Then, holding the hairpins
between her lips, she jabbed them in one by one until her
hair was secure. She recalled as she gripped the ship's railing meeting with Foscari a month ago—on God's firm
earth and not on the pitching deck of this ghastly ship.
Yes, it was a foolish and risky thing for Cesca to have

accosted Foscari after the funeral. Anyone could have seen them together and guessed she was up to no good. Even worse, when she told Foscari what she wanted of him, he could promptly have had her arrested. Neither of these outcomes came to pass. For once, luck was with her. And her own good judgment. Something about Foscari suggested he would be on her side.

Cesca had hidden in the woods behind a thicket of blackberries on the path from the Jewish cemetery to confront him as he returned from the burial. She had called softly to him as he walked past, the last person in the funeral procession. When he glanced up, she beckoned him to follow her. He broke away from the other mourners.

"Hurry!" she whispered at him. "Come on!"

If he was surprised by her behaviour, he gave no sign of it.

Cesca felt her heart racing, her mouth dry from desperation and rage. She knew she looked a mess—dust-grey clothes, dirt-streaked face from crawling around Leon's study looking for her ducats—but Foscari was evidently not a man to be disconcerted by the sight of a hysterical woman. With a jerk of his head, he tossed his chestnut hair off his face and calmly drew her farther away from the road, cautioning her to lower her voice.

"What is it you want of me?"

Cesca snatched the papers from her skirt and shoved them in his face. "Read these and tell me what they signify." As he took the papers from her, she glanced down at his shoes, an infallible sign of a man's wealth. Not as new as she would wish, but why would he trouble himself to put on his best boots to walk down a country road to a Jewish cemetery? She waited for him to demand a price in return for his efforts—a kiss, or a quick grapple in the bushes. Either of those she would happily have provided, but to her puzzlement he made no such requests. It was only later, when it was far too late, that she realized Foscari was not a man to be satisfied by fleeting rewards.

Squatting on the ground, he smoothed the first paper on a large rock and studied it for a moment. Foscari was not young, nor was he old, perhaps near to forty-five, although he still had the strong, square teeth of a younger man. The pouch of flesh on his neck, the hollows under his eyes, and his beak of a silver nose gave him the look of a stately raptor.

"This," he said, holding up the black-bordered parchment with the oak motif, "is written in Latin, which fortunately for you, I read fluently." He read the promissory note aloud with such ease, it was as though he were reading a simple broadsheet. "Leon made a loan of a hundred ducats to one Isaac . . ." He paused, then spoke with a hint of surprise in his voice. "Levy—a relative?"

"Leon's brother. He lives in Constantinople. A silk-maker by trade." Cesca knew the names of both Leon's brothers. He had complained about them often enough—their lack of attentiveness to him, their failure to heed his advice in business matters, their profligate wives.

"To whom is he married?" Foscari asked.

"Hannah Levy, a midwife." Cesca could have sworn from the look on Foscari's face that he knew this name.

He studied the second document, the one adorned with a border of peacocks' tails. Grecian urns and mating doves and flowing ribbons graced the corners. "This is the nuptial agreement Leon and Grazia signed before their marriage. That much I can deduce from the fanciful embellishments." He tapped the figure in the middle of the page. "Grazia's dowry was one hundred Venetian ducats. The rest is a puzzle. It is written in Hebrew and another language, which I believe is Aramaic. Give me a moment." He squinted and held the document to the sun. "No, it is of no use. I cannot read it, but I can guess at the gist of it because I doubt it differs from most prenuptial agreements. It probably has a number of clauses about remarriage and what happens in the event of children and so on." Foscari looked up at Cesca. "However, I suspect the provision that would interest you is that the widow, Grazia, in the event of Leon's death, is entitled to the return of her dowry. It is a common clause."

Cesca hoped she did not look as confused as she felt.

Foscari took hold of her chin and forced her to meet his eyes. "It is clear as a crow in a pail of milk."

"Not to me it isn't," said Cesca.

"Look," he said with an air of exaggerated patience. "Leon lent to his brother, Isaac, the one hundred ducats he received from his wife, Grazia, as her dowry. At Leon's death, according to the agreement, the ducats are to be repaid to Grazia. So"—he pulled a red handkerchief out of his breast pocket like a conjurer pulling a rabbit out of a hat, and wiped his brow—"Isaac now owes Grazia one hundred ducats."

The anger rose in Cesca like flames from a fire, turning her face red, preventing her from breathing. Her ducats were gone! They were worlds away, in the hands of Leon's brother.

A week after her meeting with Foscari, she had boarded the *Aphrodite* bound for Constantinople to claim what was hers.

I am the widow Grazia Levy, Cesca repeated to herself as she had so many times in the past three weeks. She wore Grazia's dress and her pearls and carried her valises. Wouldn't Grazia be surprised when she opened her cupboard to find her favourite dresses gone along with her maid? Luckily for Cesca, Grazia was a convert. Grazia might have learned the Jewish prayers and the blessings over challah and candles on Shabbat, but she looked and acted as Christian as Cesca.

Cesca's scheme was flawless, she reassured herself as the wind sprayed an arc of salt water on her dress. Grazia had never laid eyes on Isaac or Hannah. They had never laid eyes on her. Posing as Grazia, Cesca would demand the return of her dowry money. They could not refuse. It was written right there in the contract she had in her valise.

With a hundred ducats in her purse, there would be nothing so rare or so costly that she could not possess it with a snap of her fingers. Roasted meats stuffed with chestnuts, fresh mutton, warm baths in fragrant oils, silk dresses spun with golden thread!

In the interim, there were difficulties. Of course, like all the passengers, she had had food when she boarded. But Leon's ring, diamond or not, had fetched only enough for passage, not much in the way of provisions. The ship had run into unfavourable weather. Some windless days they were becalmed for hours. The crew would kedge a laborious course by rowing out several lengths off the bow in a small boat and dropping anchor. Then a sailor would heave hand over hand on the anchor line to pull the *Aphrodite* toward him, repeating the tedious process over and over, yet making such slight progress it hardly seemed worth the effort. Then there came squalls so fierce they were blown off course. The winds would claw at the sails, tear at the rigging, and snatch the tears from her eyes before they could wet her cheeks.

By the time they had pulled into the provisioning port of Valletta in Malta to take on fresh water, Cesca's hips were more slender. Her breasts, which had been firm globes of flesh, white and fragrant as peaches, when she sailed out of the port of Venice, were smaller by the time they rounded Cyprus. Cesca's trunk, once full of dried meat, fish, salted pork and beef, now sat empty; her supply of flour was wet and crawling with insects. No woman could subsist on twice-baked biscuits moving with weevils—biscuits so dry they required a cup of precious rainwater to force the crumbs down her throat. But perhaps she was doing herself a disservice. Perhaps she wasn't as unappealing as she felt. Was any woman dispassionate in taking the measure of her own beauty?

Cesca was desperate and hungry. She wedged herself between two gang-casks and a sail bag, praying she was invisible to crew or passengers while she did this awful thing, which she must do if she was to survive. The rat had been nibbling at the lace securing her pink shot-silk purse. She had snatched off her boot and given it a smart whack, then promptly put it, writhing and squeaking, into her pocket. Now, with her handkerchief covering her hand, she reached into her pocket and fished out the crippled creature. She dropped it between her feet with a soft plop and it lay there twitching.

She bent down to examine it, trying not to dwell on the sharp, pointed teeth and the tail—hairless and pink against the dark planking of the deck. She must control herself or else the energy she expended in repulsion would exceed the nourishment she might derive from this morsel.

Her mother's words came back. *To live, you must eat, my precious girl.* Yesterday she had eaten a shag, a gift from the bo'sun, if something which has been paid for in services can be considered a gift. Her stomach was ungrateful for the bird and soon it was part of the green froth swirling at the waterline.

It would be a month or so before they landed. A mere month. Not so great a length of time. Perhaps less, if God sent wind to fill their sails and, with His mighty hand at their stern, hastened the *Aphrodite* into port. Today they were making good progress. The ship was knifing through the waves, leaving a white foam in its wake. If Cesca could survive a little longer, what a future awaited her.

She squared her shoulders and fingered the wooden beads in her pocket, praying to the Virgin to give her strength. She kissed her rosary and crossed herself. Before they landed, she must fling the beads overboard. Rich Jewish widows did not swan about with rosary beads. Cesca stared at the deck, gooseflesh rising on her arms. She stepped on the creature. Even dead, it gave off an aura— of furtiveness, of clinging to walls, of pressing itself into crevices, of scurrying, nose twitching, among the crates in the cargo hold.

It was no worse than salted cod or beef—just greasier and stringier. She glanced around. Not a soul in sight. She grabbed the tail between her index finger and thumb and let it dangle within a hand's span of her mouth. She bit in, holding the carcass away from her so the blood would not stain her frock, which was Grazia's best velvet with taffeta inserts in the sleeves. Picking tiny bones off her tongue, she spit them into a tidy pile at her feet.

She felt better a few moments later. The breeze refreshed her. She gathered her skirts and began to rise from between the casks. By sheer force of will, she had accomplished what she did not think she could manage. She felt absurdly proud of herself.

A tall shadow striped her dress. "Hello, my dear," said a voice behind her. She looked up, shielding her eyes from the sun. It was the Marquis Foscari in his fine white jacket and wide-brimmed hat. His remarkable silver nose gleamed as he smiled at her.

How long had he been watching her? What was he doing

on the ship? There could be only one reason. He wanted a share in her ducats once she had obtained them from Isaac. But he was the Venetian ambassador in Constantinople. Why then would a man in his position want anything from her? Perhaps his presence on the *Aphrodite* was nothing more than an innocent coincidence?

"How lovely to have the pleasure of your company once again." He removed his hat and made a sweeping bow, as sweeping as possible between the confines of two water casks. He offered his hand.

Cesca took it, trying to look pleased to see him. Then, after hesitating longer than she should have, she said, "It is good to see you, Foscari." The sheen of robust health on his skin was like the blush on wild grapes. The perfume of food wafted from him.

"It is a hard matter to argue with the belly. For it has no ears," he commented in the Venetian dialect.

So he had seen her.

As a girl, Cesca had experienced the same rage she felt now in the presence of this rich man who no doubt pitied her. Once a week, if her mother had not the few *scudi* required for their rent, she would send Cesca to stand half naked in front of their landlord. The old man would gaze at her breasts while he drank his Madeira wine and sucked the spiced marrow from veal bones.

Cesca swallowed her acrimony and smiled sweetly at Foscari. Leaning toward him and tilting her head, she said, "What brings you on board?"

"You."

"Me?"

"We have business to discuss."

Cesca felt the blood rush to her face. So he had guessed her scheme and now here he was, greedy pig, clamouring for his share.

She would have liked to smash his silver nose clean off with the barrel stave lying in front of her on the deck.

Instead, she took his arm and together they picked their way across the rolling deck, side-stepping carelessly coiled rope and overflowing buckets, working their way along the railing of the foredeck, using the spars for handholds. She nearly stumbled into an empty hammock slung between two cannons and would have fallen if Foscari had not caught her around the waist. The sailors slung their hammocks without regard for others, settling like stray dogs where and when they could.

Foscari stood too close to her while he talked. Cesca beamed in response to his remarks about the weather, taking every opportunity to touch his hand or his arm or even his cheek to underline a point, even going so far as to cluck in sympathy when he mentioned the trouble he had finding food to please him.

Finally, when they reached the quarterdeck, Foscari cleared his throat and said, "Would you not be more comfortable in my cabin?"

She put her hand to her forehead and brushed away a strand of hair. Glimpsing her reflection in his nose, she was pleased to note that in the humid salt air, her hair had sprung becomingly into tight curls.

The exchange of sexual favours for food was an attractive prospect, but before matters proceeded any further between them, there was something she must find out. There were only two ways a man could lose his nose—from the French pox (which her mother had once contracted from a sailor from Cádiz), or in a duel. When Cesca's mother died, still a young woman, her mind was addled from the disease. If it was the pox, Cesca wanted nothing to do with Foscari. Starvation would be a kinder, quicker death. But if this injury was the result of a sword's blow, then that was a different matter altogether.

Hunger had not made her lose all reason. Men infected with the pox often treated their nether parts with a foul-scented, oily, mercury-based cream. She bent down on the pretext of retying her bootlace and sniffed. No foul odour. On the contrary, Foscari smelled of roasted meat, wine, and lavender water. One could not be too careful. She straightened.

"Perhaps you can tell me about . . ." She wasn't sure how to frame the question, but Foscari did it for her.

"What, this? Alas," he said, tapping his nose. "It happened on the Ponte degli Scalzi in Venice. I could not jump fast enough from my mistress's window to avoid her tiresome husband. One swipe of his broadsword and the tip of my nose was off faster than a pig's tail under the butcher's cleaver. A pity, but I rather like this one. It was fashioned by the Doge's personal silversmith."

She felt dizzy with hunger and gripped his arm.

"Perhaps you will do me the honour of dining with me?" He tucked her hand firmly over his forearm and rested his own on top. "My valet is setting out a meal even as we speak. Then he will depart, leaving us to dine in privacy. After we have eaten our fill, we shall discuss the business that propels us to Constantinople."

Us? She sensed Foscari was about to lay a torch to her carefully laid plans.

"I have wanted to see what the cabins in the aft deck look like," Cesca responded. She imagined the delights awaiting her in his. The hard pecorino that Venice was so famous for. Or an icy bottle of wine, perhaps? Potatoes fried in the lard of fat-tailed sheep? What liberties must she permit this man before he would part with his victuals? She would gorge herself until her stomach burst, agree with everything he said, and when they docked in Constantinople, she would lose herself in the populous city, never to lay eyes on him again.

As he led her down a narrow passage toward the first-class cabins, the wind shifted the ship so violently that Cesca was tossed from side to side, banging first one shoulder and then the other against the walls. When they reached his cabin, Foscari motioned her inside and closed the door. She took a seat in front of a table laden with food. Foscari lowered himself into the chair across from her.

What a feast! Inhaling the fragrance of the meat, she eyed the crisp skin of peacock, browned to the colour of deep molasses, honey dripping off a cake, cream sauce with yellow islets of butter floating in it, gravy swimming with morels, a roast squab, a fresh grouper, chicken baked in a carapace of salt, a joint of beef, and a flagon of wine. He had obviously orchestrated this moment, watching her grow hungry first, and then, confident in her desperation, offered this array of delicacies as bait. Was it her ducats he sought, or something else? She was too ravenous to care. There was a sulphurous taste in her mouth as though her very organs were devouring themselves. All she knew was that she must eat.

"I will strike a bargain with you, Cesca. If you tell me what you are playing at wearing the widow Grazia's best bib and tucker, sailing on this fine ship, you may eat your fill."

What plausible lie could she tell him? "I am going to visit my sister. She lives in Pera." It was the only district she could name in Constantinople. "She is governess to a rich pasha and his wife who wish their children to learn to speak the Roman dialect."

"Tsk, tsk. Such a pretty mouth, such clumsy lies." He sliced a piece of peacock, dipped it in the gravy, and popped it in his mouth. "I love well-roasted meat, don't you?"

Cesca watched as his jaws worked, savouring the flavours before swallowing. "It is hard to listen on an empty stomach." She longed to grab the entire chicken and cram it in her mouth or, better still, put her head down to the table and wolf down everything like a dog. The thought of how very rich Foscari must be made her feel faint. "I think you have already guessed my plan, Foscari," she said.

"Well, let us see." With his napkin, Foscari dabbed some grease off his mouth. "The documents, the widow Grazia's dress—forgive me if I have misjudged you—but you are impersonating the good widow Grazia to claim the return of her dower money?"

"May I eat now?" Cesca asked.

"Help yourself."

She reached for the chicken and put it to her lips, trying hard to control her desperate gulps, ignoring the smile that played across Foscari's mouth. Cesca had never eaten such tender chicken, scented with rosemary and basil and sage. She poured herself a mug of wine and drank it down in two swallows. He pulled her mug back. "Not too fast, my dear, or you will make yourself ill."

Foscari was right. Her stomach was not accustomed to such richness. She had to be careful. She looked at Foscari, who had settled back in his chair.

"And what are *you* doing on board, Foscari?"

He swallowed a bite of cheese. "It is rather a long story, but I think it will interest you. Years ago, I had a friend in Venice, the Conte Paolo di Padovani. As boys, we were inseparable. We hunted, we fished, we fought gangs on the bridges. Later, when we came of age, we visited the whores in Castello. Paolo once saved my life when I was drunk and set upon by robbers. I saved him from drowning in a canal. We were closer than brothers. When we grew up, he took over his father's trading company and ships. I became ambassador to the Ottoman Empire at the Venetian embassy in Constantinople. Three years ago, on a visit to Venice, I learned of Paolo's death. I was heartbroken."

Cesca was trying to listen and not snatch more food, but the lovely cream sauce was enticing; the meats would soon grow cold. "What has all of this to do with me?"

"Once I learned my friend and his wife were dead, I felt

I owed it to their memory to find out if their child was alive. If the child lived, then it was only right that he should inherit his father's fortune. Otherwise, because Paolo's brothers were believed dead, that lovely big estate would go to a distant relative or to some dreary monastery. I went to Paolo's palazzo on the Grand Canal. It was deserted except for the deaf old caretaker and a nursemaid, a peasant woman named Giovanna who had been with the family for ages. She told me the Conte and Contessa were dead but confirmed that the Contessa had given birth to a son before the plague claimed her and Paolo. The last time the maid saw the child, he was covered in buboes and was in the arms of a Jewish midwife. Giovanna ordered the midwife and the pox-ridden child away. She was sure the child must have died and the midwife along with him."

What on earth could any of this rubbish have to do with her? She wished he would fall silent so she could savour the grouper and the beef. There was a hard slab of pecorino hiding behind the jug of wine. Her hand crept forward as he droned on.

"I went to the Jewish ghetto, I talked to the shopkeepers, the moneylenders, the rabbi, and the neighbours. It is amazing how a few *scudi* in the right hands can loosen tongues. Before I knew it, the pieces of the story fit together as neatly as a puzzle." He paused. "The Jewish midwife was Hannah Levy."

Cesca's hand froze. She set the lovely wedge of cheese back on the platter. *Hannah Levy.* Isaac's wife. Yes, of course.

"This midwife sailed to Malta to redeem her husband,

who had been taken slave on a ship sailing to the Levant. Apparently, the Conte's son survived the plague, as did Hannah, and the child sailed with her. Neither she nor her husband have been heard of since."

"Hannah. Leon's brother's wife."

"Clever girl," said Foscari. He twisted off a wing from the squab and took a few bites. "Delicious, but full of lead shot." He spit a mouthful onto the floor. "The rabbi in Venice told me that Hannah's husband, Isaac, had a brother in Rome who was a moneylender. I visited Leon on the pretext of borrowing money. That, my dear, is when I first set eyes on your lovely face. You served Leon and me tea in his study when I signed the promissory note for my loan. How gracefully you handed us each a slice of seedcake. Leon told me about his brother in Constantinople, how he was married to the best midwife Venice had ever known, and how, despite years of unfruitfulness, their union had been blessed—seemingly by a miracle—with a beautiful copper-haired child they called Matteo. Alas, a few days after Leon told me this story, he died. When I heard the news, I went to his funeral to console his widow, Grazia— and that's when I saw you for the second time."

"You must have loved your friend the Conte very much to go to such pains." Cesca coughed, a fish bone caught in her throat.

"I did, and that is why I was most interested in the papers you liberated from Leon's study." The corners of his mouth twitched. "Imagine my amazement when I followed you"—he tapped his nose, making a hollow ring—"and watched you purchase a ship's passage to the very city where I was headed."

When Foscari first approached her on the deck, Cesca had feared he meant to demand a share of her ducats or he would turn her over to the authorities for theft of Leon's documents. Now she realized he had a use for her, something more than a quick fumble and grope in the berth of this cabin.

"What is it you want of me?"

"To arrive at an agreement for our mutual benefit." He patted her hand. "Together, my dear, we will save a Christian boy from the heretic Jews and, at the same time, we shall line our pockets with riches."

All Cesca yearned for were her hundred ducats. She had earned them by putting up with Leon all those years. Foscari could fling himself off the *Aphrodite* for all she cared. She had no need of a partner. "I already have a plan, which will require all of my cunning."

Foscari rose and stood behind her chair. "Don't refuse me."

She stiffened, afraid he would sweep a dish or serving platter out of reach, but instead he massaged her shoulders, working his fingers under the neckline of her dress.

"We are alike, you and I." He took the pins from her hair and let it fall down her back, combing through it with his fingers. "You can relax and be yourself with me, my dear."

Cesca almost laughed. Be herself? Left to her own devices, she would devour every morsel of food in this cabin, then steal every ducat in that little trunk she spied stowed under his berth.

"Just listen to what I have in mind. The Levys are Jews, living in a neighbourhood inhabited by other Jews. I would be conspicuous if I were to go there and make off with the child. You, on the other hand, if I am not mistaken, will be playing the role of Isaac's beloved sister-in-law, Grazia, which I am sure you will do admirably. Once in their house, you will confirm the child's identity and find the proof we need to establish that he is indeed the son of my dearly departed and very wealthy friend Conte Paolo di Padovani. Then, you will bring the child to me."

She needed nothing from Foscari except a bit of food to sustain her until they reached the port of Constantinople. "No," she said. Cesca licked the grease off her fingers and, reaching down, wiped her hands on her petticoats. "Unlike you, I do not have any highborn friends to fish me out of trouble should I get caught. I shall stick to my own plan."

Cesca had eaten so much she felt like a snake that had swallowed an entire donkey. She leaned back in her chair, wishing she was alone so she could loosen her stays. Slowly the terrible lassitude that hunger produces was leaving her. She was growing stronger. Her will had returned. Her hands, which had been so dry that when she pinched the tops, the skin stayed in peaks, were now becoming pliant and soft.

"A good strategist alters her tactics to accommodate new situations, just as a good sailor reefs in his sails in response to strong winds. You shall be handsomely rewarded for your assistance. My dear friend the Conte was rich as Croesus. He owned a palazzo on the Grand Canal, warehouses bursting with goods from the Levant. He possessed a villa on the Brenta River that brought an income of several thousand ducats a year. He also owned two merchant ships that sailed the Eastern Mediterranean transporting spices and silk from the Levant."

Foscari picked a blond hair off the shoulder of her velvet dress. "Imagine—life in Venice! As legal guardian of the boy, I shall reside in the family palazzo on the Grand Canal. Attend splendid parties. Entertain nobles and merchant princes. For you, silken gowns and ropes of pearls."

Cesca said, "To live in luxury, then to have it snatched away when the boy comes of age and can legally manage his own affairs? Is that not worse than not having riches at all?"

"Good heavens, Francesca. Children are such delicate creatures. Anything can happen to them."

It was the first time he had called her by her full name, and in his mouth it sounded like a caress.

"I cannot help you," she said. "I hope you understand."

"I am afraid that it is *you* who fails to understand," said Foscari. "You see, I know how Leon died. You, my dear, killed him."

CHAPTER 9

District of Eminönü
Constantinople

W HEN HANNAH arrived home in the Imperial
carriage, Isaac was standing at the gate, wearing the same look of greeting he wore when
she returned from the *mikvah* once a month, cleansed and
ready for him.

He helped her down the steps of the carriage, unfas-
tened her veil, and kissed her. The red carnations growing
in a clay jardinière at the entrance to their home gave off
a spicy fragrance. "You are tired, my *ketzele*. Come inside.
Tell me what was so important at the palace."

Once inside, Hannah kicked off her shoes and thrust her
feet into felt slippers. Isaac led her upstairs. It was late, and

Matteo was sound asleep. She threw a cloth over the parrot cage to keep the night draft away, then shrugged off her tunic and trousers and let her nightgown drift over her head. The silk was cool and smooth on her body. Isaac had ordered the nightdress from Venice. It was an absurd garment, impractical and feminine, a frothy confection trimmed with seed pearls. Hannah wore it on those twelve nights of the month—after the completion of her courses, after she had been to the *mikvah*—when the law permitted them to couple. Other nights, when it was forbidden, she donned a plain muslin gown worn thin from many washings.

Isaac took her hairbrush off the *cassone* and began to brush Hannah's hair with long, even strokes. Her muscles loosened and her eyes closed. How like Isaac to know what would relax her. They had been married fourteen years now, and still he petted and fussed over her like a bridegroom. Isaac, like the Sultan, would be incapable of performing with another woman. Hannah was certain of it. Why would he desire another woman when their lovemaking was such an exquisite exchange of pleasure?

"Matteo went to sleep without difficulty?" Hannah asked. She spoke casually, hoping to forestall his questions about her visit to the palace, which she knew would come soon.

"He refused to go to bed, so I lulled him to sleep by telling him for the thousandth time the story of my enslavement on Malta—the suffering and deprivation, how I had to eat unkosher food. He loved that part and wrinkled up his nose in the most adorable way. Then I told him how I sat in the square and wrote letters for illiterate farmers and how I rescued the cabin boy from the rigging of a ship."

This was Isaac's way of reassuring her that he was capable of looking after Matteo when she was out working as a midwife. "And then how I rescued you?" Hannah added.

"That is the part he enjoys best." Isaac put down the hairbrush, took some almond oil from Hannah's linen bag, and rubbed his ankles with it. It had been more than two years since his enslavement and Isaac still found his skin tender where the shackles had carved angry red bracelets into his flesh. He could not wrap the straps of sandals around the tender skin because the lightest pressure was painful. When he walked on the rough cobblestones of the street in the felt slippers she had made for him, Hannah noticed a slight . . . not a limp, but a tentativeness, as though he were walking on hot coals. But he never complained.

"Maybe Matteo is too young for such violent tales, Isaac. He has an overheated imagination, which you do nothing to discourage." She often wondered whether it was Isaac's stories that excited the child's nightmares. Would it not be better to tell the folktales of Nasreddin, the gentle old teacher who dispensed commonsense advice from the back of his little donkey? Or let the child tire himself out pretending to be a tightrope walker on the low rope Isaac had strung for him in the garden between two mulberry trees?

"The stories had the desired effect. He fell asleep with his blanket under his cheek." There was no need to ask Isaac which blanket. It was the one from Venice with his birth father's crest embroidered in gold thread. It was made of wool finer than anything attainable in Constantinople. She should have destroyed the blanket, which had grown worn and frayed, but Matteo loved it. Besides, it was never out of his grasp long enough for Hannah to fling it into the fire. Though Matteo was too young to understand this, the blanket was the only thing he had in his possession from the family he was born into.

"He has a desire to know about the past—his own and mine," Isaac said, picking up her hairbrush again. "And someday when he is older, we must tell him the truth about his family."

It was a discussion they had had many times.

Hannah said, "As far as Matteo is concerned, you are his father and I am his mother." Her worst fear was that someday, someone would arrive on their doorstep, a long-forgotten relative perhaps. This person would knock and announce, *I will take the boy now.*

Isaac took the teapot off the brazier in the corner. He poured two cups of steaming black liquid into glasses and handed her one. Tea was costly but they were not yet so short of money that they could not afford their nightly glass together.

"So tell me. What happened at the palace tonight?"

He wanted a full account of the events. Her stomach filled with dread. What would she say?

Hannah slipped off her nightdress and lay on the bed. "Not a confinement. Just some business with Mustafa," she said. Before he could question her further, she tried to change the subject. "Have I ever mentioned I often have dreams about babies? I find them in the wall niches of our house where the old owner used to store his turbans. I open a drawer and there is a baby staring up at me. Babies appear in the garden roosting in the mulberries, flattening their branches. I trip over babies on the floor when I get up in the night to check on Matteo. I find them swimming happily in the water in the stifling pots. Babies emerge from our silk cocoons like pupae. I swaddle and wrap and wash them all. I no sooner put one to breast than ten more appear."

Isaac laughed. "How fruitful you are in your dreams."

It was a jest, meant kindly, but in the most important aspect of her life, Hannah had not been fruitful. Her failure to conceive was a subject they trod around like a boulder in the middle of a road. After so many years of marriage, it seemed unlikely she would ever be pregnant.

"What do *you* dream of, Isaac?" Hannah asked.

"You," he said, and kissed the small of her back.

Hannah burrowed her face into the goose-feather pillow.

Isaac retrieved the *bahnkes* from the cupboard near the window. He heated the cups with a candle, inserting the flame and waiting until the cup began to smoke and turn sooty from the flame. Cradling each glass with a towel, Isaac applied them, one by one, to her back, waiting for her response—a grunt of pain if too hot or a sigh of contentment if just right. He always did this when she returned from the palace. It was as though he wanted to dispel all of the accumulated tension from her body. When he finished, there were seven glass globes spreading warmth and drawing out the pain from her back. She must look like one of those strange animals from New Spain that carried their young on their backs. The glasses tinkled against each other in rhythm to her breathing.

Their heat drew out her exhaustion. She wanted to savour the moment, to feel the tension seep out of her and luxuriate in her husband's attention. But she knew that at any moment, she would have to fend off Isaac's questions.

"Something must have happened tonight to make you so on edge."

Because she could not hide anything from him, Hannah said nothing.

"I worry about you, Hannah. Your work at the harem is all well and good, but if something goes wrong . . .? A difficult travail, a baby born with a club foot or born blind. When tragedy strikes, people always blame the one closest to hand."

Bending her leg and taking her foot in his hands, Isaac began to rub, using his thumbs to press into her arch and between her toes. "Why did Mustafa send for you?"

Isaac was not one to let a subject rest. She was going to have to tell him.

"I've done something you will not approve of," Hannah said.

"I was afraid of that." He let go of her foot.

"Mustafa asked me to verify the virginity of a young Circassian slave. She is to be a gift from the Valide to the Sultan to tempt her royal son away from Safiye. The palace needs heirs." Hannah fell silent remembering the sight of Leah, her sheared head and narrow green eyes, and her animal posture on the window ledge. Then, after Mustafa's departure, her tears and the rush of words.

"And? Did the girl pass the test?" Isaac walked his fingers up and down the backs of her thighs.

If she could not trust Isaac, there was no one in the world she could trust. "I lied," Hannah said. She lifted her head from the pillow, turned to meet her husband's gaze.

His hands stopped abruptly. "You *lied* to the Valide?"

"She's a Jewish girl, Isaac. One of us. The nomads slaughtered her mother and father before her eyes and then took her captive." The *bahnkes* cups pulled at her flesh. "I . . . I told the Valide the girl was intact."

"But she was not?"

"She was not," Hannah said.

Isaac's dark eyes looked at her, first puzzled, then angry. "How could you do this? Do you realize what the Valide will do when she discovers the truth? You've put the whole family in jeopardy." As though to busy himself, Isaac rose from the bed and tended to a candle that had gone out near the brazier. He relit it from a fire ember, but a breeze from the window extinguished it again, leaving a gamey stink in the room.

"If I had not lied, Mustafa would have sold her to one of the brothel-keepers down by the port."

"Which would have been none of your concern. The world is full of helpless creatures you cannot save," Isaac said. "Hannah, tell me this is one of your jests."

"I had no choice." She could see his face, drained of all its lightness and good humour. "Because I cannot save everyone, does that mean I should save no one?" Hannah asked. "Does the Talmud not say, 'If not me, then who? If not now, then when?'"

"For the love of God, did you even consider the consequences? You have taken a terrible risk, and for what? A slave girl."

"A *Jewish* slave girl."

"All you had to do was tell the truth and your family—your son and your husband—would remain safe."

Hannah opened her mouth to respond, but Isaac went on, his voice rising. "We are not living in your beloved, civilized Venice. Constantinople was conquered by nomadic tribesmen who swept in on horseback out of the plains of Anatolia. A hundred years ago they burned, sacked, and defeated Christian Byzantium. They were merciless then. Do you think they have changed? If you are found out, your head will be on a spike, with mine and Matteo's right next to it."

Hannah tried to quell his fears. "The Valide was kind to me. I drank sherbet with her and we talked of Venice and how we both longed for the city."

"The Valide is kind to her dogs until they shit on the floor," Isaac said impatiently. "Do you not see that your lie is a reflection on all Jews? In Venice, we were confined to the ghetto, cramped into a tiny *loghetto*. Jews were not permitted to work except as dealers in second-hand goods or as moneylenders. But here, it is different. Jews have been treated well by the Ottomans. Sultan Beyazit welcomed us after King Ferdinand and Queen Isabella expelled us from Spain. Do you remember Beyazit's words? He said, 'You call Ferdinand a wise king and yet he impoverishes his own country while he enriches ours.'"

"Isaac, do not lecture me."

"Here in Constantinople, no one thinks your birthing spoons are any more sinister than a pair of scissors." He glanced at her and then looked away as though he could not bear the sight of her face. "This tolerance for Jews could vanish faster than blood sinks into the ground after battle."

When she tried to speak, he held up a hand. "Think, Hannah. Is there a way you can set this right?" He stood towering by her bedside, looking down at her. "Can you say the girl begged you so piteously you agreed to lie for her but that you now have come to your senses?"

His tone was so harsh that she hardly recognized it as the voice that moments earlier had been speaking so lovingly. Her back was growing cold.

"Please, Isaac. Take off the cups."

Isaac went to the window and closed it, then came back to bed and pulled the cups off her back, lining them up on the floor. When he was done, he lay next to her, his back propped against the headboard.

"You know as well as I do that it is not wise to say how happy we have been. To do so attracts the attention of the Evil Eye. But I *will* say it aloud. We have been happy here. We have a son, a house—"

"—each other."

"A business. Now, with one lie, you have jeopardized everything."

"If I had not intervened, this girl—"

"—would have killed herself? Is that what you are going to say?"

Hannah felt dizzy with fatigue.

"You put the interest of a stranger before the interests of your family."

"It is called pity, Isaac."

"This is not pity, Hannah. This is idiocy. I know the difference even if you do not."

Hannah's feet were bare, her slippers on the other side of the room. She would not ask Isaac to fetch them for her.

"I do not lack compassion," said Isaac. "And I have done a number of foolish things in my life, but I would never do anything to endanger you or Matteo. You know what the palace is like—a viper's nest of intrigue. This slave girl and this lie will be found out."

"Her name is Leah."

They were silent a moment.

"Isaac, do you remember in Venice the neighbour's little brown-and-white spaniel that got out of the house and was wandering the streets when she was in heat? Every male dog from the district away came sniffing around. Remember the pack of them snarling at each other and yipping in the alley? They broke her back with their weight."

Isaac had turned away from her and gave no sign he was listening.

"Because it was too late to save the dog, the neighbour asked you to drown the poor creature in our washtub. To put her out of her misery."

Isaac said nothing.

"When you came back into the house with the dog's limp carcass in a sack on your back, your eyes were wet with tears. So it would have been tonight, Isaac, if I had revealed the truth about this girl. This child who has barely started her courses would be sold as a whore."

Finally, he turned to face her. "Your analogy is a poor one. I risked nothing in drowning the spaniel. I did a favour for the widow next door." He shook his head. "What are you going to do?"

She refused to think about Leah's future. Instead, she said, with all the conviction she could muster, "There is nothing to worry about. If the couching goes ahead, the Valide has promised me a great deal of money. I know ways to hide the truth about the girl. With that money, Isaac, we can enlarge the workshop." She spoke with a tone of finality, settling herself with her back to him.

Just as she was falling into sleep, she felt Isaac move closer to her. Their horsehair mattress squeaked as he pulled the covers over them.

"Good night, Hannah." He patted her shoulder, but did not kiss her as he usually did. "If the Sultan discovers this girl is not a virgin, it will be you who is stuffed in a sack and drowned like the neighbour's spaniel."

CHAPTER 10

MATTEO SCREAMED with glee at the sight of Möishe, who resembled a shaggy bear, carrying aloft a mothing tray. The weaver, who lived with the Levy family in a little cottage in the back of the property, lumbered to the other side of the garden, then lowered the heavy wooden tray onto a pair of sawhorses.

Hannah leaned over and kissed the top of Matteo's coppery head. "Someday, you will be big enough to help Möishe in the shop and strong enough to carry a tray like his. In the meantime, perhaps Möishe can make a special one, just for you."

It had been a fortnight since Hannah's visit to the palace. She had tried to banish the memory of Leah. She imagined a blank wall like the one from her *loghetto* years ago in the Venetian ghetto, whitewashed and unadorned. She imagined writing words on the wall with a quill and pot of ink, words that made her happy. Words like *Isaac, Matteo, challah,* and *Seder wine.* That was how she quieted her mind and erased disturbing thoughts. This morning her technique was not working. Instead, her mind projected images, like a *camera obscura*—Leah's green eyes, the glint of the knife, the Valide's unsettling gaze. Hannah blinked and tried again: *Isaac, Matteo, carnations, Iznik tiles.* It was no use.

Möishe looked at her from the other side of the garden, wriggled his eyebrows, then pursed his lips at Matteo and pretended to frown. "Are you a good boy, my son?" he called.

Matteo raced toward him, waving a stone he had picked up. He spied a mourning dove perched on a branch of a mulberry tree. "Möishe, watch me throw this at the bird!"

Möishe stepped forward and gently pried the stone from Matteo's fist. "No, don't tease the dove."

"But all the other boys do it—Hikmet and Abdul."

"My friends do stupid things too. They go to taverns, they chase bad women. So what? Are we the sheep that follow the goat to the slaughterhouse?"

Möishe tousled Matteo's hair, then went back into the workshop to sit at his loom. No one was as skilled a weaver as Möishe, who had learned his trade in Lucca but departed that city for reasons he would not reveal. Soon the thump of the loom pedals came drifting out the open door into the garden.

Hannah held Matteo's hand as he climbed onto his tightrope and proceeded to walk a few wobbly steps before jumping off. Isaac had rigged it so that it was only a few finger-lengths from the ground. He had made it out of the thickest rope he could find.

"Mama!" Matteo shouted. "It is a wonderful thing to have. A tightrope."

"Indeed it is, my son," she said, letting go of his hand and bending to pick some rosemary from the bush near the kitchen door.

The bell rang, and Hannah heard Zephra open the front door. She went to the entrance and saw her friend Ezster and Ezster's daughter, Tova. Ezster was carrying a basket of candles. Tova stood at her side, arms folded across her belly, heavy with child.

"How delighted I am to see you both." Hannah took the basket from Ezster. "Your famous candles. I am so grateful. I have been reduced to using those foul-smelling rush candles that are so hard to keep lit."

Ezster sold those candles of hers as fast as she could haul the hard, yellow wax from the beekeeper. The mice and rats did not dare nibble at Ezster's beeswax candles as they did with tallow ones, leaving holes that caused the candles to topple and set fire to curtains and baby blankets. Ezster's graceful tapers did not fuss and sputter and spit and gutter into greasy curls of smoke, casting more shadow than light. They burned clear and odourless. Her secret?

Anchor rope that she first soaked in boric acid, dried in the sun, separated, and then used for dipping as wicks. Ezster and her donkey were a common sight at the shipyards. The ship chandlers saved their old rope for her.

"We have come to ask if you would be my midwife when my time comes," Tova said.

Ezster added, "We know there is no one better in the Empire, and we'd both rest easy knowing you were there at the birth."

Hannah smiled at Ezster and Tova, who were good and loyal friends.

"Of course. I would be honoured. Just send for me. I will fly across the street as swiftly as a goldfinch."

"Thank you, Hannah," Ezster said, squeezing Hannah's arm.

Tova said, "The baby is due in a few weeks."

"I am not planning on being anywhere but here—God willing," said Hannah.

As the two women turned to leave, Tova called over her shoulder, "And bring those birthing spoons with you. I have a feeling this is going to be a large baby and stubborn like his father."

Hannah laughed. "No one is more stubborn than that man." In truth, she liked Tova's husband, who reminded her of a young Isaac.

Once the women were gone, Hannah took up her knife again and returned to the garden to finished cutting herbs.

The front door bell rang again and Hannah thought it was Tova and Ezster returning to tell her something they had forgotten to mention earlier. Matteo raced off to investigate, leaving Hannah behind in the garden. Hannah listened to the exchange of voices drifting in from the entranceway—a melodious female one and Isaac's deep bass. She heard the front door closing.

Matteo ran back to Hannah's side and tugged at her hand. "Mama, come. A woman has arrived. You must come and meet her."

Just then, Zephra hobbled in from the small orchard in the back of the garden, her apron plump with lemons, dragging her left leg bent from arthritis. Hannah gave her a bunch of rosemary to add to the capon she was about to pluck for Shabbat dinner. The old servant could denude any bird, from duck to dove, from pheasant to peacock, as deftly as a lady plucking the keys of a harpsichord. Hannah rubbed her hands on her skirt and made her way to the door.

A surprise visitor. Not Tova and Ezster. My God, Hannah thought, I must look a mess. She patted her hair, winding a stray lock behind her ear. In Venice she had always been welcoming to company. Here, because of Matteo, she was wary. Even now, after all this time, the fear of losing him populated her dreams.

Hannah stopped short before she reached the door. A graceful figure stood in the entranceway, her hand on Isaac's arm, a slight breeze from the open door shifting the blond curls at her neck. The rest of her hair was caught in a snood held in place with silver hairpins. Two valises rested at her feet. Her red dress, the pleats knife-sharp, was nipped in tight at the waist. The sleeves were loose and fluttered at her sides. The dress was an elegant sight compared to the trousers and kaftans the Mohammedan women wore. Matteo walked over to the woman and touched her dress. The woman did not turn, and stood chatting with Isaac as the sun streamed in, checker-boarding the floor.

Matteo raced back to Hannah, who swung him onto her hip. She listened as Isaac spoke in the mellow, informal tone he used for family and friends. Hannah moved closer.

Isaac was now clasping both of the stranger's hands as though about to dance a *gagliarda*. "I cannot believe I am meeting you after all these years," she heard him say.

Together they turned to look at Hannah.

"Hello!" the woman said, reaching out a graceful arm. "You must be Hannah."

Seeing up close this woman's porcelain skin and long-lashed blue eyes, Hannah realized it was possible to be too beautiful. She had to glance away, and then looked back to ascertain that her eyes had not imagined the elegant figure, the huge blue eyes set in the oval face, the small mouth, the skin as white as cream, and the cheeks blushed pink.

They moved out into the garden and stood outside the workshop where Möishe sat bent over his loom. He stared at the woman, the shuttlecock still in his hand. Tiny golden filaments of thread floated into the air, some of them settling on the guest's red dress, making it shimmer.

Hannah looked at Isaac, who stood gazing at this stranger, standing too close to her, his mouth open.

"I am your sister-in-law, Leon's wife. I am Grazia. And," she said, turning to Matteo who was also gazing at her, mesmerized by her beauty, "I am your aunt." She took a slender finger and ran it down Matteo's nose, then lightly pinched one of his cheeks.

Was this really Leon's wife? And if so, what in the world was she doing here in Constantinople, so far from Rome, and so soon after her husband's death?

Hannah wiped her hands on her apron and kissed Grazia, aiming for her cheek but kissing the tip of her ear because Grazia turned her head just as Hannah bent toward her. She inhaled the fragrance of citrus and bergamot. She and Isaac had received a letter from Yehuda, Leon's son from his first marriage, advising them that Leon had died, but a visit so soon? Had Isaac known Grazia was coming but neglected to tell her?

"Very pleased to meet you," Hannah managed to say.

If Hannah had known Grazia was coming, she would have put on her best blue dress and washed her hair. A guest such as her sister-in-law deserved special dishes, a clean house, a new coverlet for her bed, and new curtains. The spare room needed to be whitewashed. The room was not a guest room at all but more of a storeroom, piled high with mothing trays and skeins of silk thread. Was it too late to tell Zephra to prepare a special dessert of ground pistachios and spiced apricots?

"You must be exhausted from your journey," said Isaac.

In fact, she looked nothing of the kind. She looked as though she had been enjoying excellent meals and had just emerged from the baths. A garnet wedding ring, too loose on her finger, and earrings set with amethysts were her only jewellery.

Hannah tugged at the patched grey dress she always wore when she did housework, riddled with holes from the splash of lye when she made soap.

"I sailed on the *Aphrodite*," said Grazia. "A long trip, nearly seven weeks, but I find the sea air so bracing." She smiled, displaying teeth as white and even as pearls.

When Hannah had arrived in Constantinople two years ago after her sea voyage from Malta, she looked like the survivor of a shipwreck—wishbone thin, with matted, lousy hair. Matteo and Isaac had been the same sorry spectacle. This slim woman in fitted velvet seemed to have survived the voyage without so much as a grease stain on her skirt, or a tear in her sleeve.

"The sea is rough this time of year," said Isaac. They returned inside where Isaac picked up Grazia's valises and moved toward the stairs leading to the guest room.

Matteo, usually shy, surprised Hannah by scampering over to Grazia to bury his face in her skirts.

Grazia bent down so they were at eye level. She threaded her fingers through his curls. "Look at you! Such a big boy! Why, you are as tall as a bouquet of lilies."

"Matteo, can you say hello to your aunt?" Isaac said, with what seemed to Hannah to be too much insistence.

Matteo stared at Grazia.

Grazia said, "We shall be great friends by and by."

"What a pleasure to have you here," said Hannah.

If only Grazia had not arrived just now, when Hannah had so much on her mind. Grazia would be another mouth to feed, but maybe they would chat and laugh and exchange confidences like sisters. Hannah missed the company of women from her part of the world. "We have no family in Constantinople," Hannah said, "which makes you especially welcome."

While Isaac led her through the workroom and upstairs to their living quarters, Hannah hurried out to the summer kitchen in the garden to see if Zephra was finished picking beans. The old servant was adding more broth to the soup.

From overhead, she heard Grazia and Isaac walking back and forth in the guest room between the cupboard where the bed was rolled up and put away for the day, and the wall niches for storing clothes. She heard the scraping of Grazia's valise being dragged across the floor. When Shabbat was over, Zephra could clear it out and place sprigs of lavender between the bedsheets and hang the pillows out the window to air. Isaac came downstairs.

Hannah spoke with Zephra about dinner and then climbed the stairs and joined Grazia in the spare room. She had already unpacked a suitcase containing three dresses and hung them in the clothes press. They looked too big for her, but perhaps Grazia had lost weight on the voyage. Exactly how long was she expecting to stay with them?

"Leave your unpacking, Grazia. Come downstairs. Zephra will bring us some tea while you tell us of your journey. Isaac will join us in a moment. He went to talk to Möishe about some matter."

Her sister-in-law smiled and dropped the chemise she had been folding to put away in the wall niche. "I understand Ottoman ladies do nothing all day but sip tea."

Hannah laughed. "Just the rich ones with lots of servants." She turned to the door and said over her shoulder, "Come, we shall have a cup."

Hannah and Grazia went downstairs, pausing in the kitchen where Hannah asked the maid to prepare the strong black tea that she and Isaac favoured. Matteo was playing with his ball and stealing glances at the beautiful stranger who had suddenly entered their lives.

Hannah and Grazia sat under the wisteria arbour, and minutes later Zephra emerged from the kitchen carrying a tray. Isaac joined them, taking a seat on the bench next to Grazia. For a moment, the three of them were silent. Hannah tried to catch Isaac's eye to prompt him to ask his sister-in-law what it was she had come for. But Isaac did not so much as turn Hannah's way. He focused steadfastly on Grazia.

"Of what did my poor brother die?" he asked. "Yehuda did not say in his letter, only that Leon died suddenly."

"His heart gave out. His death was a terrible shock. He was at his writing desk and toppled to the floor, hitting his head."

How unusual, thought Hannah, who said, "He was a relatively young man."

"It was a terrible shock, but at least he did not suffer."

"You sailed from Venice unaccompanied? Quite an undertaking for a woman," said Isaac.

"I was not alone. I had friends on board. A couple from Rome. They were of great comfort to me. They have sailed on to Aleppo."

"I wonder that you would undertake such a voyage so soon after Leon's death," Hannah ventured. If Isaac died, she would be unable to move from the house for months, never mind endure weeks on storm-tossed seas.

"I felt I must visit you," Grazia explained. She bent forward and patted Isaac's knee. "You and my stepson, Yehuda, are my only kin, now that Leon is gone."

A strange and unfamiliar feeling rose in Hannah, one that was not at all pleasant. Was it jealousy or simply a feeling of being left out and ignored?

"It seems only yesterday that my father wrote me the details of your wedding," Isaac said, putting his hand on top of Grazia's. "And now he, too, is dead."

"I was sixteen when I married your brother," Grazia said. "So long ago! Ten years."

Their marriage had been an unusual one.

"My father wrote and told me what a lovely bride you were. I was not able to travel to Rome for your wedding, but my father's description made me feel I was there." Isaac smiled. "My father admired the bone buttons on Leon's coat. He wrote he had never seen anything so fine."

Grazia reached for her tea. Hannah was glad she was no longer touching Isaac. Had Leon captured Grazia's heart in the same way Isaac had captured hers? She would ask Grazia when they got to know each other better.

Grazia said, "Oh yes, those buttons! Leon was missing

one from his frock coat. I had sewn it on, but it popped off during the meal. He was mortified."

Isaac nodded.

"Leon ate so much lamb that night, the grease stained his suit. The Gypsy *musicians* played until dawn and then fell asleep on their feet like horses." She leaned back in her chair and played with a tendril of hair at the side of her face. "Our only entertainment at the wedding, but it was enough."

"There was something else. I am sure of it," said Isaac.

"It was so long ago. All I could think of was what was to come that night in bed."

Hannah looked at Isaac, but he did not react. It was a bold thing for a Jewish woman to say in front of a man, never mind a man she hardly knew. There had been rumours Grazia was carrying a baby conceived before the *ketubah*, the marriage agreement, was signed. The wedding had to be arranged in haste. It was not something of which to be proud. Seven months after the wedding, a baby boy was born, the birth cord wrapped around its neck.

Isaac brought a hand to his forehead. "Now I remember! My father wrote about jugglers, a troupe of five men from Edirne who tossed about lighted torches."

"Yes, that's right! An amusing display." A shadow passed over her face.

Was all this talk of her wedding saddening her? No one from Grazia's side of the family had attended, Hannah recalled, because they were so shocked by her conversion to Judaism.

Isaac blew on his tea and took a sip. "When we were

growing up, Leon protected me from street toughs in the ghetto. He was so much older, more like a father to me than a brother. As we grew up he became—and there is no tactful way to say this—difficult. I loved him, and as a child I looked up to him, but he could not have been an easy man to live with."

"He grew kinder with age," Grazia said, taking a sip of tea. "He was very fond of you, Isaac."

Tears filled Isaac's eyes.

Grazia reached out to touch Isaac's cheek. "May Leon be looking down on us as we talk."

They were silent for a moment. Matteo brought over his ball and sat cross-legged at Grazia's feet, leaning against her skirts. Grazia toyed with his curls with an air of familiarity, as though she had known him since birth.

Hannah folded her hands under her apron. Her skin was chapped, her knuckles swollen from stretching canvas onto the moth trays in readiness for the mounting season. When she had a moment, she would rub them with her own ointment made of beeswax, olive oil, and lanolin.

"You must give me a tour of your workshop," Grazia said to Isaac. "They say the silk here is the best in the world."

"May that always be true," Isaac said, rising to his feet. "Come."

Grazia placed her teacup on the little table next to her. The two of them, Matteo trailing behind, trooped into the workshop without as much as a glance back in Hannah's direction. Hannah saw Möishe eyeing Grazia again. Did all men react this way to blue eyes, white skin, and a slender waist?

"Cochineal," said Möishe, leaving the loom and approaching her for a closer look. He rubbed a fold of the sleeve between his fingers.

Hannah realized she had misjudged him. He was studying Grazia's red dress, not the woman inside it.

"Look at this, Isaac. I have not seen this hue since I left Lucca." He gave Isaac a nudge. "If I had some of that to work with, eh? The ladies of the harem would be clamouring for our tents."

Isaac turned to Grazia. "Leon had some cochineal, did he not? He once wrote to tell me that he took a pouch of it in payment of a debt from a Sephardic dyer. Do you recall anything about it?"

"Leon did not discuss business with me," said Grazia— rather tersely, Hannah thought.

"I will write to Yehuda. Maybe he knows something."

"Oh, do not bother. I will do it myself," Grazia said. "I must write him anyway to let him know I arrived safely."

They spoke of this and that and soon the shadows in the garden lengthened and Zephra emerged from the kitchen to summon them to the table. Isaac and Grazia walked back to the house, arms linked. Hannah followed, trying once again to catch Isaac's eye, but he refused to meet her glance. There were so many things that puzzled her about this unexpected visitor. Didn't Isaac feel the same way?

After Shabbat dinner, in the privacy of their bedchamber, Hannah said, "Isaac, what on earth does she want from us?"

"Hannah, she is family. *That's* what she wants from us,

love and support after losing her husband. How can you be so inhospitable and unkind?"

Maybe he was right. Perhaps she was just jealous of such a beguiling woman living in her house. But then again . . .

"Odd that she did not remember the jugglers at her own wedding."

"Why do we remember some things and not others? Why do you recall the details of every childbirth you have ever attended and I can hardly remember what we ate for dinner yesterday? Memory is a slippery eel. You can grasp one end, or you may grasp the middle, but you never can grasp the entire creature."

"You defend her because she is pretty," Hannah said. Her remark was made in jest but there was an element of truth in it.

Isaac patted Hannah's rump. "She's too skinny for my taste. If she was a heifer, I would graze her on richer pasture."

Hannah was heartened by his comment. It meant he was no longer angry about the incident at the harem and her part in it. Maybe that would just fade away and be forgotten. Hannah hoped so.

"Grazia was in a great hurry to see us. She must have departed from Rome on the first ship out of port in the spring, a week after Leon's death, without a period of mourning."

"There may be another reason she has come," said Isaac.

"I do not understand."

"I wrote to Leon last year when our silkworms died of jaundice. He lent me Grazia's dowry money so that I could replace them. He said he could afford it, that Grazia's family was wealthy, and that nothing would give him greater pleasure than to help me with my business . . . But let us go to sleep. We will talk in the morning."

They slipped off their clothes and washed in the basin in the corner. Hannah donned her silk nightdress. Isaac put on his nightshirt.

They settled into bed together, the horsehair mattress creaking under their weight.

"That is all? Talk to me, Isaac."

Hannah heard her husband give a sigh of resignation, knowing she would not let the matter rest until morning.

"Under the terms of their marriage contract, Grazia is entitled to the return of her dowry upon Leon's death. It is a common provision to ensure a widow is not left impoverished. Since Leon loaned me the money, I must pay it back to her now that Leon is dead."

So that was the reason Grazia had come. Hannah knew nothing of marriage contracts. Isaac had married her without a dowry, a fact he had the grace never to mention. "How much do you owe her?"

"A hundred ducats."

"What?" Hannah sat upright in bed. "We can never repay that. We arrived from Venice with nearly a hundred and fifty golden ducats, more than enough to purchase the house and workshop. We had some left over, did we not?"

"Shh, not so loud. You will wake Matteo." He met her eye at last. "I needed more. For equipment, for the ten hectares in Kadiköy to plant a mulberry orchard. When the silkworms died, I had to replenish our stock. There were only a few dozen healthy worms to be had. Prices were high. Then I had to hire Möishe. A silk shop must have an experienced weaver and dyer."

Hannah was reluctant to say more for fear he would frown at her the way other husbands frowned at their wives, as if to say, *You are merely a stupid woman. Finances are not your concern.*

"Why did you not tell me?"

"I worried enough for both of us. Why should you have fretted as well?"

She knew all too well the temptation of keeping the truth from her husband so he would not worry. "So Grazia has come to collect her money," she said. "Money we do not have and have no hope of getting."

How complicated and ugly everything had suddenly become. Before Grazia's arrival, before Hannah had known of the loan, she wanted nothing more than to protect Leah from the Sultan's attentions. Now, she had a chance to earn enough to pay off this debt, but only if the coupling took place between the Sultan and Leah. Now she was in the terrible position of benefitting if the couching proceeded.

"How will we ever repay her?"

"I do not know."

"What is the worst that can happen?"

"Grazia goes to court, gets the bailiffs to come and sell our house and everything we own." He spoke without hesitation, so Hannah knew he had been mulling this over.

Not long ago, Hannah had given several silver coins to a neighbour, a young widow whom she passed on the street with her children, sitting among piles of clothes and baskets of food, as bailiffs carried out furniture, clothing, sacks of flour—anything of value that could be sold to satisfy her debts.

"Grazia is my brother's widow," Isaac said. "She will agree on a compromise. Perhaps we can pay her back slowly. We will talk to Rabbi Yakov ben Asher. He is a wise man. He will decide what is best for us all. The three of us will go as soon as possible."

Rabbi Yakov? Hannah was about to protest but stopped herself before she said something she might regret. Rabbi Yakov's sermons were long and tedious. His eyes were weak from poring over the Torah all night in dim light. His hands shook with palsy. She had refused to let Isaac take Matteo to him to be circumcised. A shameful state of affairs was the result. Matteo was over three years old and had yet to make his first covenant with God.

From the garden came the hoot of an owl. That sound had once comforted her, as part of the cadence of the night, like Isaac's gentle snore or Matteo turning over in bed on his mattress or the rush of the tide entering the port at Eminönü. Now, the owl's cry sounded to Hannah like a mourner at a funeral procession.

CHAPTER 11

H ANNAH WAS IN such a state of anxiety that she
felt like a mother in labour. Rabbi Yakov ben
Asher had the power to make binding orders on
all issues, both civil and criminal. The Ottoman government
cared little about the Jews as long as peace prevailed in the
mahalle and everyone paid their taxes. But the Rabbi was ill
with influenza. There was nothing to do but wait for his
recovery, which was taking too long. Meanwhile, during the
nearly two months since Grazia had arrived, the two women
moved warily through the house, neither of them wanting
to discuss what was so present in both their minds. Hannah
went about her daily chores and watched helplessly as both

her son and her husband seemed to fall deeper and deeper in thrall with Grazia. Her influence in the household grew stronger with each passing day. She sought Isaac's opinion on a variety of matters, from whether it would rain, to what he would like for his supper. She cooked Matteo special dishes, singing him to sleep at night. She helped Möishe set up the warp and weft on the looms. Her nimble fingers rapidly unravelled silk cocoons, a tedious task.

Isaac had begun consulting Grazia in business matters, as she had a clever head for figures. She was keeping his ledgers for him, something Hannah had once tried without success. She had no knowledge of how the long columns of figures were supposed to be arranged on the page; her addition and subtraction was neither rapid nor accurate. When she added more than ten numbers together, she got several different answers. When Hannah asked Isaac why he encouraged Grazia to sit poring over his books night after night, he said, "So she could see for herself the workshop is not prospering and that we have no money to pay her."

It was not necessary to strain one's eyes over ledgers. Any fool could see Isaac's many bolts of printed silk—the entire output of his shop for the past six months—were gathering dust in a backroom just beyond the workshop. Exquisite material that shimmered like the wings of a butterfly. Fabric that would fetch a fortune in Venice languished for buyers here in Constantinople where the price was so low that Isaac could not sell it without sustaining a loss.

As for Leah, all Hannah knew—from the Valide's messenger who had arrived out of breath on her doorstep yesterday—was that the couching would take place in three days. The Imperial carriage would fetch her. As to how the girl was adjusting to life in the harem, even Ezster, with her consummate gift for ferreting out palace gossip, had no news of her.

Hannah had not told Isaac that she was soon to go to the palace. Once, she would have confided in him. Now, he was so worried about money she did not want to add to his burden.

The couching would proceed unless Hannah could think of a means to prevent it. The thought of Leah, no more than a child, coupling with the Sultan filled her with distress even if it meant Hannah would receive the Valide's gratitude as well as a rich reward. If only she had had an opportunity to counsel the girl, explain what was ahead of her, perhaps give her an opium pill to make the experience less disturbing.

A knock at the front door interrupted her gloomy thoughts. It was Myriam, the Rabbi's wife, to say the Rabbi had recovered and would see them. They were to go to his study immediately. The three of them hastily donned their best clothes and left the house, walking in silence the short distance.

First Isaac, then Grazia, and finally Hannah filed into the Rabbi's cramped study, which looked as though it had not been dusted since the destruction of the temple of Jerusalem. The Rabbi was hunched behind a table piled with books. Distracted, thin from his illness, more filled with tremors than ever, he nodded as they entered the stuffy room.

Rabbi Yakov ben Asher, rabbi of the Poli Yashan shul with a congregation of a hundred Ashkenazi and Romaniote Jews, husband of Myriam, father of five daughters, three living, stroked a beard so long and sparse that it looked like a dusty cobweb tossed over the front of his black robe. He was old, at least sixty, and his hair was more grey than black. His shoulders were rounded as a soup tureen, his skin so dry his face appeared powdered with chalk. In short, he looked like a rabbi.

Isaac had once remarked to Hannah that Rabbi Yakov was so spindly it was a miracle he could stagger with the scrolls of the Torah from the Holy Ark to the *bimah*, the pulpit. Myriam, the *rebbetzin*, had told Hannah that when she and the Rabbi joined together, they did so through a hole in the coarse blanket he threw over her first. "It is as though he is forcing himself to couple with something foul," she said through her tears. "No matter how often I go to the *mikvah*, I am never pure enough for him." Rabbi Yakov was not a man who cared for women.

The Rabbi rose and hugged Isaac. He concealed the tremor in his hands by patting Isaac's back. He looked at Hannah and Grazia, not moving to touch them. This was to be expected. He shoved some books and papers from the bench in front of his writing table.

"Sit," he ordered, as though to a group of Yeshiva students. His suit smelled of rosemary and peppermint leaves, to repel moths. Underlying this pleasant smell was the even stronger odour of smoked herring.

Hannah sat first, her mouth so dry she would have been

grateful for a sip from the water jug on the Rabbi's desk, but he did not offer it to her. Isaac sat next to her, looking as stern as Moses. Grazia sat to Hannah's left. She must have been apprehensive too, judging from the way her hands twisted in her lap.

From behind his desk the Rabbi fixed them with his sharp, black eyes. "Well, what can I do for you?"

Books teetered on his table—some opened, some closed, all well-thumbed and stacked in jagged towers that threatened to crash to the floor. Hannah had not known there were so many books in the universe and wondered if there was sufficient knowledge in the world to fill them.

The Rabbi rocked back and forth in his chair. He studied Grazia, taking in her smooth blond hair and perfect skin. If he was puzzled to see a woman dressed as a Jewess who did not appear in the least to be Jewish, he gave no sign of it. Isaac must have explained that Grazia was a convert.

When no one spoke, he cleared his throat and said, "Let me see if I can guess what has brought you here. Difficulties can come in many forms but mostly there are two varieties—those that can be solved by great lashings of money and those that cannot. I would say that from everyone's grave expressions, you three have money trouble. Am I right?"

"We welcomed Grazia, our sister-in-law, into our house a month ago," began Isaac. "We have been happy for her company. But now we have a dilemma." At the Rabbi's prodding, Isaac explained—Leon's death, Grazia's arrival in Constantinople, the marriage contract, and the debt owing to Leon and now to his widow . . .

After a few moments, the Rabbi made an impatient circle in the air with his finger urging Isaac to get to the point.

"I find myself at a loss," said Isaac. "Grazia insists on immediate and full payment."

The Rabbi stroked his beard. "The amount owing?"

"A hundred ducats."

The Rabbi whistled. "An impressive sum. Enough to buy golden *Kaddish* cups and feed all the poor Jews in the city for a year." He looked at Grazia, "Let me see this fancy marriage contract of yours."

"Leon and I signed it a few weeks before our wedding," Grazia said. She took the document from her bag and placed it on the desk, smoothing open the heavy parchment to reveal a border of peacocks, their tails draping the sides of the page.

The Rabbi rubbed his hands on his jacket and then took the parchment. "These are Hebrew characters, as you know." He pointed to the outer border of letters. "The rest of the contract is written in Aramaic." He pointed to a scrawl. "That is your signature at the bottom?"

"Yes," replied Grazia.

The Rabbi squinted. "And who is this witness?" he asked, pointing to another signature.

"I do not remember," said Grazia, shaking her head.

"You do not remember your own witness?"

Grazia rubbed the bridge of her nose. "It might have been, let me see, my father or one of my uncles or . . ." Her voice trailed off.

The Rabbi gave an impatient wave of his hand to silence her, then, muttering to himself, read aloud, moving his finger from right to left along the Aramaic script. He translated as he read, beginning with the preamble, *"In the Creator's name may they build their house and prosper . . ."* He paused at a line in the middle and looked up at Grazia. "You brought a considerable dowry to the marriage. And, yes, the contract stipulates that the money be returned to you upon Leon's death." He raised an eyebrow. "Did you and Leon have children?"

Grazia shook her head.

The Rabbi looked at Isaac. "You have been to the moneylenders?"

"Yes, and I have been turned down by everyone," said Isaac.

Grazia opened her mouth as though she wished to add something to Isaac's remark, but the Rabbi motioned for her to be quiet. He leaned back in his chair.

"And you, Hannah, what do you think about this situation?"

Hannah was startled. Since when did a Rabbi ask a woman's opinion on anything? "It is just as Isaac says," she replied. "We do not have her money, but she can live with us until the money can be found. Grazia and I get along like sisters." Did not sisters squabble at times, feel jealousy and suspicion of each other? "I would be happy for her to stay with us as our honoured guest until Isaac is able to raise her money."

"And you?" He nodded at Grazia.

"Alas, I cannot wait for Isaac to pay me. I must return to Rome."

"And what is so important in Rome?"

Grazia blushed. "I wish to remarry."

This was the first Hannah had heard of such a plan. True, life was for the living, and Jewish law frowned on a long period of mourning, but still, wasn't it too soon? Had Isaac known of a remarriage? She looked at him but could tell nothing from the stern expression on his face.

The Rabbi rose to his feet, extracted a book from a pile on the table. "All of you think this is a simple matter of debt and repayment? That all you need do is keep Grazia as a guest until her debt is satisfied? There is something of which you are ignorant." He leafed through the book until he found the page he wanted.

"Yes," he said, "this is from Deuteronomy. I will simplify for the sake of the women." He cleared his throat. "When a man dies, leaving a widow, it is the duty of the deceased man's brother to 'go into the widow,' and perform the duty of a husband. And if a son is born to her, then the child shall be named after the deceased brother." The Rabbi took a deep breath. "You have heard the Latin word '*levir*'?"

Hannah tried to concentrate on the Rabbi's words but they made no sense.

"Meaning brother-in-law?" Isaac asked.

The Rabbi nodded. "The law of levirate marriage states that a brother-in-law is married to his brother's widow, if the brother dies without heirs." He turned to Grazia. "Since you and Leon had no children, this means, Isaac, in the eyes of the law, you and Grazia are husband and wife."

Hannah felt as shocked as she had felt when years ago a rabbi in Venice had told her Isaac had been taken as a slave in Malta.

"But that is an ancient tradition from biblical times. Jews no longer practise this custom," said Isaac.

"All that remains to legitimize this union is consummation." The Rabbi spoke as matter-of-factly as if he were telling them the price of a barrel of pickled herring or a measure of lamb suet. "You may, of course, choose to have a wedding ceremony, but it is not required by law."

Hannah tried to speak but it took her a few moments to form the words. "But Isaac is married to me!"

The Rabbi ignored her and said to Isaac, "The law is for the protection of the widow."

"So I am married to *both* Hannah and Grazia?" Isaac asked, incredulous.

Hannah glanced at Grazia. At first the woman wore a look of shock, and then another unreadable expression came over her face.

The Rabbi asked, "Is there anything in your marriage contract with Hannah to prevent you from taking another wife?"

Isaac shook his head. "I married Hannah without a dowry, so there was no need for a *ketubah*."

Isaac had taken her without so much as a feather bed to her name. If only he had not been forced to mention it now in front of the Rabbi.

The Rabbi raised an eyebrow. "You must have loved her very much."

Isaac smiled for the first time since they had set foot in the Rabbi's study. "I still do."

How relieved Hannah felt, at least for the moment.

Perhaps when all of this was sorted out they could be as close as they once had been.

Grazia spoke. "This law is for my protection?"

"Can't you see?" Hannah said. "With this law, you go from one husband to the next, passed from hand to hand like a platter of lamb around the Seder table at Passover."

"Hannah," said Isaac, a note of warning in his voice.

"I will not agree to this," Hannah said, ignoring him. "I am Isaac's rightful wife. How can Isaac have two wives? Muslims—yes, their religion permits four wives if they are rich enough to support them. But Jews—no." She should not speak so. It was not a woman's place, but she no longer cared.

The Rabbi should have been offended by her outburst, but when she looked up, there was a look of bemusement on his face. "Here in Constantinople, we follow the teachings of Rabbi Eliyahu Mizrahi of Saintly Seed, who allowed such unions, especially as in your case, Isaac"—the Rabbi looked pointedly at Hannah—"when the marriage is without children." He stroked his beard. "In Constantinople a Jew can have more than one wife. Hannah, God has closed your womb. Because of you, Isaac has not been able to fulfill his obligation to go forth and multiply."

"But that is—" *Not my fault*, Hannah was about to say. *I have gone to the hocas in the market, swallowed their potions and elixirs, rubbed strange mixtures on my stomach, and slept with magic amulets under my pillow.* She said none of this aloud.

"As I have explained, if Isaac has a son with Grazia, he will honour his dead brother's memory by naming the boy after his deceased brother."

The Rabbi talked in a kindly tone, as though speaking to a simpleton.. To bear a son was the crowning achievement of every woman's life. The thought of Grazia bearing Isaac's son made Hannah feel angry and ill.

"What kind of a law marries a man and a woman without their knowledge and then keeps them married against their will? Do the first wife's wishes count for nothing?" Hannah rose to her feet.

Isaac put a hand on her arm and tugged her back into her chair.

"I apologize for my wife's behaviour, Rabbi," he said.

"Do not dare to apologize for me," said Hannah. "I can tell an unfair law even if you and the Rabbi cannot. This is wickedness! If this is the law, then I spit on it!"

"Hannah, please control yourself," Isaac said.

"My dowry is all I have in the world," said Grazia. "I came in good faith, to meet with my brother- and sister-in-law, the only family I have except my stepson, Yehuda." She wiped the corner of her eye with the back of her hand. "If the law says I am to become Isaac's wife, I will obey." Grazia spoke with a calm deliberation that Hannah admired and at the same time hated. "If I lay with Isaac and become his wife, will Hannah and I be equal before the law?" Grazia asked. "By which I mean, will we share his estate equally if he dies?"

"Yes, of course," said the Rabbi.

This was happening too fast for Hannah to comprehend. Isaac's lips on Grazia's? His arms around her? Laying together? And how could this woman, this virtual stranger, this convert, even mention, even contemplate the death of her beloved Isaac?

If this travesty of a marriage could occur, then so too could the coupling of Leah and the Sultan.

"It is up to Isaac to decide whether to accept his marriage to Grazia," the Rabbi said. "If he repudiates her, then the law in its wisdom provides a remedy—the *halizah*, the ritual divorce. A distressing ceremony but a solution."

Hannah had spoken too soon. She had let her anger get the better of her. Now she regretted it.

Everything was in Isaac's hands.

Beads of sweat had formed on Isaac's forehead. "Grazia, your money will be repaid. I have no intention of depriving you of your dowry. But I need time."

The Rabbi turned to Grazia. "When did Leon die?"

"Four months ago."

"The law provides that a levirate marriage takes effect three months from the date of death. However, I can, if you wish, order that the marriage be held in abeyance for another month. That will give you a month to pay back the dowry money. In the meantime—"

Isaac cut him off. "Rabbi, arrange the tribunal for the divorce. I will find her money."

The Rabbi held up a finger. "Isaac," he said, "do not be too hasty. Lay with this beautiful widow. Keep your silk business, keep her dowry."

"No," said Isaac.

A single word but said with such conviction. Hannah's hands began to loosen their grip on each other.

"As you wish," said the Rabbi. "If you cannot raise the money in a month, then there is nothing further I can do."

Grazia looked both confident and resigned. Hannah had seen this look on the faces of men, never on the face of a woman.

"If I am to be cheated of my dowry, then at least I deserve a proper wedding ceremony." Grazia took a handkerchief from her skirt pocket and wiped her brow with it. "If you cannot repay me, Isaac, then I shall have a wedding dinner with baked fish and potatoes and a bridal dress of white *peau de soie*, with full sleeves and gussets of satin." Her voice seemed to override the noise from the street outside: the cries of *Igde!* from the sherbet sellers, the birds overhead, and even the blows of hammer on stone from a stonecutter's workshop next door.

Hannah willed some air into her lungs.

"And you," said Grazia as she turned to Hannah, "perhaps you shall sew my wedding dress for me."

CHAPTER 12

Constantinople

THE VALIDE HAD ordered Hannah to be present tonight and so she must be.

In Venice, delicate orchids from New Spain were pollinated with a slender bamboo reed and a steady hand. In North Afrika, the lustful stallions of the Arabs required calming stable companions when they serviced their mares—a placid ewe, for example, or a shaggy herding dog. So why should the joining together of Leah and the Sultan—a man who cared nothing for the niceties of human discourse, a man who might crush her under his weight—not require the same solicitous attention?

It was a sad irony that Hannah was being summoned to

witness the Sultan's couching when she and Isaac had not so much as glanced at each other since the Rabbi's order. You could drive a horse cart through the middle of our marriage bed, she thought.

Was it Hannah's imagination or was Isaac casting covetous looks at Grazia? He had a month to raise the dowry money or Grazia would be his wife. Was he scrambling to find her money, or was he secretly pleased with the arrangement, watching calmly as Grazia cut out the pattern for her wedding dress—a dress Hannah had refused to have anything to do with.

Through her bedroom window, Hannah heard the rumble of the carriage on the cobblestones. She looked out as the Valide's personal carriage with its lacquer burnished to a dazzling blaze of gold, drawn by the bay mare, driven by Suat, appeared in front of her house. The ostrich plumes on the mare's head drooped in the summer heat; her sides were flecked with sweat. If only Hannah did not have to step into that carriage.

Hannah went to the *cassone* where she kept her best dress. *Please God*, she prayed, *help me to forge a truce with Isaac no matter how fragile. Let him believe that I am merely having tea with Mustafa and not witnessing Leah's coupling.* Hannah had never before lied to Isaac, but their relationship was so fraught with tension, she could not bear to add more. A plan had come to her earlier that morning. She had gone to the apothecary's and made a purchase, which rested in her linen bag next to a partridge egg.

She slipped on her dress and fastened her *yaşmak* around

her face. Slinging her bag on her shoulder, she walked along the hall, past Matteo's room. She peeked in, watching for a moment as he and Grazia played a game of noughts and crosses. She did not say goodbye to Isaac as she normally would, and he in turn did not see her out the door.

She climbed inside the carriage and off she went. A town crier had assembled a crowd on a street corner and was shouting out the latest comings and goings of the Sultan, the number of dead from plague and pestilence, and the arrival of the latest ships in port. Soon the carriage was gliding along the shore of Seraglio Point. It was sunset and the city never looked more beautiful than when the last rays of the sun played hide-and-seek with the waves of the Bosporus.

The carriage passed through the Imperial Gate guarded by Janissaries. The Example Stones flanked the gate, displaying the latest heads of executed subjects who had offended the Sultan. Hannah tried not to stare at the empty, gaping mouths with the bloody stumps where their tongues had been cut out. When the carriage came to a halt in the Second Courtyard, she alighted without waiting for Suat to help her down. Because she was well known to the eunuch guards at the entrance to the harem, she was admitted without difficulty.

Hannah entered the Harem and walked through the Romanesque arches leading to the baths. Sulphurous vapour filled the air. There were at least a hundred girls in various stages of undress, refreshing themselves with sweet-meats and sherbet or ladling perfumed water over each other. Hannah had once been invited to enjoy herself in the hamam, scrubbed by a bath attendant and then immersed in the steaming pool. She now knew how it felt to be a potato boiling in a pot.

Near the pools, she noticed Mustafa. He wore a long, black shift over his large, formless torso and a white turban. He smiled and waved a greeting, wobbling toward her slowly, so as not to slip on the tile floor. He enveloped her in a moist embrace. It was rather like being hugged by a well-mannered, perfumed bear.

"Afterward, you will have a glass of tea with me and a gossip, I hope?"

Hannah knew she would want to flee the palace as soon as she could, but she appreciated the kindness of his offer. "I would be delighted."

Mustafa's golden quill glimmered against his white turban. Hannah followed him down the corridor to the Chamber of the Eunuchs, where he paused at the doorway. "What an honour for you. So few outside the palace are privileged to witness such an event. Allow me a moment to change my clothes and fetch my *Book of Couchings*." Soon he was back at her side, with a heavy red volume tucked under his arm. When he noticed her glancing at it, he said, "Sadly, this is a book with many blank pages."

They were turning and turning again through a maze of corridors. Hannah lost all sense of direction and could not tell whether she walked east or west, north or south.

"Later—and I will not attract the attention of the Evil Eye by saying out loud what we are all hoping for—I will record the event in the *Book*, and we will both place our initials next to it as official witnesses." He patted his chest where his blue sapphire hung, large as a pigeon's egg. The gem was embedded in mother-of-pearl, held in place by a net of fine gold wires, creating a lifelike impression of a huge, staring eyeball. It was meant to represent the blue eye of the Greek barbarian, which Muslims believed could ward off the Evil Eye.

"Let us fetch Leah from her chamber."

If only Hannah could persuade Leah to follow her instructions, perhaps there was a chance to save her.

Mustafa clasped Hannah's upper arm. Whether to steady himself or comfort her, she did not know. "Do not look so alarmed, Hannah. Leah's first meeting with the Sultan will be a simple affair—no ladies-in-waiting, no Grand Vizier, no Valide—just us four. The Sultan may merely wish to speak to her. If he wishes more, he will toss a handkerchief at her feet to signify his desire."

"Will she find favour, do you think?"

"Desire between men and women is a mystery not even husband and wife can explain."

Mustafa was right. Often Hannah would gaze at Isaac, as he tightened bolts on the loom, for example—pliers, pincers, and hammers dangling at his waist—and would be seized by a longing so strong she had no power to resist. She would brush her breasts against him as if by accident, his eyes would follow her for a second, and soon they would be upstairs, wrapped in each other's arms. The same tools dangling from any other man's waist, even if Hannah had imbibed the strongest of love potions, would have no effect. Was it so for the Sultan?

"May I see Leah in private before she goes to the Sultan?" She tried to think of a reason that would satisfy his curiosity. "I must give her some idea of what to expect. It would not do to have her frightened."

"Who better to act as her confidante? You managed to coax her down from the window ledge. She has been docile as a lamb ever since."

Leah was tough—a mountain girl raised on rocky soil, fed on the watery soup of poverty, rendered an orphan by her enemies—but she deserved more time to remain a child. With any luck, the Sultan would simply smile at her and wave her away as he had done to so many other girls. But if he declined Leah's company, there would be no grateful smile from the Valide for Hannah and no purse heavy with ducats. And Leah would be shipped to the brothels by the docks—a terrible fate for any girl.

Once more Hannah found herself following Mustafa's swaying form, down the corridors of the Imperial Harem.

Mustafa knocked, then opened the door of Leah's room. "We have little time." To her relief, Mustafa looked only once through the doorway at Leah before shambling away. "Ring for me when you are ready and I will escort you to the Sultan's room."

Hannah entered the room and closed the door behind her. Involuntarily, she glanced toward the window ledge, remembering Leah crouched like an animal, spitting down at Mustafa. Now, Leah stood beside her sleeping mattress and rubbed her eyes, looking rather like Matteo when he awoke from a nap.

"*Shalom aleichem,*" said Hannah.

"*Aleichem shalom,*" Leah said in reply, kissing Hannah's hand and then pressing it to her forehead.

Hannah stared at the girl, refusing to believe her eyes. Thank God Mustafa had not lingered. Leah was dressed in a costume such as a dancing boy in a public tavern might wear. Instead of harem trousers held up with an embroidered sash and a tunic of fine silk print, Leah wore a *şhalvar*—loose pantaloons—and a silk shirt with a length of fabric around her waist. In each hand she held a pair of tiny cymbals.

Leah's hair, smooth and glossy, short by palace standards, was slicked back close to her head. She was clean now and smelled of cloves and cinnamon, spices much prized for their powers of seduction. Her skin was whiter too. Her slave must have been busy with lemon and lye creams, bleaching potions and depilatories. No doubt, her slave had removed the hair between her legs and hennaed her private parts. A thin stripe of kohl lined her huge green eyes.

"Why in God's name are you dressed like that?" Hannah asked.

Leah spoke quietly, careful to point her feet away from Hannah. "I bribed one of the eunuchs to bring me this costume favoured by the *köcheks*."

The *köcheks*, the "fauns of Constantinople" as they were known by the Janissaries, were boys who danced in provocative dress for the pleasure of other men. They were much loved by rough soldiers, who gave them amorous names such as "Pretty Blossom" and "Golden Love Arrow."

"Whatever for?" Hannah asked.

"The idea came to me when I overheard some of the Janissaries talking. They spoke of a terrible brawl, which broke out in Pera between two factions of Janissaries fighting over a dancing boy. So fiercely was the boy desired by both sides that fifty soldiers died in the fray."

"Surely you do not think that the Sultan has the same tastes as a coarse Janissary?" Hannah had heard rumours of some of the Sultan's unusual proclivities—but young boys?

"The Sultan has not responded to the voluptuous beauties of the harem. It is time to try a different tactic. What might excite a soldier might excite a Sultan." Leah smoothed her hair in a self-conscious gesture that saddened Hannah more than the girl's words. "I will accept my fate. If I please the Sultan, I will be safe at last."

It broke Hannah's heart to hear her talk so, resigned to a future no child should be forced to accept. She held Leah's hand. "Please, change out of those clothes before Mustafa returns. I have a plan to help you avoid the Sultan's intentions."

"You do not understand. I *must* seduce him."

Her words were spoken with such obstinacy and squaring of the shoulders that Hannah knew something was wrong. "What has changed you so?" asked Hannah.

Leah did not answer, but looked away, fussing with the folds of her *şhalvar*.

Hannah stroked the girl's hair, studying her rounded cheeks and green eyes. "I have something that will help you." She reached into her bag and held out a gold-foiled pill.

Leah looked at it. "I have no need of opium."

"You are a child. There is still a chance you can remain one a little longer." Hannah picked up the opium pill and tucked it in the pocket of the girl's şhalvar. Hannah fished something else out of her bag—a tiny, speckled partridge egg. Hannah took Leah's hand and placed the egg in her palm. "May you have strength," she said, and she whispered to Leah instructions on how to use the peculiar egg.

For the first time that evening, Leah looked like the feisty mountain girl Hannah had first met on the window ledge, spitting at Mustafa, the third-most powerful man in the Empire.

"Do you really think I can deceive the Sultan with such a ruse?" Leah asked, a new energy in her green eyes.

"Dear girl," said Hannah, "of course you can."

CHAPTER 13

Imperial Palace
Constantinople

THE HALL OF THE Sultan's Divan, designed by
the brilliant architect Sinan, was a perfect
square. The finest Iznik tiles covered the walls;
a handsome fountain splashed in the middle. In one
corner was a hearth large enough for a person to stand
upright. The pendentive dome rising above the Sultan's
divan was decorated in graceful Arabic calligraphy with
quotes from the Qur'an. In the centre of the salon was
the huge couch, strewn with silk pillows and draped in
green brocade and gold curtains. A high balcony, like
the gallery where the women sat in the synagogue, ran
the width of the room.

Hannah was in awe. She had seen so much of the harem, but never had she seen this opulent room.

Mustafa was standing next to her. He clapped his hands, making the velvet pouch hanging around his neck bounce. Four dwarfs entered the reception room bearing a huge gold filigree cage. Some said the Sultan prized these men because he was of a short stature himself and in their presence felt taller and more powerful. The Nubian eunuchs, all of whom were tall, were banished from his presence, all except Mustafa, who was permitted by virtue of his position as Chief Eunuch.

"Look, Hannah, a hundred and fourteen cooing white doves—one for each chapter of the Qur'an."

Hannah wondered at their purpose. She did not wonder for long.

A dwarf with a rounded forehead unhooked the door of the cage. The birds took flight, swooping and swirling overhead. The scent of orange blossoms filled the air. Hannah moved toward one of the doves at her feet. Fastened to its neck and to the necks of all the birds were scented pomanders, filling the room with that glorious aroma. It was as though a silk canopy had become unmoored from the ceiling and drifted down, holding her in a veil of fragrant oranges. The room glowed with the light of hundreds of candles, guttering and dripping from the stir created by the wings of the doves. Hannah stood motionless in the perfume-heavy air. The spectacle called to mind her last meeting in the Valide's apartments strewn with rose petals. Had her stomach not been in knots, Hannah would have wept with joy at this display.

Suddenly she remembered why she had been summoned and withdrew to a darkened corner. From somewhere, perhaps outside in the gardens, drifted the sound of a peasant tune from Anatolia played on a violin, the old country type of fiddle, made of a coconut shell with fish skin stretched across it.

A preternatural stillness filled the air. Mustafa froze, his red book under his arm. Even the fountain in the middle of the room seemed to pause its flow. From the far side of the room came the striking of a gong and the insistent beat of a kettle drum. The heavy timber doors, studded with iron spikes, swung open.

Sultan Murat III, Sultan of Sultans, God's Shadow on Earth, Supreme Ruler of the Mediterranean and the Black Seas, the Balkans and Anatolia, Azerbaijan, Damascus, Aleppo, Egypt, Mecca and Medina, Jerusalem, all of the Arab dominions, and Yemen, entered, borne aloft on a palanquin draped in brocade and embedded with gemstones. The bearers lowered him to the floor and he dismounted. Gathering his embroidered green kaftan around him, the Sultan climbed the two steps to his divan where he arranged himself cross-legged like a frog on a lily pad. It was an absurd image, but there he was with an enormous belly and no neck. He possessed no long, darting tongue, but instead sucked the ivory mouthpiece of a *narghile*, the water in the pipe's bowl gurgling, which a slave handed him.

The dwarfs withdrew, returning a few moments later bearing Leah on a gilded litter. They lowered the girl to the floor and helped her to alight. Hannah caught a glimpse of Leah before she turned to the Sultan. She wore a look not of seduction but of determination.

Almost immediately after being helped from her litter, Leah fell to her hands and knees, as protocol demanded. But instead of keeping a respectful distance from the Sultan, she crawled within a few feet of him, then, rising to her feet, stood before him, hands at her sides, fingers holding tiny cymbals. Her head drooped in a way that made Hannah wonder if she had, after all, swallowed the opium pill.

Musicians from the balcony at the far end of the room began playing softly at first, picked up speed, and then slowed again. As the rhythm of the music changed, Leah began to sway, delicate as a gazelle, moving her hips and shoulders. In the light of the candles, Hannah could see her luminous eyes, rimmed in kohl, gazing, though it was forbidden, directly into the heavy-lidded eyes of the Sultan.

Mustafa gave a grunt, which he quickly converted into a cough. The others in the room—the dwarfs who were about to depart and the litter bearers—gave a collective gasp, whether at Leah's costume or her boldness, Hannah could not divine.

The Sultan's posture stiffened, then relaxed. His chest rose and fell under his green kaftan, which was adorned with an embroidered peacock, one foot on a delicate peony and the other on a leaf. A smile played across his lips; his head nodded in time to the music. It was a coarse face, his lips thick and fleshy, his nose as curved as a scimitar. His head seemed large for his body and wobbled on shoulders that did not seem equal to the purpose. Hannah saw a ripple of excitement travel through him. What thoughts were passing through the dank interior of his mind?

Leah timed her movements to the beat of the music, suggestive of virginal modesty. Then, as if overcome by amorous longings, she quickened her pace. She clicked her cymbals and arched her back to show her surrender to desire. Her head tilted to one side yet her face remained as vacant as a sleepwalker's. Was she thinking of her mother and grandmother? Was she thinking of music around fires in the mountains at night—music to celebrate weddings or victories in battle, or to mark births and deaths? Or, as Hannah hoped, was Leah contemplating the plan they had formulated and how best to bring it to fruition?

Finally, Leah gave a low cry and dropped, her forehead pressed to the floor as though in prayer. Was it Hannah's imagination or did she see the girl look up and cast a knowing look at Hannah before prostrating herself again on the floor?

Hannah was close enough to hear the Sultan murmur, "Such beguiling eyes, like the eyes in a peacock's train."

Often when slothful creatures move, they move with reptilian speed. So it was with the Sultan. In one fluid motion, he withdrew a silk handkerchief from the sleeve of his embroidered robe and tossed it toward Leah. It floated for a moment, caught in a whoosh of air, then settled in front of Leah's face.

How could something so meringue-light land like a boulder hurled from the highest roof of the palace onto a stone floor? Hannah wanted to grab Leah by the hand and run with her out of the room.

Leah lifted her head, spotted the handkerchief, picked it up and wiped her brow. Then she crawled toward the royal divan. She took the Sultan's outstretched hand between her own and pressed it to her forehead. He drew her toward him.

Please, Hannah prayed silently. *Let the plan work. Let her escape unharmed, and let them both—Hannah and Leah—survive.* Hannah looked at Mustafa. Wasn't it time for both of them to withdraw?

But Mustafa shook his head and gestured to his *Book of Couchings*. "Hope must not substitute for fact. There must be no inaccuracies in the official record."

Hannah wished she could turn into the feather of a dove and float out the window to the gardens outside. The Sultan lifted Leah onto his lap and caressed her cheek, kissing her with foolish enthusiasm, as if playing with a child's doll. Then he lay back on the divan, leaning on one elbow while she arranged herself against the length of him. Leah was almost exactly his height.

Leah reached for the bowl of fruit on a table next to the divan and bit off a piece of apple. She held it between her lips and then slowly moved her mouth toward the Sultan's face. His mouth opened and he took the morsel into his mouth. Then, he motioned to have the curtains of the divan drawn.

Mustafa stepped forward and closed the red curtains. A few moment elapsed before the divan began to shudder under the Sultan's movements, or under Leah's, Hannah did not know which. Instead of watching the divan vibrate, slowly at first, then faster, then at a frantic pace, Hannah focused her attention on the doves, many of which had perched on wall sconces and on the tall pillars supporting the divan. With the movements, they left their roosts in search of more stable perches. One little hen gave her tail a twitch, and with a soft, fluty cry flew out the window.

Hannah could avert her eyes but she could not block her ears. There was a squeal, like the whimper of a frightened lamb, then a deeper sound, a quick exhalation like a boar in full rut. From the balcony, behind a filigreed tulipwood screen where the musician played softly, came another noise, a muffled cry. Hannah looked up to see the flash of blue *pelisse* and hear the swish of footsteps in felt slippers. This was the way in the palace—whispered confidences, words murmured behind upraised hands, downcast eyes concealing treachery, spy holes in ceilings, balconies connected to blank walls, passageways leading to non-existent rooms. If it was Safiye on the balcony, could anything be more painful than watching your adored husband with another woman?

After a few minutes, the salon fell silent but for two sounds: the snores of the Sultan, God's Shadow on Earth, and the scratching of Mustafa's pen as he recorded in *The Book of Couchings* the Sultan's triumph.

CHAPTER 14

District of Pera
Constantinople

IN HER EAGERNESS TO show Foscari the sketch she had laboured over so diligently, Cesca jumped from the carriage before it had come to a full stop. In front of the Venetian embassy, as grand as any palazzo in that city, a pair of turbaned guards flanked the entranceway, holding pine-pitch torches, the sap making tiny explosions in the darkness of the night. The flag—the gold lion of Venice crouching on a field of red—fluttered overhead. Cesca yanked on the bell. As she waited for a servant to admit her, she smoothed her hair. When she told Foscari her news, she was certain, he would reward her handsomely.

Foscari was right. It was against the laws of nature for a Christian child to be raised by Jews. Last night, Matteo had cried out, restless from a nightmare. Cesca went to his room to calm him. Because she was out of earshot, she sang a lullaby, "*Sleep, Baby Jesus, sleep . . .*," patting his pillow, smoothing the covers over him. Her singing, instead of quietening him, made him thrash and groan. A demon turned his body into a battlefield—a mighty conflict waged between the merciful God of the Christians and the vengeful God of the Israelites. The child's soul would know no peace in a Jewish household.

Since their visit to the Rabbi, a multitude of thoughts crowded Cesca's mind. Of course, her first reaction was shock at the Rabbi's pronouncement. What woman would not be astonished to discover she was about to marry a man she had thought of merely as a lamb to be sheared? And such an obliging lamb he was too—malleable and sweet and clearly besotted with her, judging by his glances at her when he thought she was not looking.

But in an instant she realized that marriage to Isaac could be turned to her advantage. True, Isaac had no money at present—she had seen more than enough of his account books to verify that—but the value of silk would not be depressed forever. Prices of all commodities—silk, wheat, cloves—rose and fell, so Leon had counselled her. And Isaac and Hannah's ample house, workshop, and gardens were splendid and well situated.

Besides, Cesca would not be saddled with Isaac for long. All she needed was a little more time to get acquainted with the workings of the silk trade and then she would dispose of her new husband, Isaac, in the same way she had disposed of Leon. A blow to the head accompanied by swift pressure of the thumbs to the soft tissue of the throat, and poof!

Hannah was a kindly simpleton who could easily be forced out of her home. Let her go and live in the Imperial Harem where she seemed to have found favour. When all Isaac's property and equipment was sold, Cesca and Foscari would take Matteo to Venice to claim his fortune. Cesca was a good sailor, reefing her sails as the winds of fortune blew new opportunities in her direction.

Now, as she approached the embassy steps, she fumbled open the drawstring of her pink shot-silk purse and from a ceramic box took out a bit of red powder. She smiled, then dabbed some on the fullest part of her cheeks.

A tall, fierce-looking Nubian slave opened the door. He bowed. "I am Kamet. Follow me. The ambassador is expecting you." He ushered her through the house, past marble statues of Minerva and Apollo, past the huge reception room hung with paintings, past wall sconces of Murano glass flickering with candles. She would not let the grandeur overwhelm her. She would act as though coffered ceilings and paintings of the Seven Hills of Constantinople and beeswax candles instead of humble rush lights were commonplace for her.

As she followed Kamet through the mansion, Cesca rehearsed what she would say to Foscari. No, she could not linger, she must get back home. No, she would not stop for a mug of wine, and no, she would not let him have his way with her as he had on the *Aphrodite*.

Kamet swept open the wrought-iron doors set with glass panels that led into the garden. Foscari was bent over, tearing at a loaf of bread and casting crumbs into a pond. The garden should have been dark. It was not. The flower beds were so well lit that Cesca could see every petal on the nodding heads of tulips. Even the stamens were visible, rather like queens encircled by her ladies-in-waiting. Kamet wore a yellow turban. He held out a chair for her under the arbour, but Cesca remained on her feet, gathering her skirts around her, transfixed. The lawn glowed with light so bright it appeared as though the world had turned topsy-turvy. Instead of the stars being in the heavens, they were a carpet of illumination undulating on the grass.

As her eyes adjusted, she realized she was looking at the glow from scores of candles, but they were moving. Under a rose bush, in front of a pomegranate tree, hidden behind the fountain, behind the wisteria arbour, in the distance near the stream, dots of light flickered in the night.

Cesca expected to see party guests gathered in knots, talking and drinking, but there was only Foscari striding briskly toward her, arms outstretched, a smile on his face.

"Do you like my army of tortoises?" he asked.

She bent over the closest source of light, surprised to see a tortoise, large as a serving platter, at her feet. Her hands flew to her face to stifle a cry of astonishment. On its back was a beeswax candle pressed into the shape of a yellow rosette. Now she understood. All those pricks of light were tortoises with candles attached to their shells. She hoped her awe was not too apparent.

Foscari reached her side. "How lovely to see you, my dear. I was thrilled when your messenger announced you were coming to pay me a visit tonight."

She glimpsed her reflection in his silver nose, but she could not make out her own features, just a wan face with a dusting of cochineal on the cheeks. "Even more delightful it is to see you, Foscari," Cesca said.

He bowed low and swept an imaginary hat off his head.

Cesca offered her cheek for a kiss but he pulled her into an embrace. For an instant, she relaxed against him, enjoying the muscular feel of his arms and chest. Foscari never smelled of sweat. To sweat, one must labour. But he did smell of something pungent. She was trying to identify the scent when he reached into the pocket of his waistcoat and withdrew a tiny ivory box. He dipped his little finger into it, then dotted a substance under and around his silver nose. There was that peculiar odour again. Not snuff. But what? Something fishy. Roe? Fish oil? The answer came to her— fish bladder glue to keep his nose secure on his face. Gone were the silk threads that had previously held it in place.

There was a squealing, chirping noise from behind her. From the pond in the back of the garden, five cygnets, fuzzy balls of white and grey down, waddled out of the water and stretched their necks for the crumbs Foscari had scattered on the ground.

"Join me in a glass of brandy." He turned to Kamet, who was a few paces away. "In the cellars, there is a fine cask, a gift from the French ambassador. A drop or two would be lovely." The servant bowed and then withdrew.

A moment later, Cesca sat across from Foscari under a rose arbour at a tulipwood table inlaid with mother-of-pearl. She arranged her skirts to keep them clear of the tortoises and their candles. Kamet returned with goblets of Murano crystal filled with brandy, which he placed before them. That such fragile glassware could have survived the voyage from Venice was a marvel.

Raising her glass, she said, "*Salute*, Foscari."

"To your health, Cesca," he responded. After enjoying a sip of brandy, he launched into business. "So, you have news for me?"

"I do. You will be fascinated to learn Safiye's bewitchment has come to an end. Last week, the Sultan bedded a Circassian slave girl. I heard it from one of Hannah's neighbours, a pedlar at the harem. The Sultan was as ravenous for the girl as these swans are for your bread. The other odalisques, to say nothing of his wife, are wild with jealousy."

Foscari looked amused. "I could not be more surprised if you told me the Sultan had joined the Holy Mother Church and instead of facing Mecca to pray was turning toward Rome." Foscari raised his glass. "Let us drink to the virility of God's Shadow on Earth. May he sire a legion of sons." He clinked her glass so forcefully that a drop of brandy splashed over the side and landed in her lap.

"Now, what else do you have for me?" There was impatience in his voice.

Foscari picked up a tortoise by his feet. Giving a faint hiss, the creature withdrew its head, tail, and feet into its shell. Foscari straightened the crooked candle on its back and set it down again. A moment later, the head, tail, and feet reappeared, and the creature ambled away.

It was time to turn to the true reason for her visit. "There is no doubt Matteo is the child you seek." Cesca reached into her dress pocket and pulled out a scrap of vellum folded into a rectangle with the edges laced tightly together with a strip of hide.

Foscari's eyes lit up. "How lovely to have my research confirmed! Such a tragedy when rich noble families die out. I would hate to think of the di Padovani dynasty coming to an end."

No one gave a tinker's dam when poor families died out, Cesca thought. "With my evidence, you will have no difficulty convincing a judge to appoint you Matteo's guardian."

She handed him the vellum. He unlaced it, turning it this way and that in the light, the tip of his tongue poking from the corner of his mouth as it often did when he concentrated. "This is the di Padovani crest, is it not? I copied it from the child's blanket."

"Yes," Foscari said. Holding the vellum in the manner of someone holding a valuable painting, he moved the brandy glasses to one side and placed the parchment carefully in the centre of the table. "Can you bring me the blanket?"

Cesca picked up the drawing. Hand over the blanket before they had come to an agreement? Did he take her for an imbecile? "The boy is deeply attached to it. To deprive him of it would cause his screams to be heard all the way to Büyükada."

Foscari studied the brandy in his glass, then took a sip, rolling it around in his mouth, swirling and swilling and swallowing.

Cesca said, "I have given you what you wanted—proof that Matteo is the di Padovani heir. I want your word, Foscari, that if our scheme succeeds, I shall be rewarded. I want the di Padovani villa in Maser."

Foscari choked. He rose and made a great performance of bending double and coughing. "You are mad!" he managed, before sitting back down in his chair. "Living with Israelites has not only made you greedy, it has given you thoughts above your station."

This constant jibing of Jews. Cesca had never taken the slightest notice until she began to pass herself off as one. From the *lokum* sellers in the bazaar to the *simit* vendors, everyone had some insult to offer. "When it comes to money, Foscari, all of us—Jews or Christians—are of the same religion," she said.

Foscari took another sip of brandy.

"You may be a marquis but you bargain as fiercely as a ten-*scudi* whore. It is dealing with you that has forced me to be cunning," said Cesca.

Foscari leaned forward, his silver nose riding up ever so slightly. "Tell me your plan for handing the boy over to me."

Of course Cesca had thought it through and was prepared for this question. "I shall do it during the Circumcision Parade. The Sultan, as you know, has ordered a wonderful celebration. His only son, Mehmet, has recovered from fever, so the event will take place soon. For fifty-three days, the entire city will pay him honour. Every guild will have a float, every soldier will be on the streets in full regalia. Confusion and chaos will reign. Thousands of people will travel from as far away as Edirne and Amasia to behold the splendour. It will be easy for me and the boy to get lost in the crowds. Before Hannah realizes the child is gone, he shall be on board the ship bound for Venice."

"Brilliant. Of course, you will bring me the blanket and then sail with me and the boy. I cannot be expected to tend to a young child, and I can't think of a more suitable role for you."

Foscari thought her innocent as a cabbage. "Of course I will join you—eventually." She remained silent for a long time. "And the estate?"

Foscari began tossing crumbs to the swans. Cesca rose to her feet, as if she were about to leave. Finally, Foscari surrendered.

"Fine, we have a deal, but under one condition: that you not complain to me when your grapes in the Maser estate rot on the vine and your newborn calves die from the scours. Your talents, my dear, are in the bedchamber, not in the fields. Let us finish our brandy and go into the house, where you can prove your talents to me once again."

Cesca had not counted on his quick capitulation on the matter of the estate. Yes, she would hand over the boy to Foscari, but she would keep the blanket. Without this well-worn scrap of wool, Foscari had no evidence, just an adorable little red-haired trot who could be anybody's child. She would deal with Isaac and his estate. When that was sorted out, she would follow Foscari on the next ship to Venice, the blanket and her future snug in her valise.

CHAPTER 15

District of Eminönü
Constantinople

MUCH HAD HAPPENED since that night over a month ago in the Hall of the Sultan's Divan—none of it good.

Isaac had not been able to borrow the money to pay Grazia. The price of silk continued to fall. Everyone and his dog had bolts for sale. Even the finest material went for half of what it had sold for last year. Hannah could have wept. Grazia had agreed to give them a little more time to come up with her ducats—until the Circumcision Parade for Mehmet, the Sultan's son, which was only a few weeks away.

A fortnight ago, as Hannah was drinking her evening tea under the wisteria arbour, Ezster had knocked on the back door. She would not come in but said that Leah needed to see Hannah as soon as possible.

"I should not be passing messages like this," said Ezster. "The Valide would not like it. But, Hannah, Leah looked so worried. I pitied her. You must go to her." Ezster held out a folded piece of paper. "She asked me to give you this."

Hannah's first thought was that she was astonished Leah, a simple peasant girl, could write. Hannah walked over to a candle and by twisting the parchment to and fro, managed to make out the few shakily written words, in Hebrew, the gist of which was that their ruse had succeeded and Leah was now "a girl in the eye of the Sultan." But the message went on to say that Leah must get out of the palace before it was too late.

Too late for what? Was she worried she'd be called to the divan again?

Hannah tossed the note into the fire so that neither Isaac nor Grazia would find it. Leah did not understand that Hannah could not come and go from the Imperial Harem whenever she liked as Ezster did. Hannah had to wait to be sent for.

Tonight, at last, her patience was rewarded. Without warning, Suat and his royal carriage appeared in front of her house. She was being summoned by the Valide, who wished an immediate audience with Hannah. For what purpose? Suat grumbled that the Valide did not deign to give reasons. Was it too much for Hannah to hope that she might be rewarded for her help with the couching?

Imperial Palace
Constantinople

After the long carriage ride, Hannah found herself once more walking past the tall Janissaries guarding the Gate of Felicity. She entered the harem where Mustafa, gold quill in his black turban, was waiting. He smiled and gave her a hug, as was his custom.

"May I have a word with Leah before I see the Valide?"

"I will navigate the way to Leah's splendid new apartments. No more humble dormitory for her."

Hannah followed Mustafa's comforting bulk as he explained that Leah was now so much in favour in the Imperial Harem that she had her own quarters complete with a separate kitchen, slave girls, and even a private garden.

"She is well?" Hannah asked.

"Never better," said Mustafa, bowing and taking his leave in front of the open door of Leah's apartment.

Dressed in a pair of fine silk trousers and a *pelisse* that reached her knees, Leah was standing at the window, an embroidery hoop in her hand. She raced over to embrace Hannah.

"I am happy to see you, Leah." Hannah kissed the girl on the cheek. Leah looked well. Her green eyes glowed. Her body was rounder than when Hannah had first met her two months ago. Her face had lost the sharp angles, her jaw had softened. "Ezster brought me your message. I came as soon as I could."

"You must help me, Hannah. You must transform me into a puff of smoke so I can drift out through the holes in the ceiling of the hamam and be free."

"But whatever for?" Hannah made a sweeping gesture. "What of your marvellous new apartments?" But she felt like a hypocrite for her words of enthusiasm. To be a prisoner in this golden cage was not a life she would envy.

"It worked, you know. Your ruse. The opium. The egg," Leah said.

"I am so happy for that," said Hannah as she held the girl's hand. She did not feel Leah relax. "But?" she asked, knowing Leah had more to say.

"Hannah, it was easy, as easy as slipping a pill down the throat of a child. I inserted the opium into the bite of apple, and I fed it to the Sultan. He was so transfixed, he hardly noticed the bitter taste. After Mustafa closed the curtains, the opium worked its magic. He was in a dream-like trance, hardly aware I was there. I climbed on top of him, fully clothed, and wriggled back and forth to make the divan tremble." She grimaced. "I did not forget your partridge egg filled with hen's blood. When I reached the end of my performance, I cracked it open on the sheets and the Sultan in his daze was none the wiser. The coverlet was bloody, proof of my virginity when the curtains were opened the next morning." Leah reached into the pocket of her trousers and took out her blue amulet, rubbed it against her cheek.

"You have accomplished a feat that other girls could not. I congratulate you."

"I could not have done it without you, Hannah." She kissed Hannah's hand and pressed it to her forehead. "I was born into the harsh life of the mountains, raised on whatever is left over in the pot after the men have eaten. For my mother and grandmother and all the women before them, existence was work and pain. They survived using whatever resources they had. So have I." Leah took a deep breath. "But Hannah, I must get out of this palace."

"It is impossible," Hannah said.

"There is something you don't know."

"If the Sultan calls you to his divan again, do not worry. You can repeat your performance. I have brought more opium." Leah shook her head, waiting impatiently for Hannah to finish talking.

"I am with child."

Hannah felt as though she had fallen from a great height and all of the air had been knocked from her. With child? "But you just said our ruse worked, that you didn't have to—"

Leah grabbed Hannah's hands in both of her own. "I was betrothed to Eliezer, the boy from the neighbouring village. He is the father of my child. He was murdered by the same savages who killed my family." She stumbled against Hannah's linen bag, making the birthing spoons clatter. "We loved each other. This child is the last of a long line of Jews from our part of the mountain."

The image came to Hannah of holding Leah on the birthing stool, rubbing her back, wiping her brow, and finally cutting the birth cord of her child.

Leah pleaded, "Help me escape. I am in grave danger. I have to disappear fast before the truth becomes obvious." Leah pointed to her belly and pulled the cloth of her *pelisse* tight. Hannah saw what would be abundantly clear to everyone in the palace if much more time passed—that the child Leah was carrying could not possibly be the Sultan's because she was several months pregnant. It was only the narrowness of her pelvis and the loose clothing of the harem that had allowed her condition to pass unnoticed thus far.

"You knew from the first time we met that you were pregnant?"

"Yes," Leah admitted.

Hannah thought back to Leah on the window ledge, her see-through shift, her distended belly—so, a pregnancy, not malnourishment.

"Hannah, I could not bear the thought of ending up in a brothel, giving birth to Eliezer's son on a pile of rags, dying before I had a chance to give suck to the child."

In the face of such a statement God Himself would be struck dumb. What was Hannah to do? She had a duty to help this girl and now her unborn child. But did she not also have a duty to protect herself and her own family?

"Let us think about what can be done." Hannah sat down on the divan, feeling angry with Leah's deception.

She willed herself to come up with a plan, and fast. But all she could think was that the child growing in Leah's belly would be her death sentence, hers and Isaac's.

CHAPTER 16

AS SHE FOLLOWED Mustafa's swaying backside to the Valide's apartments, Hannah thought her life was unravelling as surely as a knitted cap snagged on thorns. All she wished was to be anywhere else in the world rather than in the Imperial Palace about to face the wrath of the Valide. She slowed her pace as they approached the royal apartments. If the Valide offered Hannah a glass of white sherbet made from vanilla beans and camel's milk frozen with snow from Mount Olympus, Hannah would sigh with relief. But if the sherbet was crimson, it was an altogether different matter. Red was the colour of death.

Mustafa raised his hand to knock on the Valide's door. Hannah heard two female voices—one shrill and angry, the other low and mocking. The door was opened from within by a servant. Hannah caught a glimpse of Safiye retreating from the room through the doors leading into the garden.

Hannah followed Mustafa's lead and dropped to her knees. Eyes downcast, she tried to crawl as etiquette demanded in the direction of the Valide, who was pacing in front of her divan. She occasionally caught a glimpse of Nurbanu but because her eyes were fixed mostly on the ground, she could not read the Valide's expression. All Hannah heard was breathing and royal footsteps tapping the marble floor. She was vaguely aware of Mustafa withdrawing from the room. She crawled on. After what felt like an eternity, Hannah found herself at the Valide's feet. A slim hand covered in rings reached down and took Hannah's.

"How are you, Hannah?" The Valide spoke in the Venetian dialect.

Hannah risked meeting the Valide's eye. There was a glow to the older woman's skin that made her look younger than the last time Hannah had seen her. "I am well, Your Highness."

"You are not only the best midwife in the Empire but a breaker of spells. Soon I will be rocking a royal cradle, thanks to you."

There was no need to wonder how the Valide knew of Leah's pregnancy. The harem was filled with her informers and no doubt many had noticed the girl's blossoming belly. But the Valide's praise was merely a temporary reprieve.

How long would it be until she realized the baby was not the Sultan's?

The Valide Nurbanu rearranged herself on the divan. A tiny white dog with an aquamarine collar jumped into her lap and licked her hand. "As my father, the governor of Páros, used to say, 'A house with children is a bazaar; without them, it is a cemetery.'" It was an old Venetian proverb.

The Valide spoke matter-of-factly, but Hannah could not help thinking of the bloody history of the Ottomans who, at each accession of a new sultan, filled the Imperial mausoleum with royal princes no older than Matteo.

The Valide bent down and offered Hannah a glass of white sherbet. Hannah felt herself breathe again.

"Rise, Hannah."

Hannah rose from her uncomfortable crouch and took a seat on the divan. "I am delighted to have been of assistance." When fortune smiles, even temporarily, it is wise to say as little as possible.

"Safiye is quite beside herself," the Valide commented.

"Oh? I am sorry to hear that."

"It is of no importance. Our little shepherdess, Leah, has become a favourite of mine. I have been tutoring her—in Osmanlica, embroidery, poetry, and the playing of the lute."

"And she has proved to be an apt pupil?"

"A very bright girl. And imaginative as well. You saw how she seduced my son?"

"I was present at the couching, along with Mustafa."

"Leah was as handsome as the most beautiful of the fauns of Constantinople," said the Valide. "Do you know there is hardly a Janissary in the entire city who does not have his favourite dancing boy?" She looked at Hannah with amusement. "It is common here, my dear, more common than in Venice."

Not for the first time, Hannah had no idea what to say.

"The shepherdess may be a stringy little thing, but she has ignited the Sultan's passions by her very novelty."

The Valide was silent for a moment.

Was she playing with Hannah, waiting for her to disclose something? Testing her loyalty? It was a dangerous game Hannah found herself playing. And she was so ill-suited to it.

Better to say nothing. Hannah waited for the Valide to reveal what was on her mind. There was a reason why the royal mother's subjects approached her with such caution. It amused the Valide to feign delight, then order a subject's head chopped off with one swift blow of the executioner's axe. Hannah had heard a story from Ezster that once, when the Valide was a young woman, a celebrated artist from Venice came to the palace to paint a mural—a scene of John the Baptist decapitated, and Salome, in triumph, holding his severed head aloft on a silver salver. The Valide, displeased with the way the painter portrayed John the Baptist, ordered one of her slaves beheaded on the spot so that the artist might render John the Baptist's more realistically. The Valide was unpredictable in her capacity for both generosity and cruelty.

"I cannot tell you how pleased I am that Leah is with child," the Valide said after a time. "I have a gift for her. I am going to give her my necklace." The Valide patted her gold necklace set with diamonds, long enough to reach the ground had she been standing.

"She will be delighted, Your Highness."

"You will, of course, attend to the girl when she gives birth?"

"I would be honoured."

"I trust no one but you."

"You have only to send for me."

The Valide looked intently at Hannah for what felt like an eternity, then she said, "That is all. You may go."

Hannah bowed and in an awkward crabwalk backed out of the room, catching her heel on the edge of a carpet. The white dog yipped at her heels as she left and a slave closed the door behind her. She leaned against the corridor wall for a moment and pressed her back against the cool stone. She had escaped with her head still connected to her shoulders—for now. But if Leah remained in the palace and gave birth, the truth would be known and they would all be killed—Hannah, Leah, and her baby.

Hannah found her way out of the labyrinth of the Valide's apartments, through her private garden, through the steaming hamam where Mustafa loomed, a length of white silk cloth wound around his waist. His black toes curled over the white marble rim of the baths, his hairless pillow of a chest glistening with steam. He waved goodbye, watching her as she walked past.

The harem was the most heavily guarded fortification in the Ottoman Empire. Hannah racked her brain. Was there a way to make Leah disappear? No one had ever escaped, but a plan, a bold and perhaps disastrous plan, was taking shape in Hannah's mind. It might work, but it required a confederate. There was only one friend in the world whom Hannah could trust—Ezster.

CHAPTER 17

*Eminönü
Constantinople*

HER VISIT TO THE *mikvah* was one of the few times during the month when Hannah enjoyed a respite from the daily routine of looking after Matteo, cooking—Zephra could not always be trusted to obey the strict laws of *Kashrut*—and helping Isaac in the workshop. Hannah, face covered in deference to Mohammedan custom, walked along the street toward the ritual baths behind the synagogue to meet with Ezster. She thought of the worrying events of the day before. She could confide in Ezster, who had always been a faithful and true friend.

Hannah stepped over a pile of camel dung and dodged

a vendor selling felt slippers and confectioners selling sugary *lokum*. Hannah hoped to hear Fikret the donkey's little hooves striking the paving stones and see Tova, Ezster's daughter, so big with child that she would waddle as she led the animal along the street. They were nowhere to be seen. She entered the *mikvah*.

The air grew clammy as she descended the narrow staircase to the underground baths. This was a meeting place where the mothers of young men eyed young girls with a view to finding brides. Women with marriageable daughters loudly praised their girls' beauty and cooking skills and hinted at substantial dowries. The baths were carved from stone and fed by pure spring water. Four pillars supported a canopy of bedrock. There were three pools in the main chamber and a smaller, private bathing pool reserved for the wealthiest women.

Hannah hesitated before entering the main chamber, which was square with a vaulted ceiling. The attendant handed her a towel and a comb. The air was a mixture of soap, the musky smell of old stone and water, and the scent of candles. From farther within the *mikvah*, the echoing voices of women drifted toward her. Pray that one of the voices was Ezster.

Hannah stopped in a small antechamber to prepare herself to enter the main pool. She removed the pins from her dark hair, which cascaded around her face. She ran a comb through it, careful to untangle all knots and snarls. She cleaned her fingernails and toenails with a small, pointed stick. Each month as she performed these ablutions, she grew warm and languorous in spite of the cold of the baths, thinking of what would happen that night in bed. How different it must be for Christian husbands and wives who were free to couple at any time, even—she could hardly bear to think of it—during a woman's unclean time. She was not purifying herself for God, but for Isaac, who she hoped would eagerly be waiting for her return as he used to, even though their relationship since Grazia's arrival had been strained, even in the bedchamber.

The attendant handed Hannah soap and a washbasin. Hannah lathered herself while the attendant poured water over her. Gooseflesh rose on her arms and legs. She looked down at her flat stomach and small breasts—the body of a woman who had never borne a child and perhaps never would. A wave of jealousy passed over Hannah as she thought of Grazia. Hannah had at first been envious of her sister-in-law's beauty, hurt by the way Isaac stared at her. Now Grazia was about to become his lawful wife unless he raised her money in time. Was Isaac's lack of ardour in the bedchamber related to his feelings for Grazia? Had they coupled without her knowledge? No, it could not be. She was being foolish. Isaac had always been the most loyal of husbands. He had never given her any reason to doubt him.

Hannah's bare feet slapped the stone floor as she padded toward the bathing pool to join the other women. This was where the purest water entered the *mikvah*—rainwater captured through a special series of pipes. As she drew closer, she could hear the hearty guffaw of someone she recognized. It had been so long since she herself had laughed with such ease. There were Ezster and Tova, shivering on the edge of the pool, about to lower themselves in.

Because Tova was so self-conscious about her face, she wore her *yaşmak* even in the presence of other women. Poor girl. Before she contracted smallpox, Tova had been so beautiful that when she danced at her wedding, there was not a soul in the room, male or female, young or old, who did not fall in love with her. Even the dog scratching his fleas in the corner, hind leg moving in time to the music, raised its head to watch Tova spin and kick and toss her heels as the musicians sawed away on their fiddles. But now, her face was pocked and scarred, though her almond-shaped eyes remained lovely.

"Hannah!" Tova cried as she approached.

Hannah greeted the mother and daughter, kissing each of them in turn.

Ezster said, "*Nu*, Hannah, you are well? Business is good?"

"Yes," said Hannah, giving the white mound of Tova's belly a pat.

Jewish law requires that the entire body be in contact with the water. Tova quickly removed her veil, immersed herself in the pool, got out, and replaced her veil, which clung wetly to her cheeks. Hannah allowed herself to sink to the bottom until every part of her was submerged. This is what it must feel like to be a baby floating in its mother's womb, she thought. After a few moments, she surfaced and stepped out of the pool to sit on the edge, dangling her legs in the water.

"Will you be at the palace soon, Ezster, selling your needles and trinkets and telling your wonderful stories to the harem?" Hannah asked.

"Of course, I have more stories than a rooster has tail feathers. If I cannot remember them, I make them up."

Tova poked her mother. "You provide those girls with more titillation than the Sultan. When you open your mouth to talk, even the birds in the garden are still."

"You will accompany your mother to the harem?" Hannah asked.

"I will. Who can turn down a chance to gossip with the ladies?"

Tova would not be going to the harem for much longer. Her belly was high, well above the umbilicus—pointed, which often signified a boy. Another fortnight at the most before she sent for Hannah to steady her on the birthing stool. Hannah must put her plan into action without delay.

"You will give birth to a healthy boy, may God be listening," said Hannah.

Tova and Ezster stared at her, shocked. What a foolish, reckless thing to say aloud!

Tova was the first to recover. She kissed her thumb and looked up. "Hannah did not say that, and if she did say it, she did not mean it, and if she did mean it, she was mistaken, and because she is mistaken, she is sorry. And because she is sorry, it is as though she had never spoken at all. And because she did not speak, there is nothing to discuss."

Hannah began to apologize, but Ezster shushed her. "The Evil Eye has been placated. Anyway, we are Jews. We do not worry about such nonsense." She often forgot that in Constantinople, fear of the Evil Eye was all-consuming.

There was a long silence, during which Hannah considered how to broach the subject that was on her mind. Good, the bath attendants had left the room. She turned to Ezster and Tova.

"There is something weighing on me that I must talk to the two of you about." Ezster, for once, did not interrupt but sat quietly waiting for Hannah to continue. "Leah, the girl in the harem who sent you a note for me? She is in a great deal of danger."

"Because?" asked Ezster.

"She is with child."

"But surely that is good news," said Tova.

"Not when the baby will be born only five months after she coupled with God's Shadow on Earth, and not when I am the midwife who vouched for her virginity."

Tova gasped. Ezster looked as if Hannah had just slapped her in the face. "But Hannah, why would you have done such a thing?" asked Ezster.

"Because I did not know she was pregnant when I examined her."

"But you knew she was not intact," persisted Tova.

Hannah looked at the floor. "I did. I took pity on her, knowing if she was found out, she'd be sent to the whoremaster at the docks. Her entire family, her whole village was killed. She and her child are the last of a long line. And she is one of us. She is a Jew."

"Do you understand what you have done?" Ezster

asked. "Do you know the danger she is in? That *you* are in with her?"

"I must get her out of the harem," said Hannah.

Tova was the first to get to the point. "Why should my mother and I risk our lives for a girl we don't know?" Tova looked down at her belly. "I would like to help, but look at me. I have a child on the way and five more little ones at home needing me, plus a husband."

"I lied for the girl," said Hannah. "It is my fault. I know that. I have asked too much of you. I am sorry."

Tova and her mother exchanged looks.

"Oh, Hannah." Ezster was quiet for a moment and then said, "We will help, if there is a way."

Tova reached out a hand and took Hannah's in her own.

Hannah was speechless for a moment. When she regained her composure, she said, "I thank you both from the bottom of my heart." Then, she began to explain her plan.

Ezster's head was shaking before Hannah had finished. Ezster, who was as much a force of nature as the strong winds that blew across the Bosporus during the winter months, said Hannah's plan had no chance of succeeding.

"What can go wrong?"

Ezster ran her fingers through her wet hair. "Everything. But if you do it my way, we have a small chance." Ezster talked and Hannah listened. She concluded, "I will talk to this girl and tell her what she must do."

In less time than it takes to recite the *Shema*, the twice daily Jewish prayer, the three women had concocted a plan that was risky, but also, Hannah had to admit, brilliant.

CHAPTER 18

Imperial Palace
Constantinople

I T IS A FINE THING TO save a life, Hannah thought, as she walked through the First Courtyard. Jews believed that if you saved someone, you not only saved that person but all of his or her descendants as well. That included Leah's baby, which must have quickened by now.

The midday sun was barely past the minaret of the Fatih Mosque. *Please God,* Hannah prayed, *by sunset when this day is over and our plan executed, may we all meet at the* hoca's *stall at the market—Ezster, Tova, Leah, and me. Let there be no disasters, no mishaps, no tragedies. Let our plan unfurl as smoothly as a roll of satin ribbon.*

The sun made her feel dizzy, and with the dizziness came a loss of confidence. Why would such a ludicrous plan work? The likelihood of things going wrong when everything had gone wrong for so long overwhelmed Hannah. For a peppercorn, she would have turned on her heel and left the palace as quickly as her feet would take her. But Leah was counting on her. The timing would be crucial. They were like acrobats performing on a high-wire. They must work together as a team and perform their parts to perfection.

Hannah thought of Matteo and his low-slung tight-rope in their garden. Many times he had fallen, but with great determination he had at last managed to teeter along the entire length of the thick rope. He had persisted. So would she.

Hannah's thoughts were interrupted by the sound of buzzing. Flies were gorging on two severed heads on the Example Stones. A man's head on the western pillar was stuffed with straw, the nose bulbous, the forehead low, a filthy turban askew over one eye. His mouth was open in a rictus of a scream. The head on the eastern wall was that of a young woman, her veil drooping from one ear, her matted hair falling around her face. Her eyes were open and staring straight into Hannah's. She paused at the Fountain of the Executioner. She remembered a story Isaac had told her. Long ago, a deranged old sultan decided to replace all of his odalisques for the pleasure of selecting new ones. He ordered the deaf-mutes to strangle every girl in the harem. A week or so later, a sponge diver came across hundreds of sacks in the sea, weighed down with stones. The limbs of many of the women had come free from their sacks, and the diver witnessed the spectacle of hundreds of bloated arms waving in the currents like phantoms reaching up to embrace him. The man never again touched water, not even to bathe before prayers.

Hannah dipped her hand in the fountain and patted cool water on her forehead. Suppose Ezster and Tova could not come? Suppose they had decided the risk was too great? Suppose, and this was the most absurd of her fears, they went to the Valide and turned Hannah in for treason? As Hannah walked through the Gate of Felicity, her legs trembled. If she did not cease these gloomy thoughts, terror would cloud her thinking and render her as witless as a chicken. As she walked toward the harem entrance, Mustafa approached, keys dangling at his waist.

He greeted her warmly and said, "Ezster told me to expect you. Of course, you will have tea with me after Ezster's storytelling?"

"I would be delighted." She smiled. Her stature at the harem had grown in the months since her first visit. Hannah had become—what was the correct word? Not exactly a friend to the Valide. The word *friend* implied a relationship of equals, and of course one could not be an equal to so august a presence. But Hannah sensed she amused Nurbanu, a woman who seemed to consider the most ordinary goings-on in the Venetian ghetto as exotic as a jungle in Afrika, and regard Hannah, because she was a Jewess, as equally exotic.

Mustafa lumbered in front of her, ordering the workmen plastering the walls of the new kitchen ovens to retreat.

Men must not be present when a woman passed through the garden into the harem. One hapless young worker with a board of mortar on his head dropped his implements in his haste to depart. Hannah tripped over a trowel and stumbled. Mustafa grabbed her arm and chastised the young man. Poor fellow. Later, he would be beaten for his carelessness. She persuaded Mustafa to linger at the menagerie to watch the monkeys even though she disliked their skinny arms and clever, pinched faces. She didn't wish to arrive in the harem before Ezster and Tova.

Suddenly, from the other side of the walls of the harem, as welcome as the music of a lute, Hannah heard the colicky bray of Fikret, Ezster's donkey. Fikret always carried Ezster's bundle of candles and trinkets slung over his back, the sack as round and taut as Tova's belly. In a few hours, when they left the harem, Ezster's bundle would be empty.

It was not difficult to guess why Mustafa permitted a donkey in the gardens. Oh yes, Ezster peddled small luxuries to the ladies, and yes, she was the wife of a respected man, but it was her talent as a storyteller that gave her privileges others did not enjoy. Who could resist her sagas of Anatolia in the days before Osman I swept down from the plains—tales of daring and love, of warriors, horsemen, battles, and love matches? And, as if that were not enough, she knew tales from *One Thousand and One Nights*, and the adventures of the donkey-riding philosopher Nasreddin. Ezster always held everyone spellbound.

Hannah and Mustafa passed through the hamam on their way to the reception room. Around the pool were a series of small rooms furnished with divans and cushions for changing clothing, for depilatory treatment of female parts, for private gossiping and giggling. And dallying. Naturally, these healthy girls grew wanton and childlike without any responsibilities in their lives except to remain docile and beautiful. Of course, there were rumours about their lasciviousness. It was often jested that the cooks in the harem kitchens were under strict orders to send in no uncut cucumbers, carrots or long radishes because of how they would be used by these lusty young ladies. Hannah did not believe the gossip, which seemed to her nothing more than the fantasies of those who kept these girls in their gilded cages.

In the reception room off the hamam the audience had gathered—the Valide, the ladies, and the eunuchs. There were twenty or so girls fanned out in a semicircle around Ezster, who was settled into her cushion like a hen in a straw nest, her chicks huddled around her.

The young girls, about twenty in all, perched on cushions. Their kaftans of shimmering green and yellow and purple silks moved like butterflies in the breeze. Ezster was midstory, gesturing as she spoke. Tova held Ezster's props—her scarf and her cane—ready to hand them to her mother when the time came to illustrate the dramatic points. Mustafa stood to one side, leaning against the door leading to the baths. The Valide sat above the rest of the women on an elevated divan. She wore a white silk gown embroidered with black horses, their tails picked out in green and purple thread, so finely done that had it not been for the colours, they could have been real. The Valide smiled in response to something Ezster was saying, but everyone knew the Valide's moods could change from benevolent to furious as quickly as a falcon changes the direction of its flight.

On her right side, in the place of honour, sat Leah. The Valide personally supervised Leah's wardrobe, or so reported Ezster. The Valide had made good her promise. She had given Leah her necklace of diamonds—each one as perfect a stone as could be found in the Empire. Leah wore the necklace over a black velvet kaftan. The rise of her pregnancy pushed at the loosely bound sash around her waist, a sash of silk studded with semi-precious jewels.

Hannah felt a stab of fear. She caught Leah's eye and mouthed in Hebrew, *Have courage.* Hannah felt protective of Leah and of the small being growing within her. She hoped the baby would inherit Leah's bravery—if it survived.

The Valide finally noticed Hannah and nodded to her, her fine black eyes dancing with life. When Ezster finished her tale, the Valide said, "Come and sit. Ezster is about to begin a new tale."

By the Valide's outstretched hand, Hannah understood there was no need to crawl before Her Highness this time.

Hannah approached and bowed, then kissed the Valide's hand and pressed it to her forehead. Mustafa did the same and took his place on one of the cushions near Ezster. One would have thought that the Valide had enough drama in her own life to keep her imagination forever satisfied, but she never missed one of Ezster's sessions.

The ladies of the harem had evidently been listening to Ezster for some time before this pause. The sticky *lokum* had disappeared from the platters, the fried dumplings lay in crumbs, and the *yufka* pastry was broken and scattered. Of the pomegranate pulp, which had been beaten into sheets, then dried, cut into pieces, and dredged in sugar, all that remained on the silver serving trays was a piece the size of Hannah's little finger.

Ezster turned in Hannah's direction but did not acknowledge her. The sack by Ezster's feet sagged, no longer stuffed with her merchandise. Tova walked through the group of women, only her eyes showing above her silk *yaşmak*, as she silently collected coins for the payment of her mother's wares. Her *pelisse* was uniquely vibrant— stripes of yellow, pink, and green. Her belly was even more protuberant than it had been last week when Hannah had seen her in the *mikvah*. Hannah would not have been sur- prised if Tova began her travail right before her eyes. One more thing that might go wrong.

Ezster took a sip of tea and began a new story. "This legend of a young maiden and her lover has no beginning and no end. The maiden's lover was killed at war. After his death, the girl was transformed into a white swan, rather like the one who swims in the garden pond over there." Ezster gestured toward the fountain in the garden outside. "Did the lovers find each other again in the hereafter? I like to think they did."

The Valide's eyes were fixed on Ezster. "Was the maiden very beautiful?" she asked.

Kübra, the slave girl, entered and, bowing low, offered Nurbanu a tray covered with balls of ground pistachio nuts and honey flavoured with saffron. Nurbanu waved her away.

"Was she beautiful, you ask, Your Highness?" Ezster repeated. "Is there a heroine in the world who was not thought more beautiful after leaving this earthly world for the next? There are no plain heroines or homely heroes."

There was a murmur of agreement among the girls.

Ezster held up a finger upon which she wore a ring set with a citrine—not a valuable stone, but one that brought the bearer good luck. Hannah hoped it would work today. Ezster went on to tell the story of the beautiful maiden, but Hannah was too anxious to pay close attention. Before she knew it, Ezster had begun another tale.

"Now for a story about one of our illustrious neighbours from Araby. We have seen such types many times traversing the city in their caravans," she said. Then, remembering these girls had never been permitted to leave the harem, she added, "Or you would have seen if you had ever shopped in the markets." They all waited while Ezster swallowed a piece of *lokum*. "An Arab and his camel were crossing the desert with a cargo of spices," she began, dusting powdered sugar off her hands. "The Arab pitched his tent one cold night and went to sleep. The camel put his nose inside the tent and said, 'Master, it is so cold outside that icicles are forming in my nostrils. May I please keep my nose in your tent tonight?' The Arab agreed and went back to sleep.

"A short while later, he heard a voice say, 'Beloved Master, my forelegs are numb from cold. Can I put them in the tent as well?' The Arab agreed and went back to sleep. A dark shape pushed through the tent flap, and, bending its head low, nuzzled him with soft lips."

Ezster paused long enough in her recitation to accept from a servant a bowl of beet soup, fragrant with ginger and cumin. "In the middle of the night," she said, "the camel once again awakened the Arab. 'Good sir, my hind legs are frozen. Can I place them in the tent?' The Arab agreed. With a grunt, the camel collapsed next to him, squeezing the Arab so vigorously that the Arab was forced through the flap of the tent and pushed into the desert. For the rest of the night, the poor man froze outside."

Everyone laughed—everyone, that is, except Hannah. It was as though Ezster were speaking directly to her about Grazia, warning her that Grazia would shove her out of her own house and take possession of everything Hannah had ever cherished—Isaac, Matteo, her livelihood.

Ezster took a taste of soup and smacked her lips. Every eye in the room was upon her. After patting her mouth with a cloth, she continued. "The Arab rose with difficulty the next morning because he was stiff from sleeping out in the cold all night. He prepared a soup of dried lamb in a watery broth. The camel started to plead, 'Kind sir, just a taste. I have been having terrible dreams and crave the solace of some of your fine soup.'

"The Arab, furious with the beast, picked up the pot of soup and hurled it at the camel, covering him from head to chest in the boiling liquid." Ezster rose from her cushioned stool and approached the Valide's divan. Pulling back her arm, Ezster tipped her bowl of beet soup over the Valide's gown. The Valide leapt to her feet. "'There!' the camel-driver shouted. 'Have the only thing I have left and then leave me in peace. It is better to starve alone than to be harassed by such a creature!'"

The bodice of the Valide's lovely robe had turned a shocking red. "What have you done?" she screamed.

Hannah gave a cry, ran over to the Valide, and, with a cloth from a nearby table, began to mop at the stains. The Valide pushed her away and signalled for Mustafa.

Ezster, looking as though she were about to burst into tears, said, "I am so sorry, Your Highness. I do not know what possessed me. I was caught up in the story." She was performing her role as the shamed storyteller perfectly. Her hands, usually never still, lay as motionless as a pair of dead doves.

The Valide stood stock-still, her mouth compressed into such a grim line that her lips disappeared. The women around her grabbed cloths and began rubbing her kaftan, which only made the stains grow larger. While everyone was thoroughly distracted, Hannah nodded in the direction of Leah, who slipped away from the Valide and toward the hamam.

The red stain on her bodice made the Valide look as though she had been stabbed. She glared at Ezster. "I have had enough for one day. Leave this instant. You shall return another day with better stories, and a new white gown to replace this one that you have ruined." She turned and left the room, Mustafa following in her wake.

No one looked at Ezster. The odalisques moved uneasily

away from her. Many drifted to the hamam, where they commenced bathing. Through the archways and pillars, Hannah could see a few moving in twos and threes toward the private dressing rooms that ringed the pool, supported by a slave on each arm to keep them from falling off their pattens.

Seeming to recover herself, Ezster called out, "Tova! Where are you, my daughter? We must be going."

A pregnant figure dressed in a brightly striped *pelisse*—yellow, pink, and green—emerged from the area near the hamam, eyes downcast, a veil covering her face. The girl walked over to Ezster, picked up the empty sack by her feet and slung it over her shoulder.

Ezster reached for her cane. The girl then took Ezster by the elbow and the pair made their way to the door. No one gave them a second look. To do so would be disloyal to the Valide.

Arm in arm they walked, the pregnant girl and Ezster, through the hamam to the gardens. Hannah allowed them a head-start and then followed several paces behind. Once in the garden, the two women proceeded to an orange tree, where Fikret's reins had been tossed over a branch. The pregnant woman took Fikret by the bridle. The donkey jerked its head and gave a little buck at her touch. Ezster offered him a turnip from her bag and slapped his hindquarters, sending up puffs of dust. Two eunuchs, decorative swords tucked in their sashes, led the women past the Sultan's menagerie toward the First Courtyard, never once daring to meet their eyes.

Hannah followed from a distance as they marched along, moving through the rose gardens and past the marble fountain jetting rainbows of water into the air. For a moment, the women and the donkey resembled an exquisite Persian miniature. Finally, they disappeared through the gate.

What a performance! By the time the muezzin issued the cry for evening prayers, they would all be together at the *hoca*'s stall in the market, ready to make their way home.

Hannah returned to the reception room to gather her belongings. Mustafa, back from escorting the Valide to her apartments, unlocked the harem gate for Hannah. "Such a terrible thing. The Valide is so upset," he said. "But she will recover. In a few weeks, the harem ladies will clamour for Ezster and the Valide will welcome her again."

Hannah felt a stab of guilt. Ezster was indeed a true and loyal friend to sacrifice several weeks' earnings for the sake of Hannah and a girl she did not know.

"Shall we have tea?"

Hannah put her hand on Mustafa's arm. "I am too upset." That much at least was true. "May we have tea another time?"

"Of course," Mustafa replied. "But let me send you home in a carriage, Hannah. It is unwise for you to be wandering about on your own."

"A walk will do me good."

Mustafa raised an eyebrow.

"I need fresh air," Hannah said, wrapping her *yaşmak* around her face, leaving only her eyes uncovered.

"Peace be with you, then."

"Goodbye, Mustafa. Let us forget this afternoon as soon as we can."

A few minutes later, having exited the palace, Hannah was walking along Seraglio Point. She smelled the breezes coming off the Bosporus. As she neared the markets, the fragrance of flower blossoms turned to the smell of fish. Cobblestones bit through her sandals, horse and camel dung clung to the hem of her skirts. She felt faint at the stench of the wool-makers street lined with rancid sheep fleeces spread out on airing racks to dry in the sun.

No matter. Everything was going according to plan. Kübra had been bribed with a garnet ring to lie about Leah's sudden disappearance. She would say that the girl, overcome by melancholy for her murdered family and convinced she was carrying a princess and not a prince, had flung herself from the highest palace walls. There would be no way to verify her story since Leah's body would be dashed on the rocks below. Robbers would strip her body of its silk clothing and jewels, then toss her into the sea.

Hannah hurried through the spice market, her skirts brushing against the glass bottles filled with wriggling leeches, powdered toadstools, and ginger soaked in the urine of pregnant camels—cures for fever, catarrh, and madness. She dodged piles of merchandise—copper cook pots, pottery dishes, wooden spoons. The gnarled, beseeching hands of beggars plucked at her, and she was overwhelmed at the sight of mothers with babies more dead than alive, and lepers missing fingers and toes. She emptied her pockets of small coins, knowing that even if she managed to sleep tonight, these scenes of human misery would haunt her dreams.

Through a series of intricate twists and turns, she reached the *hoca*'s stall. The old woman was bent on her rush mat, telling a young woman's fortune. Pieces of molten lead simmered in a pot of boiling water. The old woman scooped them out with a ladle and tossed them in a pot of cold water. They sizzled. Steam rose. The lead hardened into twisted pieces. From these shapes, the old woman could divine the future of the young woman who squatted before her—whether her husband would be unfaithful, how many sons she would bear, and how she could cure the persistent sty in her eye. The old woman peered up at Hannah, grinned, and gestured by pinching two fingers together to signify that she should wait a moment so that she too could have her fortune told.

Hannah looked around, allowing her eyes to grow accustomed to the dim light. Young tea boys rushed by, serving from brass trays; merchants shouted out the virtues of their wares. From the minaret of a nearby mosque came the keening of the muezzin, calling the faithful to evening prayer. Fear began to rise in Hannah. She had not felt so frightened since she was a child and fell into the Rio de la Sensa in Venice, nearly drowning before a gondolier fished her out. She searched the area around the *hoca*'s stall, only to be greeted by a sea of unfamiliar faces.

Ezster, Tova, and Leah were nowhere to be found.

CHAPTER 19

Constantinople

S HOULD HANNAH WAIT? She did not know how
long she'd been standing there, the panic engulfing her.
Where were Leah, Ezster, and Tova? The sun was sink-
ing low in the sky. Isaac would wonder where she was. The
merchants were packing up their wares and closing their stalls.
Stray dogs gathered around the food vendors, eager for the
scraps that the proprietors tossed them at the end of the day.

Finally, Hannah heard the clip-clop of hooves and
Fikret with Tova on his back came into view. Leah and
Ezster followed.

"I was so worried!" Hannah said, as soon as they were
within earshot. "Are you all right?"

"We're fine," said Ezster. "Just fine. Tova bribed one of the eunuchs to unlock the gate when we were leaving, but once in the First Courtyard, she slipped on a patch of mud and twisted her ankle."

Hannah, concerned, said, "Are you really fine?" She reached over to touch Tova's prominent belly.

"Yes, Hannah," Tova said. "All is well."

Hannah was greatly relieved. In the grand scheme of things, a twisted ankle was nothing. These three women were standing before her, all of them alive.

"Once we were outside the gate, Leah was waiting for us," said Ezster. "A eunuch heard Tova's cries of pain and sprang forward to help. I intercepted him and took Tova's arm, and Leah took the other. Together we hoisted Tova onto Fikret. It did not take long for the eunuch to become suspicious. I gave him my day's earnings so he'd forget the sight of two pregnant women dressed in identical striped kaftans."

Both women were still dressed in matching garments. Tova said, "Leah planned to change into her own kaftan someplace out of the way. But with my little mishap, she didn't have an opportunity."

"I'm so glad you are all right, all of you," Hannah said. "But we must get out of here before we are noticed."

Leah had been very quiet throughout this exchange. Now, she looked at the women and spoke. "Before you go," she said, "I want to say how wonderful I think the three of you are and how grateful I am for your help." Tears sprang to her eyes, and she pushed her veil higher on her face to hide them. "You have saved my life. And the life of my unborn child."

"And mine," said Hannah.

Leah took Hannah's and Ezster's hands and kissed them. Then she reached up to Fikret's neck and patted Tova's hand. Not knowing what else to do, Leah bowed her head and stood still before them. Only then did Hannah realize Leah had no idea what was to happen next.

"Leah, you are coming with me. To my house. We will keep you there until your confinement."

Leah looked up at Hannah. Clearly, she did not know what to say. All she could manage was a sincere "Thank you, Hannah."

The four women exchanged quick farewells and promises to keep in touch, and then Hannah and Leah made their way home.

❧

When they arrived, Hannah opened her front door as usual and ushered Leah through.

"Who is she?" Grazia said, appearing almost immediately in the entrance, Matteo trailing behind her.

Hannah explained that Leah was a girl from Manisa, rescued from the slave markets because she was pregnant. From her face, Hannah was sure Grazia would ensure the entire neighbourhood knew the details of the new slave girl's arrival. For once, Hannah was grateful for Grazia's overactive tongue. It meant the neighbours would not discover Leah's true identity.

Grazia turned on her heel to go. With Matteo following

close, she made her way toward the kitchens, where she would no doubt inform Zephra of the new arrival.

Hannah was more concerned about Isaac's reaction to Leah's sudden presence in the house. She did not have to wait long before her worst fears were confirmed. Isaac was carrying a tray of silk cocoons, walking toward the stifling pot in the workshop. He stopped suddenly when he saw the pregnant woman before him, dressed in a colourful kaftan.

His face grew set and white. "It's her, isn't it? The slave girl you lied for," he hissed.

"Please, Isaac, it is only for a little while. She is with child. In a few months, as soon as she has her baby . . ."

Isaac was unravelling the silk cocoon in his hands. He flung it to the ground, where it fell into a pile of sweepings.

"I want nothing to do with her or her baby." He said this to Hannah, refusing to look at poor Leah, who stood in the doorway.

Hannah had never defied Isaac in all their married life. Bargaining, calculating, and scheming were something she did in the marketplace, not in her household with the husband she loved.

"After the baby's birth, I will send Leah to the countryside. Ezster has a sister, Naomi, in a nearby village. I'll tell Naomi that Leah is a widow, her husband killed by the Yürüks. Naomi will find Leah a husband." Hannah was babbling now, unable to stop herself, even though she knew that her words were only driving Isaac further away.

"I will not have her here," he said.

"Is this not my house as well as yours?" Hannah countered.

"Make other arrangements. Surely, there are other families in Eminönü who would take her in."

"By 'take her in'—you mean like a stray dog? Isaac, for the love of God, she's carrying a child. Have you no compassion?"

Hannah refused to back down even though she felt sick and weak. She woke up every morning feeling nauseous and remained that way most of the day. Food repelled her. She was growing thin. She had to force herself to eat so much as a piece of dry bread. Isaac stormed from the room. Had she not allowed Grazia to join the household? She was not going to send Leah away. Instead, she escorted her upstairs and settled her in a small room in the attic.

Isaac, her rock, her font of love, warmth and good advice, did not so much as meet her glance that evening when Zephra served their tea. Zephra and Möishe eyed Leah quietly, believing the lies about her being a pregnant girl from the slave market brought home to help in the workshop. Later that night, Isaac would not touch Hannah in bed, nor even say good night, so great was his anger.

A week later, Isaac was still not speaking to Hannah except to convey the most necessary details of day-to-day life. Around the house, he ignored Leah completely. Neither Leah's rounded belly—her confinement was not far off—nor her eagerness to help around the house and workshop made him soften. Grazia, for her part, stayed far away from the girl and regarded her with equal parts suspicion and fear. So far, no one except Isaac had guessed the truth about Leah. No carriage had arrived at her doorstep summoning Hannah to the palace. Ezster had not been to the harem since the afternoon they rescued Leah and so could not bring Hannah up to date on whether Kübra's story was believed. But if anyone had suspected Hannah, she would have been dead by now, and Leah along with her. This, if nothing else, gave Hannah some hope.

Her marriage was another matter altogether. When she looked at Isaac's face over the breakfast table, at the lips she had kissed with such passion, at the dark eyes she had gazed into so many times, at the lean muscular body she had curled around so many nights, she realized she and her husband had become strangers to one another.

He claimed to be struggling to find Grazia's dowry money, but how hard was he trying? Was he trying at all? In her heart, Hannah feared he simply did not love her anymore.

Zephra, meanwhile, confessed to Hannah that she'd seen Grazia put several drops of her menstrual blood in Isaac's tea, the traditional way to make a man fall in love.

Her spell was working, Hannah thought as she watched Grazia and Isaac from the kitchen window. In the garden, Grazia was trimming Isaac's beard—a curiously intimate thing for her to do—and Isaac appeared to be enjoying it. He sat very still with his eyes closed and his chin jutting forward. Grazia's breasts were level with his face.

Leah had begun to play with Matteo, who seemed to enjoy her company. Like an older sister, Leah picked him up and swirled him in the air, her filmy trousers billowing out behind her. Her hair had grown to below her chin in the weeks since Hannah first met her in the palace. With the growing bulge in her belly, she no longer resembled a boy but a lovely, graceful young woman. Sometimes, when Hannah hugged her and felt Leah's belly pressed against hers, her own womb responded with a slight wrench, as though a taut string were connecting them.

When Grazia finished Isaac's trim, he thanked her and made his way to the workshop. Grazia took her scissors and, ignoring Leah, said to Matteo, "Let's cut some daisies, shall we?"

Matteo left Leah and scampered to Grazia's side. Together, they cut and braided a pile of daisies. Holding up the plait to gauge its length, Grazia nodded, then fastened the ends together to make a garland, which she handed to Matteo. Watching, Hannah recalled an old proverb of her mother's: "She fondles the lamb so that she might steal the ram."

Matteo raced toward the kitchen with the wreath on his head. He burst in with a jerky trot, knocking a tinderbox and flint off the table. "Look what Mama Grazia made me," he said, one eye obscured by the wreath.

When had Matteo begun to call Grazia *Mama?* Hannah straightened the garland, picking a flower petal out of her son's hair and flicking it out the window. "How nice," she said. She told herself it was a good and fine thing that Grazia cared for Matteo and he for her. She was his aunt, after all.

Hannah watched Matteo from the kitchen. While he played, she went to the sitting room, where she began to stitch a pair of trousers for him to match his blue wool waistcoat. The wide and floppy legs of the garment pooled in her lap. She must remember to order a matching pair of tough cowhide boots from the boot-maker for the muddy streets. Boots and breeches and baking bread and making soap? What did any of these household details matter anymore? If they could not pay Grazia soon, none of these chores would be Hannah's concern. Her husband and son would be lost to her.

Isaac entered, not acknowledging her presence. He took a seat at his desk and opened his black ledger. His ink-stained fingers moved over the book. He wiped his quill with a pen rag and set it down on his desk. Hannah was surprised when he spoke to her.

"Grazia has become devoted to Matteo."

Isaac was as unobservant as most men. He did not notice that Grazia played with Matteo in a way that seemed too studied. He did not observe how she hugged him too often and fussed over him excessively. How she spooned into his mouth special soups and stews that she cooked herself.

"Grazia bathes him, changes his clothes, and prepares dishes for him that I do not know how to prepare," Hannah said. "Matteo seems to prefer her company to mine." Just as you do, she thought.

"You do not appear to be well," he said. "It seems to take all of your will to rise in the morning, and to dress yourself and Matteo." His voice sounded kind but his words were terrifying.

"You have one wife who is vigorous. That should be enough for you." How sour she had become. If only she could hold her tongue.

"Hannah, how can you say that? She is not my wife any more than Leah is my daughter."

The words stung, as all of Isaac's words did of late. Hannah knew she was distraught and should defer the conversation until she was feeling more composed. But how would she ever have any energy when she could not sleep at night? How could she look well when at any moment she expected a knock on the door and the squad of deaf-mutes to take her away? How could she rest when Grazia was taking over the running of the household? Grazia had even started giving orders to Zephra.

"We used to work together, Hannah, like two horses drawing the same cart. Now you pull one way, I pull another, each of us determined to take different paths," Isaac observed.

"Everything was different before Grazia arrived."

"And before you brought Leah into the house."

It always came to back to this impasse.

His words made Hannah feel sicker and more alone. "When Leah's baby is born, I will find a family far away to take her in and find her a husband. You will see, Isaac. It will all work out."

But the thought of Leah gone dismayed her. Hannah had grown to love the impulsive, energetic girl. It was Grazia she wanted to be quit of.

"And have you raised the money yet for Grazia?" Hannah asked, knowing he had not. "Perhaps you are not trying very hard because you enjoy her company more than mine."

"Hannah—" Isaac began, but she cut him off.

"She is beautiful and—"

"You have nothing to be jealous about. Yes, she is beautiful but in the way a statue is beautiful. I do not desire her."

"No? Every time she enters the room, every time you hear the rustling of those Venetian silk skirts of hers, you get a look on your face."

"That is not true!" He rose to his feet and paced back and forth. "You are being unreasonable, Hannah."

Hannah could not help herself. "You think she will bear you a son as I have failed to do."

"I want more children. That much is true. The rest is not. Is that so terrible?"

If he had taken a knife and plunged it into her heart, it could not have been more painful. Hannah began to cry, hot, angry tears pouring down her cheeks.

Isaac put away his ledger and his ink pot and quill, and left the room.

A few hours later, after putting Matteo to bed and banking the fire in the stove, Hannah, exhausted, retired but was unable to find comfort on the hard pallet she had fashioned for herself on the floor of their bedchamber. She got up and returned to their bed, where Isaac lay snoring. She crawled in next to him and tentatively wrapped her arms around him. From the corner of their room, Güzel the parrot fluffed her wings, then coughed in a perfect imitation of old Zephra, who suffered from catarrh. Hannah had forgotten to cover the bird but was too tired now to get out of bed.

There was a low purring noise, like folds of velvet being rubbed back and forth against itself. Hannah sat up in bed to listen, staring through the blackness of the bedchamber. On the window ledge was the silhouette of a cat backlit by the moon, eyes narrowed, back arched, ready to spring at Güzel. Hannah had no wish to wake up to a feather-strewn floor. She flung back her covers, grabbed a fire poker, and ran to the window, but the cat scampered down the wisteria vine and away into the night. Hannah returned to bed after shutting the window. After a time, she finally drifted off to sleep.

It was dawn when Hannah heard Leah's agonized scream pierce the air, then a whimper, then silence. She pulled on her old blue *cioppà* and grabbed her linen bag with her birthing spoons. She looked over to see if Isaac had heard Leah's cry, but his side of the bed was empty.

CHAPTER 20

District of Eminönü
Constantinople

NOT FOR THE FIRST TIME in her life, Hannah prayed a baby would be born alive. This baby, conceived in the mountains of Circassia, the last of a long line of mountain Jews, must not be smothered in its mother's womb nor strangled on its own birth cord, may God be listening. Leah, after all that had happened to her, should be allowed at least this: a lasting legacy of her village, her people, and the young man she had loved.

Hannah took the stairs two at a time to Leah's room in the attic. When she opened the door, she saw Leah writhing on the floor, clutching her belly. In the pink light of dawn, Hannah saw the mound of her child pulsating through the thin cotton of her shift. Hannah knelt next to her, placing her bag on the floor. The birthing spoons clanked as they jarred against glass vials of oils and tinctures, tin boxes of herbs.

A makeshift lamp—a slab of limestone with a chipped-out reservoir for holding a knob of fat—sat next to Leah. The rope wick was smouldering, charred to a stump, casting more shadows than light. Hannah snuffed it out. It was nearly daylight anyway. She pulled the door to the attic closed and worked quietly so as to not disturb the rest of the household.

Leah was not due for several weeks. Early babies slipped out more easily than full-grown ones, but they had little chance of surviving. If born in the fall and winter months, they rarely lived to see spring.

"Has my time come?" asked Leah. "Isn't it too soon?"

"Much too soon."

Hannah took the bottle of almond oil from her bag and lifted up Leah's nightdress. She rubbed some oil between her palms and stroked Leah's abdomen, palpating to determine the position of the baby. The head was already well descended into the birth canal.

Hannah must deliver this baby alone. Isaac had made it clear he wanted nothing to do with the birth. And Hannah did not trust Grazia to be present. What if, in pain, Leah said something to reveal her true identity? Hannah could not call for Zephra. The old woman looked on Leah with suspicion, believing she had been brought to the house to replace her.

Hannah massaged Leah's belly to relax her. How like a daughter Leah had become. She urged the girl to breathe, hoping she would not shriek quite as loudly as she had and wake up the household. Grazia was a sound sleeper, but no one could sleep through the screams of a labouring mother.

The girl looked ashen and hollow-eyed. Her hair was hanging loosely around her neck. Hannah drew several packages of herbs from her bag. "This is valerian and black haw. I will prepare an infusion with boiling water from the brazier. It won't take long, but it has to steep a few minutes." The herbs might stop these contractions. It was the only hope of forestalling the birth.

Leah reached for Hannah, gripping her hand between her own.

"Whatever happens to me, I want you to know I am grateful for your kindness."

"Try not to talk."

Leah reached up and put her arms on Hannah's shoulders. "I want you to promise me something."

There was a spasm; Hannah felt the girl's belly harden against her hand. Leah twisted in her arms and gripped her so tightly that Hannah almost felt it was her own travail. It would be a powerful herb, indeed, that could stop these birth pangs.

In a voice so low Hannah had to bend her ear to Leah's mouth, the girl said, "If I die, take care of my baby."

"You will be fine," said Hannah. She had often heard such words from young mothers. The pain of giving birth frightens a girl, making her soft and beseeching. "Of course I shall raise your child if it comes to that. You are a daughter to me, a much-loved daughter. Now, I must prepare the herbs."

Hannah took the kettle off the brazier, poured boiling water in a bowl, and added the herbs. With a wooden spoon, she stirred the mixture, submerging the herbs. After the herbs had steeped sufficiently, Hannah carried the bowl of steaming liquid and set it down on the floor next to Leah. She thought of Isaac. Perhaps he had left before Hannah was awake to deliver a few skeins of silk to the Armenians next door? Hannah refused to contemplate other possibilities. She must concentrate on Leah and her baby.

Hannah reached out a hand and stroked Leah's belly. The girl's hips were barely the span of a man's hand. With such a childlike form, she could struggle for days and not manage to push out the child.

"Where is the birthing stool?" asked Leah.

"It is right here behind that curtain." She hauled it out into the centre of the room where Leah could see it.

The chair was shaped like a chicken's wishbone with handles at either end for the labouring mother to grip. The handle of the carved wishbone turned up into a backrest. Isaac had fashioned it for Hannah, hoping that one day she might make use of it herself. On the back, Isaac had painted a pair of turtle doves mating in mid-air, although Hannah knew the thoughts of a labouring mother were far from love and marital congress as she struggled and sweated to expel her baby.

Hannah took the herbal potion and blew on it to cool it, then coaxed Leah to sip as much as she could manage.

Leah soon grew hot to the touch. Her eyes lost focus, darting around the ceiling of the attic like a sparrow searching for a place to light. A puddle of water appeared between her legs. The herbs were not taking effect. Hannah debated whether to give Leah a dose of cramp bark in a cup of warm sweet wine, but decided it was too late. The travail was proceeding. Hannah felt as powerless to stop it as she would be to halt a runaway horse.

Leah's legs were filling with fluid. Her lovely, sharp-featured face was turning as puffy and white as pastry dough. Hannah pressed a thumb into the top of the girl's foot, held it there for a moment, then took it away. The indentation remained. Hannah had seen this condition before. A feeling of helplessness and frustration came over her.

"Let us get you on the birthing stool," said Hannah. "You will be more comfortable."

Hannah raised Leah from the floor by grasping her under her arms. She helped her toward the chair. To Hannah's surprise, Leah remained calm and, moreover, did as she was told. Hannah managed to get Leah to lower herself to the chair and grip the handles. Even with her huge belly, the girl felt light, hardly more substantial than Matteo.

Leah said, "My mother did not have the luxury of a birthing chair and a midwife as kind as you. She appeared home one late afternoon from high up in the summer pastures with my baby brother strapped to her back."

Were there no women in Leah's village helping their sisters and neighbours through their travails? Was life in the mountains nothing more than a comfortless test of endurance from birth to death?

"After, the mother cooks and eats the placenta to give her strength."

The custom of eating the placenta was common among the nomads, but Hannah had never heard of the practice among Jews.

"If the baby is not wanted," Leah went on, "they leave it in a crevice for the wolves and return home with empty—" The girl's tongue was swollen and protruded from her mouth, making it difficult to understand her speech. She let out a groan and clutched at her belly.

If Leah were still in the harem, this would be a festive occasion like Safiye's confinement. Jugglers and acrobats would amuse and distract the crowd, if not the mother. An astrologer would draw up the baby's chart. The lead ladler would predict the baby's fortune.

"Leah, relax, breathe. If you are tense, you will only make it more difficult."

"Make it stop, now!" Leah pleaded, the pain overwhelming her.

The girl's body was stretched as tightly as the strings of a *klezmer*. Hannah knew there was little she could do, but she went around the room opening the window and all the dresser drawers. This would help ease the baby's passage into the world. All cooking vessels should be turned upside-down to prevent the Angel of Death from finding a hiding spot.

During the next hour, Hannah sang songs to distract Leah. Between pangs, Hannah told her the tale of a maiden who loved a silly young knight who cared only for his horse. The knight fed oysters to his mare night and day.

Leah seemed unable to remain upright in the birthing chair and so Hannah helped her to lie down on the floor. When the pains came closer together, Hannah examined the mouth of the womb. It had opened nicely, but the sharing bones still would not permit the passage of the baby's head. Not even her birthing spoons could help in this situation. As each strong pang came and went, Hannah feared that the pressure of the contractions would cause the infant's head to bend back, snapping its neck. It was no good telling Leah not to push. When the urge to push came, there was no resisting.

Hannah could hardly bear to think of what she would be required to do to save Leah's life if something did not happen soon—take out her crochet, an evil pointed instrument, and pierce the baby's skull, dismember it, and pull out the severed limbs until the womb was empty and the floor strewn with tiny body parts.

Hannah brought a paper twist of ground pepper out of her bag to make the girl sneeze, which sometimes helped to hurry the birth. She held it under Leah's nose. Nothing.

More time passed.

There was one thing that could be done to save the baby, but she could not resort to it yet. Hannah had seen death in many forms—plague, murder, and childbirth. She would never grow accustomed to it.

Gradually Leah's green eyes grew dull. When Hannah moved her hand in front of them, the girl did not blink.

The girl's pulse was much too rapid. Her body grew rigid. She was icy to the touch.

It would be a kindness to give her an opiate, but Hannah doubted the girl could swallow a large gold-foiled pill. All she could do was stroke Leah's hair and hold her as her breathing slowed and grew more shallow and eventually stopped. Was it God's will that Leah die? No. Surely, God was not so unjust.

She fumbled through her linen bag for a hand mirror and held it to Leah's lips. Nothing. No breath at all. Hannah closed Leah's eyes.

The poor baby, ill-fated from conception, would soon be dead too. Was it right that this be so? Without a mother's love, what chance was there for this child? A crippling grief overcame Hannah. Despair hung in the room as pungent as the smell of blood. She dropped to her knees and rocked back and forth, head in her hands.

I murdered my son's uncle, Hannah thought. I caused my sister Jessica's death. I have failed to keep the love of my husband. I have failed to give him a child. Now I have one more failure to add to the reckoning.

Hannah rose to her feet and started to draw a sheet over Leah's body and face. Just then there was a ripple along the surface of the girl's belly, like the twitch of a horse's hide when a fly alights. Hannah considered. Was failing to act not just as wicked as placing a pillow over the face of a living infant? For the rest of her life, Hannah would strug- gle to forget what she did next.

She pushed aside the sheet. She oiled Leah's belly from

breast to umbilicus. She took up her iron knife. *Guide my hand, God.* Hannah made a horizontal cut above the umbilicus from hip bone to hip bone. A tracery of red blossomed on the white belly, a gaping mouth opened. Such a small girl, so much blood. Hannah placed the sheet on Leah's chest, then reached inside the belly with both hands and lifted out the womb. Hannah manoeuvred it onto the sheet. It was the colour of a ripe plum, round and bursting, mapped with a network of veins. With the tip of the knife, Hannah made a small incision. Watery blood flowed like wine from a ruptured goatskin.

Hannah wiggled her fingers into the small cut and ripped open the womb. The sound of tearing flesh made the bile rise in her throat. This was not Leah, a girl she had come to love and admire, she reminded herself, but a vessel of flesh and muscles cradling a child, a child waiting to be liberated, a child with a will to live.

Through the tissue and blood and sinew, tiny curled legs and a bottom emerged. Hannah groped, trying to gain a good purchase. When she found the shoulders and had hooked two fingers under the armpits, she pulled. The baby slipped from the womb. Hannah was panting as violently as Leah had done a few minutes ago. The child was blue.

Hannah turned away from Leah's body, upending the baby. With the heels in one hand, she gave the child a vigorous whack on the bottom. The baby choked, screamed, and turned scarlet with fury. Hannah placed the child on a cloth on the floor and took up her iron knife. She severed the birth cord, then sank to her knees. Gradually, she felt her pulse slow and her breathing grow more regular.

She shielded the baby, tucking it to her breast. The child's first view of the world must not be its mother's mutilated corpse. Still kneeling on the floor, struggling and slipping in the blood, Hannah used one arm to pull the sheet over Leah's face. *God,* prayed Hannah, *guide me. Tell me what I am to do with this motherless child.*

The baby was whimpering softly. "It is all right, little one. You have made it safely into the world. No need to dunk you in a cold bath to coax you to breathe."

A dense fatigue swept over her. With her hand, Hannah cleared the baby's mouth and face, washing off the sticky white grease that coated all newborns and protected them from the waters of the womb. Like many babies born too soon, Leah's was covered with a golden down like the hairs on a bee's legs. The child was small but not impossibly small. As Hannah rocked it, she glanced between its legs. A girl.

A wet-nurse must be found. A grave dug. The placenta buried. She had not the energy for any of it. Who would see to everything? The only thing of which she was certain was that someone else would need to take care of these matters. The girl Hannah had hoped would become like a daughter to her was dead, and her baby, the last of its mountain tribe, an orphan.

CHAPTER 21

Constantinople

STANDING AT THE WINDOW, Hannah once again
saw a carriage pull up in front of her house. There
could be only one reason for the Imperial carriage
with its little mare snorting, harness bells tinkling, plumes
dancing in the breeze.

Several weeks had elapsed since Leah's baby was born.
In that time, Tova also bore a child—a vigorous, healthy
boy whom she named Benjamin. Jessica, as Hannah had
called her, had grown plump and healthy on Tova's rich
milk. She began to gurgle. When Matteo held her carefully
on his lap, she waved at him and tried to pull his hair. Isaac
had grown fond of the child, fussing over her when she

cried, taking her to Tova's house when it was time for her to be nursed.

But in spite of all the joy the children brought, it was still a house in mourning. Leah's death hung heavy in their hearts, even Zephra and Möishe who had avoided her company, believing she brought bad luck upon them, felt her loss. Isaac, who even in happier times kept his feelings to himself, looked sad and weary, although he called for the Rabbi to bury Leah and covered the mirrors for *shiva*, the period of mourning. Zephra no longer whistled tunelessly as she scrubbed the pots. Möishe no longer teased Matteo and tossed the ball for him in the garden.

Grazia, meanwhile, had become more insistent that her money be paid and refused to grant any further extensions. They had until next week or she would insist her marriage to Isaac proceed. Soon, Hannah feared, she would have no husband, no son, no home.

Suat dismounted and knocked on the door. Hannah, the baby on her hip, opened it. "I have orders to fetch you," he said. "The Valide wants to speak with you."

"About what?" asked Hannah.

"Her Highness wishes you to bring the baby."

So the Valide knew. Hannah felt her entire body grow cold.

Suat turned and returned to the carriage, climbing into the driver's seat.

Hannah had no time to run or hide. Only Grazia was home. She appeared now in the front entrance.

"What is going on?"

"I've been called to the palace."

"I'll take the baby, then."

"No," Hannah said. "She's coming with me."

Grazia looked about to argue, but seemed to think better of it and withdrew into the house.

It was horrible to think that the last familiar face Hannah might see was Grazia's. Hannah wanted to say a last goodbye with Isaac. She wanted to throw herself in his arms and cry, *The Valide has found me out. I may never see you or Matteo again. Don't let me go without hearing you say 'I love you' one last time.* But there was no Isaac to confide in and kiss goodbye. He was at the market and was not due home for at least another hour. Perhaps it was better this way, because what, after all, could he or anyone do to help her out of this situation, a situation entirely of her own making?

The neighbours craned their heads out of their windows to get a better look as Hannah and the baby climbed into the carriage and old Suat clucked to the horse and they pulled away. Hannah hugged the baby against her chest as they rode.

It seemed impossible that this infant born in tragedy could be so beautiful. The baby's eyes, as green as Leah's, darted from side to side, trying to focus on Hannah's face. Bracelets of fat encircled her wrists. Hannah jiggled Jessica in her arms in time to the swaying of the carriage, wondering at the baby's fate, and her own. The movement would soon have the infant sleeping.

Mustafa was waiting at the entrance to the harem when they pulled up. His eyebrows were drawn in a scowl, his shoulders stiff. The golden quill in his turban trembled in disapproval. He greeted her without his customary smile and offer of tea. He cast a dismissive look at the baby. Her staunchest ally in the palace had become hostile.

Without preamble, he said, "I will take you to her." He beckoned Hannah to follow him to the Valide's apartments.

When they passed through the marble columns, the floor was strewn with fresh rose petals. The infant was now asleep in Hannah arms, oblivious to her opulent surroundings, the walls lined with Iznik tiles and gold-embroidered tapestries. What did any of this beauty matter, if the Valide was about to order their executions?

Mustafa knocked on the doors of a formal reception room and when the doors opened, he dropped to his knees and crawled toward the Valide, who wore a kaftan of rich cerulean blue. Tucking the baby under one arm, Hannah got down on her knees and crawled, as best she could, to the royal divan, leaving in her wake a swath of exposed marble floor as her skirts swept away the rose petals. Hannah did not dare meet Nurbanu's eye.

The Valide's white lap dog scampered from her arms, knocking over a small table holding an Iznik ewer and a tray of pastries. The pitcher shattered into dozens of pieces. The dog, unconcerned, commenced to gobble down the pastries.

The Valide snapped her fingers and ordered a slave to attend to the mess. Then she turned to Hannah, who had approached as far as she felt she was proper. "You and I have much to discuss."

There was no escape from this huge room with eunuch guards at all the doors. There was no way to explain how Hannah came to have this baby.

"Yes, Your Highness," Hannah said, still afraid to raise her head. The baby had done nothing wrong. Surely the Valide would not order the execution of an innocent child?

"Be seated." The Valide gestured to a nearby cushion.

Hannah was surprised by the invitation and immediately stumbled to her feet, arranging herself on the cushion, still holding the baby tightly. Nurbanu's eyes came to rest on the child. She crooked a finger to beckon Hannah to hold the child so she could see her.

"And what have you named this little thing?"

"I call her Jessica," Hannah replied. "After my sister." She had planned to ask Rabbi Yakov to say a *brokhe*, a blessing, over the child and bestow the name Jessica in blessed memory of Hannah's dead sister, but Hannah had not been able to bring herself to do it just yet. Was it right to give such an ill-fated name to the baby? Her sister had died by bloodshed and so would never be at peace until she found another body to inhabit. Hannah hoped Jessica's spirit would find repose in this baby and protect it.

The Valide sighed. "All that nuisance for a girl."

Nuisance? What exactly did the Valide know? Hannah couldn't help thinking of Leah's white body, the knife, the hasty funeral, the lusty baby, her own tears.

The Valide leaned over to examine her. "It has been so long since I held an infant." She reached out and took the sleeping babe in her arms, bent over and kissed her round cheeks and silky black hair. "Does she resemble the Sultan, do you think, Hannah?"

The Valide was playing with her. Hannah was certain of it. "She is so young. It is too soon to tell who she looks like," she ventured, hoping she wasn't making a fatal mistake.

"Nonsense. Many newborns are the very image of their fathers." The Valide tucked a corner of the blanket around the baby's feet. "How old is she?" She peered more closely. "I would say a few weeks. Would that be right?"

Hannah nodded.

"So that means . . ."

Hannah watched her mentally calculate, counting off months.

"She was conceived a good while before my son ever laid eyes on little Leah." The Valide studied Hannah, daring her to make a reply.

"She was born very early," Hannah said. "It is a miracle that she survived."

"You do not think I am so stupid as to think this child is the Sultan's?"

There was no answer except a truthful one. Hannah was about to speak, but the Valide held up a hand to silence her.

"The child is mine, of course. I owned Leah; therefore, I own her child." The Valide cradled the baby even closer.

Would the child be raised in the palace, taught to embroider and play the flute, or would she be executed? Hannah imagined both of their heads on the executioner's block.

"She has grown very dear to me, Your Highness," said Hannah. She had to suppress the urge to snatch the baby from the Valide and race out of the palace.

"So I gather from the way you gaze upon her." The Valide lowered the child to her lap. "Convince me why I should not take her from you."

Hannah paused, considering carefully. "The child is of no interest to anyone but me."

"You acknowledge she is not my son's child?"

"Yes, I do." Hannah's confession was tantamount to asking for her head to be impaled on a spike and displayed on the Example Stones.

"Since you have been forthright, I will be forthright with you," the Valide said. "I knew before Leah was within the harem walls an hour that she was pregnant."

Hannah could not believe her ears.

"Unfortunately, by that time the Sultan had already glimpsed her and could talk of nothing else. Imagine my dilemma. I was thrilled he had taken an interest in a female other than his wretched wife. I needed Leah to break Safiye's spell. Once she did, he would be free to pursue other girls. But protocol demanded that Leah be confirmed a virgin. Mustafa had to record this proof in *The Book of Couchings*."

The Valide rocked the baby on her lap. "Any of the palace midwives would have told me the truth about Leah. But I wanted someone with a soft heart, someone who would pity the girl. So I summoned you. I knew you would lie to protect her from being sold into a brothel. What I had not reckoned on was that you would arrange matters so that my son would think he had couched the girl when he had not."

Hannah recalled the swish of a silk *pelisse* she had heard the night of the couching and the sound of a gasp coming from the balcony above the Sultan's divan. At the time, Hannah had suspected it was Safiye and felt sorry for the Sultan's wife having to witness such an event. But it had not been Safiye; it had been the Valide.

"You know Leah is dead?" asked Hannah.

The Valide looked at Hannah, bemused or angry—Hannah could not tell. "There is little that happens in the city that I do not know." The Valide gave a little shrug. "Inventive little Leah did her job well even in doing nothing. My son is now as licentious as a goat. After the so-called couching with Leah, his royal chamber has been visited by many young women. Three odalisques are now pregnant. Soon, babies will be raining from the heavens, filling dozens of cradles."

Hannah was confused. What need had the Valide for this child of Leah's when soon she would have many grandsons and granddaughters? The Valide planted a kiss on the baby's soft, pink cheek and passed her back to Hannah. There was a spot on the Valide's blue kaftan where the baby had wet her. People had been executed for far less. When the Valide saw Hannah looking at the stain, she smiled.

"Never mind, it is good luck when a baby makes water on you."

Nurbanu fixed her steady gaze on Hannah. "Very few of my subjects have ever lived after lying to me, but I intend to spare you. After all, you will never reveal the details of what you have done. In the end, your duplicity has served me well."

Hannah was so relieved she wanted to do cartwheels on the cold tile floors or throw the white China porcelain vases of red tulips out the casement window. Of course she did neither. "Thank you, Your Highness. I will say nothing, ever. I am most grateful."

Hannah did not want to spoil the moment, but she had to ask. "Did you know all along that Leah was staying with me?" The baby was getting hungry; she was growing restless in Hannah's arms.

"Yes, but I told the Sultan that Safiye, in a jealous rage, ordered the girl's death. I told him the deaf-mutes had killed her and that her body would never be found, nor would anyone be able to trace Leah's death back to Safiye, so richly had she rewarded the killers. The knowledge made her repugnant to him." The Valide showed her square, white teeth. "Life in the harem is so complex."

"Indeed it is," Hannah responded. Poor Safiye. "You are the very soul of benevolence," she managed to say. Once the words were out of her mouth, she feared they sounded sardonic. But the Valide accepted the remark as a genuine compliment. Hannah rocked the baby, hoping she would not cry. There was no need to try the Valide's patience further.

"I should not reward you when you lied to me, but as you have pointed out, I am the soul of kindness. I shall allow you to keep her. But no one must ever know she is Leah's child."

The relief Hannah felt at hearing these words made her voice catch. "Of course not," she said. "I will say that she is a poor orphan, the child of a slave girl I found in the market and took pity on."

"Good. I have a contact in the city, a fellow Venetian who brings me tidbits of news from time to time. I hear you require a hundred ducats to pay off a certain . . . debt." The Valide stroked the white dog that had crawled back on her lap.

Hannah thought of Isaac. With a hundred ducats Grazia could take the money and leave on the next vessel bound for Rome.

"Tucked behind that vase of carnations is a velvet purse." The Valide inclined her head toward a table beside Hannah. "Accept it with my gratitude," she said.

How Venetian the Valide was in her subtlety, giving a gift indirectly so as not to embarrass the recipient. Hannah did not know what to say.

"Go on."

With one hand, she reached out and took the pouch. It was heavy. "Thank you, Your Highness."

"I know you will use this money wisely. You may go."

Hannah carefully moved the baby so she could tuck the purse into the pocket of her skirt. A sudden joy filled her. If she had been standing instead of seated, her knees would have given out. She looked at the Valide one last time and then tucked the baby under one arm and crawled backwards, awkwardly, from the room, the pouch of ducats clinking against her leg.

Just as she had struggled to rescue Isaac from the Knights of St. John in Malta so long ago, now she would save him again. And their marriage.

CHAPTER 22

District of Eminönü
Constantinople

IT WAS ALREADY DARK when Hannah returned
home from the palace. She went straight upstairs.
Isaac was seated upright in bed, his nightshirt opened
at the neck. "Oh my God," he said, jumping to his feet.
"It's so late and I thought the worst. I thought . . ." He
took her and the baby in his arms, resting his chin on the
top of Hannah's head. "I thought . . ." he began again,
but could not go on.

"I know," said Hannah.

"I wasn't even here to say goodbye when you left. You
could have died alone thinking I didn't care for you anymore."

In the doorway, hesitant to move into the bedchamber, stood Möishe and Zephra, both smiling. Möishe said, "Your head is still attached to your shoulders, I see." He could turn the grimmest subject into a joke.

Zephra entered and patted Hannah's cheek. "I am so happy you are alive."

Behind Möishe and Zephra, in the shadows, stood Grazia. She made no move to come into the bedroom, and from the look on her face she was not as happy as the others were to see Hannah and the baby.

"A joyous occasion," she said finally, and then retreated downstairs.

Zephra and Möishe followed her.

"Such a lovely child," Isaac said.

"The Valide gave her to me. I will raise her, if you agree." A tone of defensiveness had crept into her voice.

"Hannah, I am sorry about the way things have been between us—so strained, so difficult. We will raise the child together. You and I."

Hannah felt a stir of hope. She looked down at the baby, their baby. The tiny face, the rounded cheeks, the mouth like the bud of a rose. She looked so much like Leah, it broke Hannah's heart. The Valide had almost certainly noticed the resemblance but had not mentioned it.

"And, Isaac, I have the money to repay Grazia."

He turned to her, a puzzled look on his face.

"The Valide gave it to me."

"Are you jesting?"

She passed him the baby and took the velvet purse from her pocket. She shook it so the coins jangled.

The look of pure happiness on Isaac's face made Hannah regret her earlier suspicions.

"I do not know what to say." Isaac laid the baby down in her cradle and gave it a slight push with his hand. "I was so afraid of losing you, Hannah. I saw us drifting further and further apart until there seemed to be nothing I could do to stop it. I never wanted Grazia. All I wanted to do was placate her to buy us more time. I was trapped."

Hannah began to see all of Isaac's actions in a different light. He had not been fawning over Grazia after all, but was merely trying to keep her at bay.

"Shall we tell Grazia the news together?" Hannah asked, taking his hand.

They found her in the garden, tossing a ball to Matteo. Grazia had not been looking well of late. Her mouth was tight. She was not taking the usual care with her appearance. Today her dress was creased and her hair had been arranged in haste.

"We have your money," Hannah announced without preamble. "Now you can sail home and remarry."

Grazia stared at her and then at Isaac, an unreadable expression on her face.

"Aren't you overjoyed?" Isaac asked, his arm around Hannah's shoulder.

Hannah showed her the velvet pouch. Grazia took it, weighing it in her palm. She did not look like a woman who had just been handed a fortune.

"Where did you get this?" Grazia asked.

"It does not matter," said Hannah.

"Aren't you happy?" Isaac asked.

"Of course, I am overjoyed. It is just so unexpected." But when she tried to smile, her lips remained closed and tight.

Matteo wrapped his arms around Grazia's legs and buried his face in her skirts.

"I am happy, of course I am. It is just that I shall miss you all so terribly." Grazia fondled Matteo's ear. From the chicken coop in rear of the garden, the rooster crowed three hearty *cock-a-doodle-doos*.

"Isaac will ask the Rabbi to arrange for the divorce," said Hannah.

Grazia took Hannah in an embrace. "Dear clever sister-in-law." She kissed her on both cheeks. "I am so very pleased that you will remain Isaac's wife."

There was such a note of insincerity in Grazia's voice that Hannah wondered why Grazia had bothered to say the words at all.

The following day, Hannah, Isaac, and Grazia went to the Rabbi's study, where two other rabbis were present. Under the direction of Rabbi Yakov, Grazia untied from Isaac's foot a sandal specially designed for the ritual divorce ceremony and hurled it across the room. She then spit on the ground in front of Isaac, declaring, "My brother-in-law refuses to raise unto his brother's memory a name in Israel; he will not marry me."

Isaac, as the ceremony demanded, responded, "I do not wish to take her."

Hannah noted with relief the elation in his voice as he said the words.

Grazia continued at the urging of the Rabbi: "Marriage to you would be an abomination." She said it without conviction, but Hannah didn't care.

Then it was over.

They walked home together, Grazia lingering a few steps behind Hannah and Isaac. Isaac cradled Jessica in his arms. He brushed against Hannah from time to time and smiled at her, making jokes and teasing her.

"So I am to be deprived of the happiness of having two wives to scold me and order me about?" Grazia made no reply, not even a smile.

When they reached their house, his face took on the tender look it got when he was thinking of making love to her. She was glad she had been to the *mikvah* recently and so was ready to receive his love. She felt the old Isaac coming back to her, and she accepted him as easily as she might envelop herself in a cherished cloak.

That night was hot and so muggy that Isaac suggested they sleep under the stars. In the middle of their garden was a secluded space formed by arching willow trees and carpeted with moss. On summer nights when their bedchamber grew unbearably hot, they often slept there.

When Isaac made love to her, he let her reach her fulfillment first. When it was his turn, he called out her name. When Isaac had persuaded her to marry him, he had promised no one would ever love her as much as he would. Falling asleep beside her, holding her in his arms, Isaac had kept that promise. *Thank you, God,* Hannah prayed, *for returning my husband to me.*

❧

At dawn, as they were waking up under the willow, Isaac said, "Good morning, dear wife." He kissed her on the forehead and drew her closer. They made love again, tenderly, and later, still in each other's arms, discussed their plans for the day ahead.

Isaac said, "Grazia wants to take Matteo to the parade to celebrate Prince Mehmet's circumcision."

Hannah wiggled out from under his arm and sat up. "The streets will be packed with thousands of people. What if he gets tired and has to be carried? What if he stumbles under the wheels of a cart? I think it is wiser if we all go."

"But baby Jessica needs you here," said Isaac. "And Möishe and I have work to do on the looms. Matteo will be thrilled to have Grazia all to himself before she takes her leave. It is only for a few hours."

"I suppose you are right," Hannah said with reluctance. She should not let her dislike of Grazia interfere with Matteo's love for his aunt.

"It will be a spectacular event," said Isaac. "This will be a day he remembers for the rest of his life."

CHAPTER 23

IT WAS LATE AFTERNOON and Hannah was chopping
onions for a beef stew. Matteo and Grazia should have
returned hours ago from the Parade of the Circumcision.
Of course, Matteo would be enjoying the jugglers, the magi-
cians, and the bears, but Hannah worried that Grazia would
exhaust him. Grazia would let him drink too much sherbet
and buy him dozens of sweetmeats, which he adored. Oh
well. How often was a prince's circumcision celebrated with
a parade lasting fifty-three days?

The house seemed deserted without the boy's exuberant
cries. By this time in the afternoon he could be counted
on to fling his bedsheet over his shoulders like a cloak and

charge up and down the stairs. Other days, he would be in the garden practising walking his tightrope.

Before Hannah took the baby to Tova's to be nursed, she must go to Grazia's room to find Matteo's old swaddling bands. Lately, a few ordinary items had gone missing. It must be the work of the *djinns*. This morning, it had been Matteo's blanket. Matteo had been inconsolable and sobbed throughout breakfast. He flung himself from his chair, refusing to sit at the table or eat his bread until Grazia searched the house and came back with the blanket.

"Where was it?" Hannah had asked.

"Oh," Grazia said, "in the garden."

Odd. Hannah hadn't seen it there, but no matter. Matteo was overjoyed to have it back and sat clutching it to his chest.

Now, Hannah held the baby upright, patting her back while she climbed the stairs to Grazia's room. The sleeping mattress was neatly rolled up and put away. The cupboard doors were closed. The curtains were blowing through the open casement window.

Something was very wrong. The bottles and jars of creams and scents and oils that were always arranged on the low table under the window, Grazia's precious blue enamelled box containing red powder—all gone. The room had been used by the previous owners as a storeroom for turbans. The walls were lined with niches. Grazia had used these for storing odds and ends—gloves and shoes and a hat. Now they were empty.

Hannah searched the closet for her suitcase, but all she found was dust.

"Isaac! Isaac!" she called. "Come, quickly."

Moments later, she heard Isaac bounding up the stairs.

He came in, his hands and the front of his apron stained green from dye. "What is wrong?"

Hannah paced back and forth, holding the whimpering baby. "All of Grazia's things are gone."

Isaac surveyed the barren room and looked into the closet. "There must be a simple explanation."

Hannah stared at Isaac, wanting to shake him. "Isaac, she has Matteo. All her clothing and personal effects are gone. Do you not understand? She has taken Matteo!"

"What? But . . . why?"

Why could not Isaac, who was so much wiser in the ways of the world than she, realize what had happened? "We have no time to waste!" Hannah's voice was so loud that the baby began to cry, reaching a crescendo that made it impossible to hear what Isaac was saying.

Zephra came into the room. "Please take her to Tova for a feeding," said Hannah. Jessica's angry pink face nodded over the old servant's shoulder as Zephra left the room.

"Isaac, we must look for him—and fast."

"But there must be some expl—"

Hannah interrupted. "Isaac, no." This was not a Talmudic debate about how many angels could dance on the head of a pin. Now was the time for action. A thought struck her. "This morning, when they left, Grazia insisted on taking Matteo's blanket." Hannah could not explain it, but there was something about Grazia's insistence that had disturbed her. Matteo's blanket—the only thing that linked him to his natural parents.

A look of alarm crossed Isaac's face. Finally, he was beginning to see.

"We will find him. Don't worry," he said.

They hurried to the front door, where Isaac took his *berete* from the hook. Hannah slipped on her sandals. She called to Zephra to tell her they were going out, before remembering that she had already left with the baby for Tova's house. Hannah wrenched open the front door and together they ran out.

"They must be heading through the crowds to the docks," Hannah said.

"It will be impossible to get through the crowd in a carriage. Let us go by foot."

Several streets later, they encountered the parade. "Isaac, how will we find them?"

Hand in hand, Hannah and Isaac squeezed through the crowds, ducking past the various guild floats, including the chalk-makers'. The men riding on top of the wagon were crunching chalk in their hands and using handfuls of it to whiten their faces. A band followed in their wake, playing eight-fold Turkish music.

A cart lumbered by, drawn by massive draught horses pulling the silversmiths and their forges. Which of the many floats would Matteo insist on seeing? The carpenters building a wooden house? The bricklayers raising a wall? The silver thread-spinners? The saddlers? The felt-makers? The confectioners' guild that flung their sugary delights into the crowd—Lips of the Beauty, Hanum's Finger, and Ladies' Thighs?

Thousands of people were milling about, mothers holding babies in their arms, fathers carrying children on their shoulders. She spotted a red-haired boy, arms extended to catch a piece of marzipan thrown from the confectioners' float. Her heart nearly stopped. But he was an older child, five at least, and not as handsome as Matteo.

A mime spotted Hannah and Isaac rushing through the forest of people and followed them, stroking his beard in imitation of Isaac. Isaac tossed a coin at the man, trying to get rid of him, but it only encouraged the mime and soon he added ribald gestures to his act.

They pushed and shoved, Isaac shouting for people to move aside. It was too much movement, too much, too fast. She stood for a moment to catch her breath.

Isaac pulled her arm and they raced along the Street of the Armourers, side-stepping a cart piled high with cooked sheeps' heads. In the distance was the blue expanse of the Bosporus. Now Hannah had a stitch in her side. She cursed herself. Just when she needed all of her endurance, she seemed to have none.

"Are you all right?" Isaac asked, slowing.

"Of course," she said. "I am fine."

Hannah pressed her fist into her side, grabbed Isaac's hand, and carried on.

CHAPTER 24

Circumcision Day Parade
The Old City
Constantinople

C ESCA HAD NOT WANTED to steal Matteo from the only mother he had ever known any more than she had wanted to kill Leon, but God had ordained otherwise. She walked along Caddesi Selçuk. And there in the distance was Foscari, waiting at the *simit* seller's, just as arranged. What greater proof did she need of God's approval? She approached him, dragging Matteo by the arm. The boy was exhausted from excitement over the wonderful sights of the parade.

"Hello, Foscari," she said, taking in his handsome face and the thick hair that had grown too long and now curled over his collar. "You are looking well."

"As are you." Foscari beamed at the boy and said, "We shall see some marvellous sights, you and I. Perhaps the sponge divers' float? Or maybe the confectioners'? You look like a boy who enjoys sweets."

Matteo grinned, clearly fascinated by Foscari's silver nose. Cesca smiled brightly and stared at it too. It was as though his silver nose were a fortune teller's crystal ball in which she could see her future. There was her villa in Maser, with its apple orchards, rich pastures, and honey-coloured cows. Since that evening at the embassy, everything had fallen as neatly into place as pleats in a silk dress. The dower money had dropped from the heavens into her lap. The absurd divorce had saved her the trouble of murdering Isaac and claiming his paltry estate—a trivial loss. Cesca had bigger fish to catch. She had Hannah's hundred ducats, an enormous sum. She was free to sail to Venice. And Matteo could keep his precious blanket, thus avoiding a tantrum. They would all be reunited soon enough at the docks. The villa would soon be hers.

Cesca paused a moment, deciding how best to phrase what she was about to say next. "Foscari, there has been a slight change in my plans. You'll be pleased to hear that I can sail with you after all. And soon," she added. Without Isaac as her husband, there was no reason to remain in Constantinople. It would be a relief to go to Venice, where she could understand the language. She would not have to pretend to be someone she wasn't, constantly vigilant lest she make a slip and mention the Virgin Mary or eat cheese with a piece of roasted meat, or violate some other preposterous dietary prohibition.

Cesca spoke in a low voice so Matteo would not hear. "I shall look after the boy during the voyage."

Foscari did not look as pleased as a man should look at the prospect of several weeks of a beautiful woman's company aboard a small ship.

"And the blanket? Where is it?"

"Where it always is, in the boy's pocket."

"Very well then." Foscari studied Matteo for a moment. "Such a handsome little trot. Quite the image of his father." He held out his hand. "Let me see that blanket I have heard so much about."

Matteo backed away.

Cesca bent down to him. "It's all right, my son. You do not have to give it to him now."

To Foscari, Cesca said, "Don't worry about the blanket now. You'll frighten him. We'll have plenty of time for that later.

"You be a good boy, Matteo. Enjoy the parade and don't leave the Marquis Foscari's side. He will buy you any treats you want."

The boy finally lost his shyness and spoke. "But Mama gets angry when I eat too much *lokum*."

"Today is a special day, and you can have anything you wish. I will meet you later for a special adventure."

"All right, Mama Grazia."

"I shall meet you at the embassy later," she said to Foscari. "You will purchase passage for me?"

"Yes," he said. "Of course."

Cesca kissed Matteo and told him to be a good boy. Then she left to reclaim her valises from where she had hidden them and take them to the docks.

⚜

An hour later, Cesca marvelled at her own stupidity. What use had Foscari for her with both the boy and the blanket in his possession? She raced down Caddesi Istiklâl toward the Venetian embassy. She had trusted him simply because he had promised her the villa. She must be more calculating if she was ever to become the owner of a grand villa. But—perhaps it was not too late.

Cesca fought her way to the embassy, past floats, squeezing through the crowds. By the time she finally saw the Venetian flag, the golden lion on a field of red flying high over the walls of the embassy, she was faint from the heat. She hurried up the street, praying to see Foscari ordering his servant, Kamet, to load his valises onto a porter's cart. Then they would all proceed together to the docks.

Cesca pulled on the bell at the entranceway, not a tentative jerk like last month but a desperate tug. No one came to the door. Kamet was probably in the garden, out of earshot, or helping Foscari to pack. She yanked the bell cord harder. The two guards on either side of the doorway turned to glance at her and then looked away, no doubt amused by her appearance, her hair coming unbound, her mud-spattered skirts. They were tall and fierce-looking and wore black turbans. It had been a different pair altogether when she had been here before.

A yellow street cat wandered over and sniffed at her shoes. She hissed at it and it slunk away. At last, she heard footsteps and the door swung open, framing a tall, fat Nubian wearing a blue turban. This slave had whiskers that grew down the sides of his face. It was not Kamet.

He waited for her to speak.

"I wish to see the ambassador. Will you tell him Grazia is here?"

"The *bailo* is not in residence, Madam. He is in Venice on business and has been there for several months." The servant spoke in the Venetian dialect.

Did he mean that Foscari had already departed for the docks? No. He clearly said the ambassador had been away for months. "That is not possible. I saw the Marquis Foscari a few hours ago." The Venetian flag flapped in the wind above her head like the sails of a ship.

"The ambassador is Andrea Ridolfi, and I assure you, Madam, he has been gone for many months. Perhaps you mean the embassy of the Franks on the next street?"

The impertinence of the servant took her breath away. "You brainless creature. I am talking about the *bailo* Foscari—tall, well-proportioned, and wearing a silver nose. He has a little boy with him. Fetch him at once."

"I have been serving here for many years and know what goes on under this roof." He moved to close the door. "There is no man here with a silver nose, ambassador or not."

"What of Kamet? A Nubian servant who wears a yellow turban?"

The slave paused, holding the door halfway closed. The guards in the entranceway sidled closer to Cesca, making her uncomfortable.

"Kamet worked here for a short time but was relieved of his duties some time ago. Where he went, I do not know." The slave wiped a rivulet of sweat from his brow. "Good day."

Cesca found herself staring at the closed, heavy oak door of the embassy. She hammered on it with her fists until the two guards on either side ordered her to stop, and she gave up.

She turned and walked down the street, a wide one filled with carriages and flanked by mansions. What did it all mean? Was Foscari *not* the ambassador? She was filled with rage and humiliation. When she caught up to him, she would make him pay. She would see him hanged as the mountebank he was. She strode along so rapidly she tripped over a sleeping dog in the road and fell to her knees.

A liveried servant from an adjacent house helped her to her feet. "Tell me," she said to the servant. "Have you seen a man with a silver nose, coming and going from that place over there?" She pointed to the flag fluttering over the embassy.

The servant shook his head. "I am out here in all weather. Never have I seen such a person."

She continued on. The muggy air and the mud on her skirts weighed her down. Her thoughts went in crazy directions as she tried to make sense of the situation. She was certain the *Medusa* had not yet sailed, but suppose Foscari planned to sail on a different ship? Suppose she arrived at the *Medusa* and he had not bought passage for her? What if Foscari alone claimed Matteo's fortune?

No. She would not have it. She could buy her own passage. After all, she had her hundred ducats. She reached into the pocket of her skirt where she had carefully placed a thin silk wallet. She fumbled desperately for it. The wallet was gone.

CHAPTER 25

The Hippodrome
Constantinople

MATTEO HAD BEEN plucked from the earth. Nowhere in the crowds outside the Hippodrome could they find him. Hannah and Isaac entered the stadium, the oval race course built centuries ago by the Romans for horse and chariot races. Ancient monuments still remained in the middle of the track: the Obelisk of Thutmosis III, hauled all the way from Egypt, as well as the Serpent Column, both of them taller than the mast of a ship.

The noise of the firecrackers in the arena was so overwhelming that at first Hannah did not hear the voice behind her. But then it came again, high-pitched and insistent. She felt a tug on her sleeve. It was Mustafa shouting above the clip-clopping of a cavalcade of solemn-faced Janissaries on horseback.

"Hannah! I thought it was you. Come with me. The Valide will be delighted to see you . . . and to meet your husband." He turned to Isaac and bowed slightly. "You must join the Valide in the Royal Kiosk."

"It is a great honour, Mustafa," Hannah said, breathlessly. "But we cannot."

Isaac explained. "Our son has disappeared. We fear he has been kidnapped."

Mustafa looked alarmed but did not ask for more information. Instead, he said, "All the more reason to see the Valide."

Hannah and Isaac exchanged looks. He was right. If anyone could help them now, the Valide could.

Mustafa took Hannah by the arm and Isaac followed close behind. They hurried through the crowds toward the far end of the Hippodrome, where the Royal Kiosk had been erected high above the open field so that the Sultan and the royal family could preside over the entire event. "You can see everything from the Royal Kiosk—the acrobats, the wrestlers, the magnificent floats of the goldsmiths and arrowsmiths. The Kiosk is so high, you might even be able to spot your little boy," Mustafa said.

Mustafa, Hannah, and Isaac climbed the stairs of the Kiosk, ascending higher and higher above the crowds and confusion of the parade.

When they reached the top, Hannah felt dizzy and held on to Isaac's arm. It was as though she were a swallow looking down from far above onto a miniature city below. Surrounding the Royal Kiosk were *nahils*, gigantic artificial trees made from a framework of balsa wood and decorated with fruits and flowers, human and animal figures, even models of ships, all of which were fashioned from beeswax. Some *nahils* stood as high as the minarets of Hagia Sofia. Private homes had been demolished to make way for these imposing structures as they were carried aloft through the streets by a hundred Janissaries.

Sultan Murat III was seated on a gold cushion at the front of the Royal Kiosk. He watched the parade as the one thousand and one guilds of Constantinople marched past. He did not notice Hannah and Isaac entering because he was busy throwing gold coins to his pages and the other young men passing below. The Sultan looked no more handsome than he had the night of Leah's make-believe couching, but he seemed to be making an effort to appear benign, rather like a fierce grandfather trying not to frighten timid grandchildren. God forgive her for this thought, but his large middle draped in a girdle of diamonds reminded Hannah of the elephants in Venice that Christians decked out for Lent celebrations.

Near him sat the Valide, veiled, her shoulders not touching the back of her gilded throne. She wore a shimmering red kaftan, which made her black hair look even darker and richer. On her hand was a ruby the size of a sheep's eyeball. Safiye sat on the Sultan's left with little Ayşe on her lap. Safiye touched her husband's hand, but he brushed it off on the pretense of reaching for a glass of sour-cherry sherbet offered by the Superintendent of Sherbets, a portly man who in spite of the unseasonably hot weather was wearing a great deal of silk and fur and velvet.

The smell of roasting meat drifted up from the ovens in the square below. During the celebrations, the palace fed the public twenty roasted oxen a day. Before the oxen were cooked, live foxes, jackals, and wolves were sewn into the oxen and then released in front of the crowds. When they bounded out from the carcasses, the spectacle caused much hilarity and more than a little panic in the crowds.

Mustafa rushed ahead, approached the Valide, and whispered something in her ear. The Valide turned. She nodded at Hannah and Isaac and beckoned them forward. Thankfully, in the small confines of the Royal Kiosk, subjects were not required to drop to their knees and crawl.

"How lovely to see you, Hannah," the Valide said.

How difficult to read the thoughts of a face hidden behind a veil, even a veil as diaphanous as a silk moth's wing. The Sultan, to Hannah's relief, continued to take no notice of them. Hannah took the Valide's hand, kissed it, and pressed it to her forehead.

"I am delighted to see you. And this, Your Highness," she said, turning to Isaac, "is my husband."

"I have heard a great deal about you, Isaac. It is a pleasure to meet you."

Isaac bowed low but knew well enough not to take her hand, nor did she offer it.

"Mustafa tells me you have lost your son in the crowds, Hannah."

Hannah looked gratefully at Mustafa, who was standing, dignified and silent, behind the Valide's throne.

"We are so worried. I have no idea where to find him." She was afraid to say the worst—that she feared Grazia had taken him with her on a ship bound for Venice.

"I shall help you search for him."

How exactly would she be able to help? There were so many people in the Hippodrome, it would be like searching for a gold coin in a sack of wheat.

"The Kiosk is heaped high with gifts of every description—crystal, Chinese porcelain, Syrian damask, Indian muslin—all thanks to the Sultan's viziers, Kurdish beys, and foreign ambassadors. Somewhere in this pile of trinkets is a spy glass." She turned to Kübra, who was standing in the corner. "Would you find it? The one from the Venetian ambassador?"

Kübra disappeared with a bow and a moment later returned carrying a long, cylindrical brass instrument that would have looked more at home on the deck of a brigantine than in the delicate hands of the Valide.

"Try it," the Valide said, passing it to Hannah. "You hold this end to one eye and close your other eye."

Isaac stood at her elbow, anxious. Hannah did as instructed. As if by magic, all things in the distance appeared closer and sharper.

Gradually her eyes grew accustomed to the strange magnification, which was like peering through a goblet of water held up to light. She saw a troupe of wrestlers rolling on the ground, their bodies slick with oil. She saw dancers and fire-breathers and a man leading a string of zebras tied together like black and white beads on a necklace. She saw the carpenters' float—watched as the joiners erected a small wooden house on the immense wagon.

And then, stretched high between the Obelisk of Thutmosis III and the Serpent Column, she saw a thick hemp cord. Two acrobats wearing thin, leather-soled shoes walked along the taut cord, starting from opposite ends, intending, Hannah surmised, to meet in the middle. One of the tightrope walkers carried on his back a charcoal brazier. An audience had gathered underneath them, clapping delightedly. It seemed that as part of their act the acrobats planned to cook a meal while balancing on the tightrope.

Hannah felt a rush of excitement. Was it possible that Matteo had seen the tightrope walkers and even now was watching them? Hannah was certain—this is where she would find Grazia and Matteo.

"Your Highness, I have a feeling you may have helped us find our son. May my husband and I be excused?"

"Of course you may," the Valide said. "Good luck, Hannah."

Hannah raced for the stairs, realizing even in her state of panic how rude it was to turn her back on the Valise. She called over her shoulder, "Come, Isaac!"

CHAPTER 26

The Hippodrome
Constantinople

HANNAH AND ISAAC nearly tripped and fell in their haste to get down the stairs. At the bottom they dove into the crowd and elbowed their way to the tightrope acrobats. Just as Hannah had suspected, there was Matteo! "Isaac, there he is!" she cried as she made her way to him. Hannah thought her heart would leap from her chest from the joy of seeing his chubby cheeks and blue eyes. But Matteo was holding the hand of a strange man with a silver nose. When he saw his mother, he tried to twist out of the man's grasp, but was held tight.

Isaac shouted to the man, "What are you doing with my son?"

The man's face was turning red with the exertion of hanging on to the child. "I hardly think he is yours."

Isaac grabbed Matteo's free arm but still the man wouldn't release his other. Matteo began to scream and kick.

"Papa! Papa!"

"Let go of my son!" Isaac commanded.

"He is not your son," the man said.

Mustafa, who had followed Isaac and Hannah, arrived on the scene huffing and trying to catch his breath. Hannah watched helplessly as her son was yanked in opposite directions, fearing his arms would be pulled from their sockets. He looked terrified and began to sob.

"Please!" Hannah yelled. "Whoever you are, let my son go!"

A crowd began to gather around them, drawn by the odd spectacle of the man with the silver nose, gleaming in the sunlight, and the little boy being used in a tug of war.

"His shoulder will be parted from his body!" Hannah cried.

"Release him now!" Isaac growled.

And just when Hannah feared the boy would be torn in two, everyone around them fell to their knees. Hannah turned to see the Valide and her entourage of eunuchs approaching, and she bowed low. The strange man and Isaac stopped pulling and stared, dumbfounded, while Matteo pulled free and ran to Hannah, wrapping his arms around her waist.

"Your Highness," said Mustafa. "What brings you here?"

"I could not help but observe this commotion from the Royal Kiosk. Nothing escapes my notice, especially"—she held up the brass spyglass—"with this clever device. May I ask what on earth is going on?"

Hannah, Isaac, Matteo, and the silver-nosed man stood before her as Mustafa explained. "Your Highness, this man claims that this boy does not belong to Hannah and Isaac."

"That's correct, Your Highness," said the silver-nosed man. "This child is the son of a nobleman in Venice. His father and mother died in the plague, and these Jewish kidnappers stole him—a Christian child—and brought him to Constantinople, where they have been raising him."

The Valide's eyes widened. She stared right at Hannah. "You took a Christian child and have been raising him as a Jew?"

"Your Highness," Hannah said. "When I was in Venice, I was midwife to Matteo's mother. Soon after his birth, she and the Conte died of the plague. But the boy's uncles wished to kill him so they could inherit the family fortune. I protected the child and took him away. There was no one else to care for him. I brought him with me to Constantinople. This much is true. Isaac and I have raised him as our own ever since."

"This is a dreadful state of affairs," said the man. "It must be remedied, Your Highness. The child must return to the city of his birth and his fortune must be restored to him."

Isaac spoke up. "Your Highness, we are the only parents that Matteo has ever known. Without my wife's intervention, my son would have perished long ago."

The Valide was quiet for a moment, then said, "Isaac, you may be right that the boy would have died, but that doesn't mean you can claim him. And you, Foscari . . ." She turned to the man with the silver nose. "What in the name of heaven would make you go to such great lengths to retrieve this boy?"

"My undying love for the di Padovani family," Foscari answered.

The Valide looked dubious. "Well, this is a new side of you, Foscari. I've never known you to be quite so altruistic in your motives."

Hannah saw Mustafa lower his head to hide a smile.

"With respect," Foscari replied, "beyond my compassion for the boy and my abiding love for his deceased father and mother, there are political considerations that motivated my actions. The matter goes far beyond Matteo and his family's estate. Tension is high between Venice and Constantinople, as you know, Your Highness. If it came to light that a Christian child had been kidnapped, brought here, and raised as a Jew, it might be enough to touch off a nasty incident."

Had she saved Matteo from death and raised him as her own, only to have him taken by this man and used as a political pawn? It was too much for her to bear.

Suddenly, from behind her Hannah heard a familiar voice. She turned to see a figure dressed in travelling attire—a long, dark blue *pelisse* and *yaşmak*—approaching the Valide. Above her veil, the woman's eyes shone bright and determined. She walked over to Foscari, eyeing him as though she wanted to claw at his face.

The Valide said, "And who might you be?"

"I am Grazia Levy," she announced.

"It is customary," said the Valide in a voice that could chill sherbet, "to bow before me."

"I am so sorry, Your Highness," said Grazia, dropping to her knees. "I have come to claim my nephew, Matteo, and to return to him what is rightfully his."

"Yet another party claiming this unfortunate boy? And what exactly do you mean by that?" asked the Valide, her face tight with disapproval.

"Foscari asked me to verify the boy's identity. And I have. I have proof that he is indeed the heir to the di Padovani fortune. Foscari and I plan to take him together to Venice."

Grazia called Matteo to her side, and the boy immediately ran to her and hugged her skirts. She reached into Matteo's pocket and pulled out his blanket, which she held up for all to see. "This is the boy's blanket. He has had it since birth. And this," she said, pointing out the crest in the middle, "is the di Padovani coat of arms."

"You see, Your Highness? Just as I claimed," Foscari said.

Grazia eyed Foscari suspiciously. "But Foscari is not the protector he pretends to be," she said. "After he is appointed guardian and appropriates the di Padovani estate, he plans to kill the child!"

Hannah felt as though a knife were lodged in her heart. Kill Matteo? The boy loosened his grip on his aunt's skirts and ran into her arms. Hannah held him tight. He smelled of soap and sugar.

The Valide looked at Grazia. "I do not know who you are, but I do know Foscari. For years, he has kept me informed of various matters going on in the city. He is a man of . . . shall we say . . . flexible principles. But I do not believe him capable of harming a child."

"He stole Matteo from me this morning when I was showing the boy the sights of the parade! I searched high and low for them. I went to the embassy and asked for Ambassador Foscari, only to learn that there was no such man. I even went to the docks, thinking he had put the boy on board the *Medusa*. I had almost given up hope of finding him when I spotted him here, near the tightrope act."

The Valide shook her head. "Really, Foscari? So you are an ambassador now?"

Foscari said nothing.

"I suppose that ridiculous nose of yours serves some purpose?"

Foscari put a hand to his face and touched the silver appendage.

"Take it off," the Valide ordered.

"But Your Highness—"

"Now!"

Foscari inserted a finger under a corner of the right nostril and then the left. He gave an abrupt tug and off it came. Hannah looked away, afraid to see a stump suppurating with pus or at the very least a badly mangled lump of cartilage. She took a moment to compose herself, and then raised her eyes.

His nose was a perfectly ordinary appendage, typically Venetian—long and thin with flared nostrils. Without the silver beak, his bare face looked almost indecent. He looked like an entirely different man. That, she supposed, was the whole point.

The Valide said, "I assume once you boarded that ship you were going to remove that monstrosity so no one would connect you with the abduction of a child from the Jewish Quarter of Constantinople?"

Foscari stood silently, his shoulders squared. He gripped the silver nose in his hand.

Grazia said, "He is an abductor of children, Your Highness! And a thief. He stole my hundred ducats."

"I am no more a thief of ducats than I am a thief of children!" Foscari retorted. "This woman extracted from me a promise to give her the di Padovani villa outside Venice in exchange for her help. And she is no more Grazia Levy than I am an ambassador. She is a pretty Christian housemaid with loose morals and a greedy nature. She is also the murderer of one Leon Levy, brother to Isaac. May I have the pleasure of introducing. . . . *Francesca?*"

Dear God, thought Hannah. Now it made sense. Grazia often stumbled over the Shabbat prayers that should have been second nature to her. Hannah had attributed that to the fact Grazia was a convert. But Grazia did not even know the details of her own wedding. And she had never acted as a widow—there had been not a trace of grief in her words or attitude whenever her husband's name came up. Long ago, Hannah had thought that Grazia was not who she claimed to be, but the idea was so preposterous she had put it out of her mind. How could she have been so naive?

Isaac's voice was cold with rage. "You are not my sister-in-law? You sailed from Rome for the sole purpose of fleecing me, of taking my house, of becoming my wife, of kidnapping my son? And you killed my brother?" Isaac made a move toward Grazia, but the Valide held up a slender arm, which stopped him in his tracks.

"I think I have heard enough," the Valide said, and turned to address Foscari first. "You have booked passage on the *Medusa*?"

Foscari nodded.

"For you and for this imposter?" The Valide nodded in Cesca's direction. Cesca started to protest but the Valide silenced her.

The Valide said to Mustafa, "Send my Janissaries to escort these scoundrels to their ship. I have no authority to detain this woman for a crime committed on Venetian soil, but I shall inform the Venetian authorities that one of their most cunning citizens is on her way back home. I am sure she will be greeted with all the welcome she deserves." She turned to Foscari. "And as for you, 'Ambassador Foscari,' allow me to thank you for your service to me over the past years. I see now that your loyalty knows no bounds. Truly, I wish you a good voyage on the storm-tossed seas. It is a dangerous trip, so do be careful."

There was an implied threat in the Valide's words. Hannah was grateful it had not been directed to her.

"Sometimes," the Valide said, looking at the Janissaries standing near the tightrope acrobats, "people have a way of slipping off ships and returning to stir up more trouble."

"I shall see that does not occur, Your Highness," said Mustafa, "if I have to buy her passage with my own money."

"And the boy?" asked Foscari. "He should come with me."

"The boy remains here," snapped the Valide.

Not for the first time that afternoon, Hannah felt relief. She hoped it would last. She prayed she would remain Matteo's mother. She prayed Isaac would remain his father. She longed to see Matteo grow to be a man.

The nearby Janissaries came forward and led Foscari and Cesca away.

"Wait a moment," the Valide ordered, and everyone stopped.

"The ducats, Foscari?"

Foscari reached into his pocket and pulled out a silk purse.

"Mustafa, please hand that purse to its rightful owner."

Mustafa walked the few steps to Foscari, took the wallet, and returned to place it in Hannah's palm.

"Isaac," the Valide said, her tone softening as she turned to him. "I have heard that you craft tents that are as light as meringue and as red as the blood of the lamb?"

"Very poetically put, Your Highness," said Isaac.

"I shall order a dozen of your tents for harem excursions to the Princes' Islands."

Isaac bowed. "It would be my pleasure to serve you."

"And now," the Valide said, "about this boy. About Matteo . . ."

Hannah held her breath, and saw a muscle twitch in Isaac's jaw.

"I think that in the spring, you and Isaac must take the boy to Venice and see to this business of his inheritance. I will send you with a letter explaining that you and Isaac saved the child's life and are, if not his natural parents, mostly definitely his rightful adopted parents."

Hannah would have fallen to the ground if Isaac had not caught her in time—so great was her relief to feel Isaac's hand clasp hers. But how was she going to explain that she could not travel in the spring?

She steadied herself and prepared to speak the truth. "Thank you so much for declaring Matteo our son," Hannah began. "But begging a thousand pardons, Your Highness, I cannot sail in the spring."

"Why ever not?" the Valide asked.

Hannah put her hands on her stomach. Must she tell the Valide what she had not even told Isaac? There was no other way. "Your Highness, I am with child. My confinement will be in May."

Isaac turned to Hannah in disbelief, tears of joy in his eyes. Regardless of the Valide, Mustafa, and the many servants and subjects present, Isaac took Hannah in his arms.

From around them rose the crowd's cheer. "Look, Mama!" Hannah felt a tug at her skirts and looked down at her beautiful boy. Matteo pointed up. The acrobats were preparing a meal on the tightrope. Midway between the Obelisk of Thutmosis III and the Serpent Column they had set up their charcoal brazier and were cooking.

Isaac put his hand on his son's shoulder while with the other he held Hannah tight. He sniffed the air. "Circassian chicken with walnuts," he said.

"Cooked in the full view of everyone in the Hippodrome," the Valide added.

Hannah said, "What could be better?"

"What indeed?" said Isaac.

ACKNOWLEDGEMENTS

To Nita Pronovost, my talented editor, whose impeccable judgment has kept me from my own folly on more occasions than I care to contemplate. Her meticulousness and patience have been unfailing, her instinct for plot and pacing sublime.

To the indefatigable and resourceful Beverley Slopen, my agent, adviser and manager of my overblown expectations. Her good common sense, humour and friendship have been a continuing source of support.

To Martha, Ben and Sam, who taught me everything I know about childbirth.

To my wonderful sister-in-law Barbara Vance, my cyber-genius who navigates the misty shoals of Facebook and Twitter with aplomb.

To Gay Ludlow and Roland Lougheed, videographers extraordinaire.

To the Jewish Book Council of New York, a wonderful organization that acts as *shadkin* between reader and writer to such brilliant effect, keeping alive the love of reading.

To Adria Iwasutiak, my publicist, who has promoted my books with such flair, imagination and zeal and, like all true professionals, has made it look so easy.

To Terri Nimmo, who designed the magical book cover. To Kiara Kent for her helpful editorial support.

To the talented Jordan Hall of the Booming Ground program at the University of British Columbia.

To Dr. Minna Rozen of the University of Haifa, Israel, and Dr. Ashley Krisman of Vancouver.

To my many friends and family who encouraged me by their support, love and expertise: Katherine Ashenburg, Pam Barnsley, Sandy Constable, Caitlin Davis, Carla Lewis, Sharon Rowse, Lynne Fay, Wendy Matthews, Gale Myers, Shelley Mason and Jim Prier, Diane Sanderson, Diane Saarinen, Catherine and Terry Warren, Alice Rich and Adrian Palmer, Ruth and Von Peacock, Kübra Uçar, Gayle Raphanel and Guy Immega, Jacqueline Brown, and Doreen and Don Reimer, and, of course, to Beryl Young, my wise friend and invaluable mentor.

And to readers everywhere who urged me to write a sequel.

HISTORICAL NOTE

Many of the incidents in *The Harem Midwife* are true. Many of the characters are historical figures—Murat III, the Valide, Safiye, Ezster Mandali.

Ottoman history is a motherlode of dramatic events requiring little embellishment. The story of the deranged Sultan Ibraiham having his entire harem strangled for the pleasure of selecting a new one is true, though it took place in the mid-1600s. His squad of deaf-mutes strangled six hundred women and dumped them in weighted sacks into the Bosporus.

Murat III's bewitchment by his wife, Safiye, was a source of great consternation to his mother and sister, who managed to break the Sultan's spell with the purchase of a young slave girl.

So successful was their ploy that Murat III went on to father 101 children.

The story of the Valide ordering a slave's head cut off for the benefit of an artist is inspired by an encounter that took place between the Venetian painter Gentile Bellini and Sultan Mehmet II, who, displeased with Bellini's depiction of John the Baptist's decapitation, demonstrated the process on a slave.

A letter from the Valide to the ambassador complaining of the large white dogs he sent to her is paraphrased from a letter written by the Valide Nurbanu to the Venetian ambassador.

Readers will forgive me, I hope, for taking liberties with a few dates in service of the plot. Most conspicuously, the famous Circumcision Parade for Mehmet II took place in 1582, not 1578. Note, too, for those who have visited Istanbul, that what is referred to as the Imperial Palace in this book is now called Topkapi Palace.

GLOSSARY

✦

aigrette: a jewelled stickpin designed to keep the turban in place. Mustafa had an elaborate filigreed gold *aigrette* set with rubies and diamonds.

bahnkes: placing heated cups on the body to draw out pain and tension. The cups are heated with a candle.

bimah: a raised platform in a synagogue from which the Torah is read.

Bismillah: an Arabic phrase meaning "in the name of God, the most compassionate."

börek: a family of pastries made of a thin flaky dough known as phyllo, with varying fillings.

brokhe: a Jewish blessing.

buzkashi: literally "goat grabbing." A game played on horseback, the object being to wrestle the headless carcass of a goat or a calf from the opposing team and race with it to the goal post. The game is played in countries such as Afghanistan, Uzbekistan, and Turkestan.

cara: a term of affection in Italian, meaning "dear."

cassone: a chest, which may be rich and showy or very simple.

catarrh: a persistent inflammation of the mucus membranes.

chopine: high, treacherous shoes worn by Venetian women of fashion, designed to keep them elevated from the mud of the streets. The height of the *chopine* was emblematic of the social standing of the wearer; the higher the shoes, the higher the woman's status.

cioppà: a Venetian term for loose-fitting dress.

djinns: tiny demons made of fire that tormented and interfered in everyday life, causing endless misfortune.

dolma: grape leaves stuffed with ground meat, rice, or herbs.

gagliarda: an athletic and popular Renaissance dance.

gözde: a girl in the eye of the sultan.

halizah: a ceremony to dissolve a levirate marriage, for example, a marriage between a widow and her brother-in-law. The widow removes the brother-in-law's shoe, a specially made sandal, and he is released from the obligation to marry her.

hamam: steam bath or sauna.

hocas: witches.

Janissaries: an elite private corps of soldiers who guarded the sultan.

kaddish: the Jewish prayer of mourning.

Karagöz: a type of marionette theatre, popular at the harem.

keriah: a ritual of mourning; the cutting of garments to show grief for the dead.

ketubah: a Jewish prenuptial agreement. Many beautifully adorned examples of these marriage contracts can be found in museums, such as the Jewish Museum in Paris.

ketzele: a Yiddish term meaning "little kitten."

klezmer: Jewish music—lively and spirited, often played at weddings and dances.

köchek: the "fauns of Constantinople," as they were known by the Janissaries, were very handsome young males, often provocatively cross-dressed in feminine apparel, who danced for the entertainment of other men.

lapis lazuli: a semi-precious blue stone found in many parts of the world. The finest examples come from Afghanistan.

loghetto: a tiny, cramped, one-room apartment in the Venetian ghetto.

lokum: Turkish delight—sticky candies dusted in confectionery sugar.

mahalle: an Arab word meaning "district," "quarter," or "ward."

mezes: hot or cold appetizers, usually served as snacks or as the prelude to a meal.

mikvah: a ritual bath where Jewish woman cleanse themselves after menstruation.

nahils: a festive decoration and form of art used during certain ceremonies in Ottoman tradition. It is a highly decorated artificial tree fashioned from beeswax or coloured paper. They were a sign of power, and accordingly were as big and extravagant as possible.

nargileh: a water pipe used to smoke flavoured tobacco.

nazar boncuğu: an amulet believed to be protection against the Evil Eye. In modern Turkey, it is common to see *nazars* hanging in houses, shops, and offices and worn as jewellery.

odalisque: a female slave, a candidate for the sultan's affections.

Osmanlica: the language of the Ottoman Empire.

pattens: high, wooden shoes designed to keep the wearer off the wet, hot floor of the steam baths.

plov: rice.

shul: a synagogue, the Jewish house of prayer.

rebbetzin: a rabbi's wife.

repoussé: a metal-work technique in which metal is shaped by hammering from the reverse side to create a design.

scudo: a Venetian coin of small denomination.

Shabbat: the Jewish day of rest, the seventh day of the week. It begins a few minutes before sunset on Friday until the appearance of three stars in the sky on Saturday night.

Shabbat goy: a gentile servant who performs tasks not permitted for Jews to perform on the Sabbath.

şhalvar: loose trousers worn by Turkish women.

shiva: a Jewish period of mourning lasting seven days.

tallis: prayer shawl worn by men, fringed and reaching below the knees.

Talmud: refers to the "six orders" in the Oral Law of Judaism. The Talmud has two components—the *Mishnah* and the *Gemara*.

tughra: the seal (or monogram) of the sultan, written in calligraphy.

yali: a handsome country house, especially on one of the Princes' Islands in the bay of Istanbul.

yaşmak: a veil worn by Muslim women wrapped around the upper and lower face so only the eyes are exposed.

yeshiva: a Jewish educational institution focusing primarily on the study of the Torah.

yufka: Turkish bread, thin, round, and unleavened.

FURTHER READING

꒦꒷꒦

Ashenburg, Katherine. *The Mourner's Dance: What We Do When People Die*. North Point Press. 2004.

Brox, Jane. *Brilliant: The Evolution of Artificial Light*. Mariner Books. 2011.

Croutier, Alev Lytle. *Harem: The World Behind the Veil*. Abbeville Press. 1991.

Faroqhi, Suraiya. *Subjects of the Sultan*. I.B. Tauris. 2005.

Freely, John, and Hilary Sumner-Boyd. *Strolling Through Istanbul: The Classic Guide to the City*. Tauris Parke Paperbacks. 2010.

Goodwin, Godfrey. *The Private World of Ottoman Women*. Saqi Books. 2007.

Greenfield, Amy Butler. *A Perfect Red: Empire, Espionage, and the Quest for the Color of Desire.* Harper Perennial. 2006.

Hanimefendi, Leyla. *The Imperial Harem of the Sultans: Daily Life at the Çirağan Palace During the 19th Century: Memoirs of Leyla Hanimefendi.* Peva Publication. 1994.

Hutter Epstein, Randi, M.D. *Get Me Out: A History of Childbirth from the Garden of Eden to the Sperm Bank.* W.W. Norton Company. 2010.

Inalcik, Halil, and Donald Quataert, eds. *An Economic and Social History of the Ottoman Empire, 1300–1914.* Cambridge University Press. 1995.

Kia, Mehrdad, *Daily Life in the Ottoman Empire.* Greenwood Press. 2011.

Lewis, Bernard *A Middle East Mosaic: Fragments of Life, Letters and History.* Modern Library. 2001.

Peirce, Leslie P. *The Imperial Harem: Women and Sovereignty in the Ottoman Empire.* Oxford University Press. 1993.

Polk, William R. *Neighbors and Strangers.* University of Chicago Press. 1997.

Rozen, Minna. *A History of the Jewish Community in Istanbul. The Formative Years 1453–1566.* Brill Academic Publishers. 2002.

Sancar, Asli. *Ottoman Women: Myth and Reality.* Tughra Books. 2007.

Wertz, Richard W., and Dorothy C. Wertz. *Lying-In: A History of Childbirth in America.* Yale University Press. 1989.